HEATHER MARY

HEATHER MARY

By

J. M. SCOTT

E. P. Dutton & Company, Inc.

NEW YORK, 1953

C. 3

LIBRARY OF CONGRESS CATALOG CARD NUMBER: 52-12336

- BL

To

Duet

HER SKIPPER AND THE REST OF THE CREW,
REMEMBERING OCTOBER—NOVEMBER 1949

A foreboding of disaster, and a chilling, uncanny feeling of mystery runs through this weird story of the sea in which Richard Charrington and a crew of four set sail from England for Bermuda in the *Heather Mary,* a small yacht. The members of the crew are inexperienced, and although they have been acquainted with their skipper, they are not his close friends. But they have all been devoted to Heather Mary, his deceased wife.

Gradually, through each man's recollections the story unfolds, and the gaps in Heather's life are filled in, pieced together in snatches as the crew struggles to keep the small craft on its course in the raging seas.

HEATHER MARY

CHAPTER 1

AT 7:15 A.M. on November 1, 1947, a Seven Continents Airlines
Skycruiser left Bermuda for the Azores with twenty passengers
and a crew of seven. At 8:20 she sent out a routine position check.
She had then covered 150 of the 1754 miles. The weather was
known to be stormy, with strong winds in some areas, but since
her captain made no mention of this it was taken for granted that
the conditions were not dangerous. At 9:15 A.M. she announced
that she was switching over to the Azores frequency. That was
the last message received from her.

She failed to reach the Azores at the scheduled time. Four hours'
spare fuel had been carried, but this margin of time passed without
news of her. That meant that she had come down in the Atlantic.

Questions were later asked in the Press about the delay in putting the rescue scheme into operation. Admittedly some hours
were lost owing to confusion between the Bermuda and Azores
stations who had both believed that the air liner was in communication with the other. But directly this was resolved every available aircraft with the necessary range was mobilized. Every ship
in the area—liners and cargo vessels—were asked to keep a sharp
lookout. Units of the United States Navy joined in the search.
Even a number of private yachts put out from Bermuda and the
Azores.

But two factors reduced the chances of success. First, small and
rapidly moving depressions made the whole ocean more or less
stormy. Wave crests, scalped by the wind and blown along in a
horizontal curtain of spray, made it infinitely more difficult to
locate wreckage or rafts. Besides, there was a great deal of low
cloud. The second factor was the extent of the possible area. The

machine might have come down anywhere between her position at her last message and the Azores. One thousand five hundred miles by, say, fifty miles—to allow for drift with whatever winds or currents were encountered—meant that an area about as great as that of England and Scotland had to be combed. And after forty-eight hours, when the weather had begun to calm, this possible area had enormously increased. It was probable almost from the start that this would prove another unexplained disaster. The aircraft would have sunk within a few minutes, and those aboard her might not, among such waves, have had time or opportunity to man the safety rafts.

None the less, the search was continued into the third day. Owing to the thick weather, aircraft had proved of little value, but there must have been some fifty vessels—from naval ships to liners and fine yachts—beating up and down in the stormy sea. None of them found any trace of the disaster.

Then a signal was received from the *Morning Pride*, a small freighter which was not searching but on passage between Kingston, Jamaica, and Liverpool. The message gave a position on the outer fringe of the search area, and read: "Picked up twenty-six survivors presumed of S. C. A. aircraft. Master."

Public interest which had begun to die down flared up like gasoline thrown on embers. But during the next twenty-four hours there were more speculations than facts in the newspapers. The names of the twenty passengers and seven crew had already been confirmed and published. Twenty-six survivors meant that one was missing—unless the number were wrong. If one were missing, how had he or she died? Presumably in the crash. And how had the rest survived?

The *Morning Pride* was bombarded with questions. Her radio operator, who had plenty of other duties, answered only a few. Twenty-six survivors was correct. But they were in no condition even to tell their names, let alone describe their experiences. The final message read: "Further enquiries will be dealt with in Liverpool. Master." So the identity of the missing person remained unknown while the little freighter steamed northeastward at a steady seven knots.

She was not left alone for long. A United States destroyer which had been in the search was ordered to make contact with the

Morning Pride and take off survivors; and a seaplane chartered by a news agency flew out to get the story.

Pending the court of enquiry, the Captain and crew of the aircraft refused to make any statement. So the story came from the passengers.

Although the weather was rough almost from the start they "seemed to be getting along pretty well." But about two hours after leaving Bermuda they flew into a thunderstorm and "fell into an air pocket deep as a volcano." The aircraft dropped several hundred feet and struck the water. There she was helpless as a butterfly in a river, and the waves began to batter her.

The crew acted promptly and efficiently. Oil was jettisoned. This stopped the waves from breaking, thus making it possible to launch and inflate the pneumatic life-saving apparatus. This consisted of several small floats of the survival equipment type developed during the war and two large rubber rafts of amply sufficient size to carry everybody on board. The Captain decided to use only the large rafts, but, to prevent these from being damaged by bumping against the aircraft, they were allowed to drift out to lee to the extent of their painters while the passengers were pulled out to them on the small floats.

In the course of this operation an accident happened. One float broke free with a woman passenger on it. A line was immediately thrown, but she failed to grasp it. Before more could be done the light float was swept out of reach by the wind and was lost sight of among the waves. Apart from this most unfortunate occurrence the disembarkation was safely completed in the short period before the aircraft sank.

The two rafts were bound together and those on board them secured in their places by canvas belts. The craft were unsinkable and fitted with canopies which kept out much of the spray. They carried food and water for several days. Theoretically there was no danger provided they were found before these supplies were exhausted. In fact, there was no risk of finishing the food because nobody was inclined to eat. Seasickness was the mortal danger. If the wind had not modified when it did nobody would have survived. As it was, their recovery after having been picked up was remarkably rapid. One survivor was sufficiently resilient to describe his experiences as " three days in a cocktail shaker."

After the thrill of the rescue, interest naturally turned sympathetically to the girl who had been lost. Her name was Mary Brown. It took a day or two to discover her story. She had been a saleswoman in one of the leading West End fashion houses, but all her interest and ambition were in the cinema. When her father died, leaving her about £1,000, she decided to gamble it all on a visit to Hollywood. Several people had told her that she had a film face, she knew how to wear clothes, and she believed that she would catch the eye of a director and become famous overnight.

This extraordinary novelette story almost worked out as it should—but not quite. She did catch somebody's eye. But after a brief association he gave her not a contract but an air ticket home. So she set off upon her return journey with her little fortune gone, unknown as she had been before. It was cruel irony that now she had passed beyond ambition her name was on everybody's lips and her curious pleasantly ugly face—high cheekbones, wide cat's eyes and big mouth—was pictured in every newspaper.

After two further days the search was abandoned altogether. It was not worth risking other lives by continuing to look for a float scarcely larger than a doormat.

But Mary Brown lived on in people's thoughts. That a girl like the tens of thousands of others who hurry to business every day should risk everything to make her dreams come true, should lose the gamble and meet an end like that, caught the imagination. How long had she remained alive and what had she thought about? Perhaps lightheadedly she had imagined she was acting a scene in a film. . . . .

Nowhere was the story of the crash and its sequel followed with more interest than on the liners which were during that period at sea. I will give an account of what happened in this connection on board the *Lucullus*, a luxury passenger ship of twenty thousand tons then homeward bound from New Zealand. I was one of the passengers.

We were in the Pacific when the S. C. A. Skycruiser came down in the Atlantic. But when an indication of the search area was published, many of the passengers realized that our ship would be bound to pass through it. They wanted to know if the *Lucullus* would join in the hunt.

The ship's officers with their usual patience pointed out that the area was more than three thousand miles away. The search would be over one way or another before we could hope to join it.

That was discouraging. Yet there was always a crowd round the bulletin sheets, and the radio officer was continually being asked if there were "anything new." As one passenger put it, even if we could not ourselves hope to make the rescue we felt a kinship for men and women in peril on the same element as ourselves. Besides, one never knew—strange things happened at sea.

The twenty-six survivors were picked up before we reached Panama. Then we heard the full story. Even in the heat of the canal there was a great deal of discussion about the unfortunate Mary Brown. But this topic did not last for long when the *Lucullus* sailed into the Caribbean. After all, the subject was not inexhaustible and there were plenty of interests on board—the swimming pool, gossip, the cinema, the wonderful meals, concerts, dances and, for those who liked that sort of thing or couldn't say no, every kind of deck game. By the time that the liner had passed beyond the islands and was fairly into the Atlantic the incident of the Skycruiser was as good as forgotten.

On the evening of November 12th, those of the passengers who had gone on deck to watch the sunset noticed that the white and green wake of the *Lucullus* was curling to one side. Why were we changing course? A passenger suggested that it was something to do with the great circle route.

But soon the truth was buzzing round. A chartered aircraft flying that day between Trinidad and Bermuda had reported seeing "a yellow object." Its position was given. The two or three ships, including ours, for which this position was not far off course had been asked to investigate. The *Lucullus* would reach this spot at about eight o'clock next morning, almost certainly before any other ship.

Such were the facts. The passengers made a great deal of them. Although the position was, said the ship's officers, several hundred miles from where the Skycruiser crashed, and although the yellow object might have been wreckage or a patch of seaweed it was taken for granted by most people that it was Mary Brown's float. Starting from that premise discussion in the bar went on until very late that night. One line of talk was that there would be no one on the float. Almost certainly she had been washed off, and if not she would have jumped overboard when she went mad from thirst or fear and loneliness—"a sort of claustrophobia." Another line was that the will to live would keep her clinging to the float until the end and she was probably still on it. Therefore it would be a good thing, for the sake of the women passengers, if we did not find it. The third line of talk was, or pretended to be, the most responsible. Horrible or not, it would be best that we should find both float and body. That would write *Finis* to the sad affair and prevent any possibility of legends and rumors. Besides, Mary Brown could then be given Christian burial.

The talk had reached this solemn morbid stage when a blaring explosion of noise made several of the glasses spill. The *Lucullus* had sounded her fog horn.

One man who had just come in from the deck remarked that it had been misty for the last hour or more—which made another say crossly that in that case the fog horn should have been used before. An officer told him that a well-equipped modern vessel did not depend for safety on her horn. But the placidly discursive mood had been destroyed, and everybody went to bed.

From seven o'clock next morning the passengers began to come on deck and take their places at the rail. It was still misty in patches, and calm. White clouds, no longer airborne, lay helpless on the oily water. They moved and wavered slightly, giving occasional glimpses of a longer view—then seemed to close together again as the liner steamed slowly on.

It was infuriating not being able to see properly. And yet—as one lady said—Nature has her sense of the dramatic. The mist was like a theater curtain which might rise at any moment.

The mist did not rise like a curtain but broke up into separate woolly masses which moved over the smooth dunes of the swell as slowly as grazing sheep. Thus we would get a view of one stretch of water which directly afterwards was closed as another vista opened up. There must have been a breeze but it was not perceptible from the deck.

At about half past eight a sailor who had been posted at the masthead, which was above the ceiling of the mist, gave a shout and pointed to the port side.

We could see nothing, but a launch which we had been towing cast loose and left the ship. It vanished into the mist while we strained our eyes after it, listening to the noise of its engine as it grew fainter and fainter with distance.

The *Lucullus* had stopped her engines but was of course still moving. I suppose it was because of this and the slight drift of the mist that we got so suddenly and briefly a clear view to port.

The launch was approaching a tiny yellow thing about a mile away. With binoculars we could make out that it was a float but at that distance could not be certain if there were anybody on board it or not. The launch was signaling with a lamp. The mist closed again.

For a minute or two we lost even the sound of the launch's engine—presumably it had stopped by the float. Then we heard it again, growing stronger as it approached. By this time the passengers who were lining every inch of the rail were talking with the greatest excitement. Everybody wanted to know what the launch had signaled. But the officers who until now had been friendly and co-operative, although a trifle patronizing, had suddenly become preoccupied. Their calm superiorty had deserted them. They hurried through the crowd, deaf to all questions, went to the bridge or radio cabin or whispered among themselves.

Without them, the most extraordinary and horrific rumors began to circulate among the passengers. But I don't believe that any of us expected what we saw when the launch materialized out of the mist.

Between the sailors in the sternsheets were two figures wrapped to the ears in blankets. There were two of them—not one.

I remember how the jabber of excitement started slowly, uncertainly, then burst into pandemonium. Although neither figure could be recognized as a woman one must be Mary Brown. And someone—some creature which seemed human—had joined her in the middle of the Atlantic to keep her alive.

I forced my way below, but before I could reach the sick bay the door had been closed and a guard set. The guard would say nothing. I think it was at that moment that I formed the resolution of discovering the whole story—which I shall tell.

CHAPTER 2

"THIS is the last time I shall be in a train". . . . More and more he had been thinking in that way, shedding the habits and incidents of what had been his life. But he had given up saying it aloud. "This is the last week I shall be at the office". . . . It had begun to annoy them there. They had ceased to look at him with admiration and startled wonder and had begun talking in a sinister way about his future. Damn the future. When the trip was over he would have done something worth while and that was the best form of capital. It was a sort of duty to take a chance like this.

All the same he had postponed telling Elaine. But she guessed that he was planning something. Women always did seem to know what was at the back of your mind when you were trying to be particularly loving. So he had told her—and suggested that to make the most of the time remaining they should behave just as before. But since then there had been no real pleasure in kissing her. It had been like tearing off sheets from a calendar, or rather tearing something painful from each other—a sort of rite that had to be gone through.

She had never reproached him. She had not come to see him off. He hadn't expected it and it was a relief anyway. . . . The whistle blew. He leaned out of the window to see the last of Paddington.

As the train began to move Elaine appeared from somewhere and put a small parcel into his hands. She said, "Oh, Toby," and then seemed to glide backwards into the crowd with her little face smudged with tears. He stared desperately after her; then, losing her, withdrew his head and plumped down violently upon his seat. An old gentleman opposite said quietly, "They're very brave." Toby looked fiercely at his shoes. He had thought he was the one who was being brave.

Also, as the train started, square shoulders and a close cropped, well groomed head protruded from a first class carriage window. "So long, old girl." An arm waved.

"Look after Richard," a woman called back, standing slight but self-reliant on the platform, used to saying good-by.

"He'll have to do the looking after," the man shouted. But she could not have heard him for she had already turned away.

He sat down and picked up *The Field*. The index finger of his left hand stroked his small military mustache as he read.

In the next carriage sat a man who did not look out of the window at all. He leaned back in his corner, his eyes closed but—from his expression—not asleep. When the train started he smiled.

He was short and broad and bony. He might have been something of an athlete in his youth. Now it was difficult to guess his age within ten years—about forty-five. His hair was gray, long and curling except on the crown of his head which was bald as a monk's. His face was colorless and tired. When he opened his eyes you saw that they were intelligent and blue. They looked at the people in the carriage with interest but without curiosity. He seemed a reposeful, kindly, sympathetic person.

From the last window of the train a big man leaned out dangerously far, waving and calling, "Good-by, Tilly," to a sturdy young lady who for some distance kept up with his carriage shouting, "Good-by, Dad." Then moving as carefully as he could among the legs of the other passengers, he returned to his middle seat, pulled up his trousers an inch or two and sat down. He took out a handkerchief and blew his nose. Then he remained sitting bolt upright and staring straight ahead.

The elderly lady in the opposite seat had been admiring him— such a big, handsome, well-preserved man. But his straight stare embarrassed her. In fact he did not see her at all. He saw only a wide and ever moving seascape and his chest heaved and his eyes sparkled as he looked at it.

The train reached Brixham late in the afternoon and the four people who have been mentioned all got out of it. They were only names to each other, and it was by chance that two of them met.

The soldier was arranging with a porter to take his valise down to the harbor when the short, broad, monklike man asked if he could share the barrow.

"Of course, sir."

The square man studied him a moment, "I think you must be Colonel Harding?"

"Yes. Are you—?"

"Boyd."

They shook hands. After that they scarcely spoke until they were following the porter down the street, but Harding's first impression had been favorable.

"You know, Professor—" he began.

"Mister," Boyd corrected.

"But Richard Charrington said you were a professor at—I'm sorry—somewhere in the Midlands."

"I was, but in this country the title does not survive the appointment."

"Then I suppose your substantive rank is Doctor," Harding laughed. "In any case I was darned glad to hear you were coming on the trip."

"Why?"

Confound the fellow, Harding thought. He said, "You are too modest, Doctor. Of course I'm glad. This will be a formidable trip and I'm a complete duffer myself about anything that concerns the sea—"

"So am I."

"You can't be."

"I haven't been in a sailing vessel since I was a boy."

"But you're a physicist, aren't you? You know the theory."

"So does the child who drops a feather into the windward end of a puddle."

"The Atlantic Ocean is a formidable puddle," Harding said, looking doubtfully at the shorter man who looked back at him in a quietly interested way. Then the soldier laughed, his loud two-syllable laugh which was like an order to himself to change his mood. "Never mind, Richard Charrington is an expert and no doubt the other two are pretty good. What are their names?"

"Carlyle and Yeoman."

"Know them?"

"We haven't met. Commander Charrington told me of them in his last letter."

"You know Richard pretty well, I suppose."

"He first wrote to me shortly after the war ended about that tragic affair of his wife. Since then we have met I suppose half a dozen times. I very much appreciated his invitation. It happened to fit in perfectly."

Harding would have liked to know why this fellow ten years older than himself and not so fit by the look of him, without yachting experience and a mere acquaintance of Richard, should have jumped at this peculiar method of going to Bermuda. But he did not feel that he could ask. Instead he said:

"No doubt we'll all know each other well enough before we arrive." And when Boyd did not answer, he added, "You knew his wife?"

"Yes, for a short time."

"Damned shame. She was the loveliest creature that ever stepped."

They had halted by their barrows of luggage, where the main street branches right and left to fringe the inner harbor. The porter had gone to enquire about the yacht. There was a lot of shipping in the basin—mostly fishing vessels but with a few yachts, some large, some very small. The two men stood looking at the forest of masts, smelling the odor of the port, hearing the sea birds.

"I wonder which is the *Heather Mary,*" Harding said. "I hope that one, she looks steady."

"I've got some very good pills," Boyd said. "The kind they used on D Day."

"Were you in that?"

"No. I was in a reserved occupation."

At that moment the porter returned and told them that *Heather Mary* was in the outer harbor. They must walk round the basin. They were about to move on when a big man in an overcoat and a black hat approached them as respectfully as it is possible to do with a suitcase in each hand. He said:

"Excuse me, I didn't mean to eavesdrop but I couldn't help overhearing you mention *Heather Mary.*"

"That's all right," Harding said. "You one of the galley slaves?"

"I'm Jack Yeoman."

"Splendid. I'm Marcus Harding. This is Doctor Boyd."

"I'm sure I'm very pleased to meet you."

"Lucky we have run into you," Marcus Harding said when Yeoman's luggage was on the barrow. "The Doctor and I wouldn't have been able to recognize the yacht."

"She's a yawl, isn't she?"

"Yes. But we don't know what a yawl looks like."

Yeoman glanced from one to the other. He seemed doubtful how to take this remark.

"You know a lot about sailing ships?" Harding asked.

"I've always been interested in them."

"You know what ropes to pull to make the boat go where you want?"

"I hope so."

"I'm sure you do. And no doubt this other young fellow does too —Carlyle, I mean."

"Are you concerned about this voyage?" Boyd asked suddenly of Harding.

"Not in the least—particularly with Richard Charrington as skipper. But I've done only one job all my life. I'm not used to tackling things I'm no hand at."

"You expect to sail the yacht yourself?"

"To help at it. We'll none of us be passengers, you know."

"I shall. I'm on a rest cure," Boyd said.

"A what? You're joking."

"Not at all. I've been ordered a complete rest for three months."

"Surely a small yacht is hardly the place for that."

"On the contrary. I couldn't stand the idea of a nursing home. If I had stayed in my house I would have worked—I couldn't have avoided it. But on a little boat crossing the Atlantic without even a book in my luggage. . . . That's why, as I told you, I was so grateful when Charrington invited me."

"Richard knows this?"

"Of course."

Harding laughed. "Then I'm certain it's all right—just like Richard."

"There she is! That must be her," Yeoman shouted, pointing. While the two men had been talking he had discreetly gone ahead. Now, coming up with him where he stood on the sea wall they had a view across the great bight of salt water which stretches from Berry Head to the Bill of Portland. It looked like open sea and it was stippled with white waves. But the foreground, the outer harbor, was protected by the long, low stone mole. This white arm sheltered a score of yachts which bowed and swayed and nodded as if in animated conversation. But the yacht towards which Yeoman's arm was pointing rode at anchor by herself, away from the gossiping cluster. Harding who knew nothing about yachts, knew at once that she was in some subtle way superior to all the others. *Heather Mary*. His mind went racing off into the past—*Heather Mary* would naturally be superior.

Yeoman was staring with glittering eyes, his big chest heaving as if he had been running. Boyd stood with his short legs apart, looking intently across the water with half-closed eyes.

"How do you know that yacht is *Heather Mary?*" he asked.

He had to repeat the question. Then Yeoman answered breathlessly, "I've seen her photo. I wouldn't forget, would I ?"

"She's very small." Marcus Harding said. "By the way, Porter, what do we owe you?"

When the porter had gone he asked the others, "What do we do now? I wonder if the Skipper is aboard."

"Presumably, since he did not meet us at the station," Boyd said.

Yeoman suggested diffidently, "We might hail her—you know, *Heather Mary*, Ahoy!—all together."

They did. The Ahoy went well enough, but none of them made much noise over the name.

For a moment afterwards the scene in the evening light was as peaceful as before. The three men stood in a row with the little town behind them, embarrassed by the noise they had made. The group of yachts in front continued to bob and curtsy to each other. Then a figure appeared from the hatch of *Heather Mary*. He stared towards them under a shading hand. Then he waved his arm, hauled up the dinghy, got into it and began to pull towards the shore.

Until he had covered three quarters of the distance he never once glanced round and yet he kept direction almost exactly. Boyd noticed this and wondered by what two marks the rower might be steering. But as the dinghy came closer, with a white mustache alternately growing and being shaved from her bow, Boyd became more interested in the man who propelled it. His shoulders rose and fell and swung back with the power and assurance of a piston.

One oar was thrust forward while the other was pulled back and the dinghy snuggled against the jetty as a pin does against a magnet. Charrington stepped out and greeted them.

Boyd and Yeoman, who before had seen him only in town clothes, greeted him now almost as if he were another person. But it was the conventional figure which had been false. This man in a peaked cap, thick reefer jacket and sea boots was genuine and exactly right. He was nearly six feet tall. His thick shoulders were slightly rounded and this had the effect of thrusting his head forward. His nose was aquiline, his mouth firm, his brows heavy and his eyes deep sunk. His face was vigorously alive and carelessly charming as the sea in sunlight. As he shook hands with each of them his dark eyes glowed with pleasure.

"Where's Toby Carlyle? Wasn't he on your train?" he asked. "But, of course, none of you've met him. He ought to find his way here, though, so we'll give him five minutes."

Charrington took a pipe from his pocket, filled and lighted it. He asked about their journey, asked Marcus Harding about his wife Meg and their children, Jack Yeoman about his daughter Tilly, Boyd about his work—"You've handed everything over. Good. That's the last time we mention it. You're going to have a complete rest—plenty of good hard manual labor. You'll be a new man in a week."

"You've been disguising yourself already, Richard," Marcus said.

"What d'you mean?"

"Your beard—"

Charrington's hand went to his chin which was whiter than the rest of his face.

"It made me look too much like Captain Kettle. I'm a pleasure yachtsman now. For the rest of my life I shall sail with the wind."

"But you'll stay with us in Bermuda for a bit? Meg would never forgive you if you didn't."

"Of course. The yacht will need a fit-out there in any case. Well, no point waiting any longer. We'd better go aboard."

He stowed the luggage. "We're a full load, but don't be alarmed —she's steady as a lifeboat."

The little dinghy had only a couple of inches of freeboard, but two minutes later they came safely alongside *Heather Mary* and, careful of the paint, scrambled aboard.

Charrington took them below at once.

"Closet and oilskin locker," he said, pointing with either hand as he reached the foot of the companionway. "Aft is the skipper's cabin and chart room." He pushed open double doors in front of him. "The saloon. Marcus, you and Boyd had better doss down here. In the fo'c's'le yonder—we'll call it the forward cabin—there's a couple of hinged cots. It doesn't look much—the chain locker cramps it a bit—but if you're sleeping no one sits on your face at meals. Suit you, Jack? You bed with Toby when he turns up. Well, gentlemen, this is your home for the next hundred days so make the most of it. Get your kit stowed. Most of the lockers are full of food tins but there's some space here and there. I've a few little jobs still to do before we are ready for sea—That's why I couldn't meet you. I'll get them finished, then we'll have some grub."

CHAPTER 3

CHARRINGTON left them to themselves while he was occupied about the yacht. They were glad of this. They had evidently brought far too much kit and they found difficulty in stowing it away in the space available—to leave anything lying about in the perfect neatness of the saloon and forward cabin was not to be thought of. But somehow or other they got it out of sight and after half an hour or so the three of them were sitting on the settees in the saloon talking in a desultory way and waiting for their next cue.

"What's Richard doing?" Marcus Harding asked.

"He's on deck," Boyd answered. "He said he didn't want any help."

"One feels so damned useless doing nothing. I say, Yeoman, be a good fellow and go up and have a look. You know the form."

Yeoman obeyed at once. In a few minutes he came back and reported.

"He's going through sails and ropes and things."

"Do you think we could help?"

"He said not. I helped him to haul the dinghy on deck. He said he'd be down directly."

No one spoke for a minute or two. Then Harding laughed. "This reminds me of my first night in an officers' mess."

Boyd raised his eyes and looked at him but did not speak.

"I was as scared as a debutante of doing the wrong thing," Harding went on. "Now I want to be useful but not to make a fool of myself and merely get in the way."

"Don't you think it would be a good plan to take a rest while you can?"

"No doubt you're right. But I've lost the knack of doing nothing." Harding paused, his head bent, thoughtfully stroking his mustache. Then with sudden activity he took out his cigarette case, tapped and lit a cigarette.

"You've set the fashion, Doctor. No doubt we'll know each other inside out before this trip is done but you might as well hear at once why I signed on. Since a month I've been out of the Army. I'm a free lance now."

"Were you tired of being a soldier?" Boyd asked.

"Tired? Good God, of course not!" Harding exclaimed, coloring. Then he laughed and said more quietly. "I've been in the Far East since the last year of the war. When the Battalion was ordered home I sent in my papers. Not that I'd enjoyed jungle fighting— Lord no! But, well, a home station seemed pretty flat and I felt my wife deserved a break. She was in the Foreign Office from the start till '45—no Cook's touring for her. London all the time— blitz, doodle-bugs, V 2's. Then looking after the kids I've hardly seen. She needs a holiday. I don't know what I shall do later— farm or something. But we've taken a house in Bermuda for the winter."

"Charrington is going to stay with you in Bermuda?" Boyd asked.

"Yes, that's the idea."

"You know him well, I suppose."

"Pretty well. My wife has known him for years. Her people

live ten miles from Heather's home. When Richard asked me on this trip it seemed to me a lot more worth-while than going by liner—I've spent too long on troopships. Meg—my wife—was damned sporting about it." Harding dropped his voice. "Tell the truth, I believe she's been worried about Richard since, since— You do know about his wife?"

"As much as anybody, I believe," Boyd said gravely.

Marcus Harding stared at him for a moment. Then he turned to Yeoman. "You know about Mrs. Charrington? Excuse me asking point-blank. I only want to make sure nobody drops a brick."

Yeoman started. He had been listening attentively to all that was said, turning from one speaker to the other. But he was embarrassed at being brought into the conversation.

"Why, yes. I knew Miss Heather—I mean Mrs. Charrington— very well. I can't help calling her Miss Heather because I knew her before she was married, and still more afterwards in a way— not really personally of course, except sometimes in the war, but the Morrisons have always been clients of Kingsgate and Simms and when the father died. . . . You understand in the war most of the partners were away and there was a good deal in the estate that had to be explained to her. Oh what a lovely lady she was. And to think—"

Harding stopped him with a gesture, hearing footsteps on the companionway. The narrow double doors of the saloon were thrust open and Charrington came in. He sidled between the table and one of the settees, sat down and began to jab tobacco into his pipe. His hawk-like face was excited, as if he had something pleasant to tell them.

"Sorry to leave you alone for so long. I still had a good many jobs to finish. The lists and counter lists one makes on these occasions! But I've just performed the ceremony of ticking off the last item."

"We've been feeling guilty sitting on our backsides and not helping," Harding said.

"My dear Marcus, you needn't have. As I told Jack Yeoman, it was no good your coming in on preparations at this stage. You'll get plenty of opportunities to earn your passage later, I promise you. Much better that you should get to know each other, as I'm sure you've been doing."

He looked round at the three of them with aggressive, smiling eyes. Harding met his stare with an appreciative nod. Yeoman looked down. Boyd smiled—not at what had been said, for he had scarcely listened, but because he had suddenly realized what Charrington's expression—now and when he had picked them up in the dinghy—reminded him of: it was the expression of the boxing instructor at his school, an ex-champion heavyweight, when sparring with a favorite pupil.

"And now," Charrington said, "we deserve a tot—I for finishing several months of work and you for trusting yourselves to the result of it."

He opened a locker and took out glasses and bottles.

"Jack, you're the senior, what is it to be—rum, gin or sherry?"

"Whatever you can spare best, sir," Yeoman said.

Charrington stood with a bottle in each hand, his head thrust forward. "We might as well get this clear at once. Somebody has got to be skipper on every craft and I'll give such orders as are necessary. But you aren't a pressed crew. You are my guests and I'm your host, Richard or Skipper or anything you like—except Sir. What d'you want, Jack, rum, gin, sherry?"

"Gin, please—Skipper." Yeoman was beaming.

"Water?"

"Yes please, Skipper."

Charrington went forward into the galley. There was the squeak and sigh of a small pump and he returned with the filled glass. He held it to the light.

"I watered yesterday. Good plan to test the stuff—with spirit in to make it healthy . . . What's your tipple, Marcus? And you, Boyd?"

A minute later Harding said, "This fellow Carlyle—what happens if he doesn't turn up?"

"We'd have to wait, blast him. But he'll turn up all right. He's young—that's his trouble." Charrington finished his drink with a movement like an uppercut. "You must excuse me. From tomorrow one of you will be cook, but tonight I intend to set the standard myself."

He went into the galley, closing the forward double doors behind him.

"There's a leader for you," Harding said.

After that remark neither he nor the others spoke much during the next half hour. They sat sipping their drinks and thinking their own thoughts while the purr of a pressure stove came from the galley. Meanwhile the yacht lay peacefully at anchor. She was not still as a house is still. She was alive. She influenced the thoughts of her crew. Tomorrow she would begin her journey. . . . The three men looked about them at the saloon, a room less than three paces by two in extent. The settees which bordered the two sides were the tops of food lockers. The settees themselves became sleeping bunks at night. Everything was designed with an eye to utility and the saving of space. The other compartments had been built on the same principle—the galley which was the size of a cupboard and through the middle of which the mainmast passed, the fo'c's'le or forward cabin which was also the chain locker and bosun's store, the minute closet, and presumably the skipper's cabin as well—everything was as small and neat and intricate as a cunningly made toy. And this would be their home for a hundred days and nights.

"How are you getting back, Yeoman—from Bermuda I mean?" Harding asked suddenly.

"I'm not."

"What d'you mean? You don't object to my asking, do you?"

"Of course not, Colonel. I'm grateful. But I'm really not meaning to come back. I'm emigrating, you see."

Boyd changed his position on the settee.

"You see, Doctor—" Yeoman turned gratefully towards Boyd's reposeful face, away from Harding's frankly puzzled stare. "I've always wanted to live on a coral island."

Boyd nodded, as if he found this the most natural wish in the world.

"Yes, I've dreamed about it since I was a kid," Yeoman went on. "As I grew up I got to realize it wasn't likely, to say the least of it. A coral island for a solicitor's clerk—I ask you! And when I married I—well I didn't forget but I sort of filed it. Then my dear wife died. God forgive me, it came up again. But I soon realized my girl Tilly was my responsibility in her place. Then along came Commander Charrington to thank me, he said, for helping his wife in business matters while he was a prisoner. I saw him several times—he was so friendly, and him being a sailor

I told him about my old ambition. Then he told me about this trip and offered to take me. Bermuda's a coral island and there are jobs there. As soon as I find one I'm going to send for my girl."

"And you will save the passage money," Harding said.

"Yes. But that's not why I'm excited. What an adventure for *me!* You should have seen their faces, the people at the office and the fellows I met at lunch and in the carriage traveling."

The forward doors opened and a good food smell came in. "Put up the flaps and lay the table, someone," Charrington's voice shouted. "Cloth and cutlery in the port locker, plates and glass to starboard."

The narrow double doors closed with a bang. Glad of something to do, Harding and Yeoman got in each other's way laying the table. Boyd drew up his legs and watched.

Charrington appeared with a couple of plates in each hand. "*Moules marinieres,*" he said. "Toby will miss a good dinner if he doesn't hurry."

The sea-blue shells were gaping wide as the beaks of hungry baby pelicans, lying in wine sauce, sprinkled with parsley; and a fragrant steam was rising from them.

The crew had been expecting something heated up out of a tin. They were silent. Charrington said nothing as he put the plates in front of them, but from the light in his eyes he was conscious of the effect he had made.

Suddenly he straightened up, listening. From the quiet night outside came the creak and splash of oars. Then there was a bump. In a moment Charrington was on deck. They heard his voice, violent as an explosion.

"Mind my paint, confound you!"

There was a pause, and the grumbled apology of the boatman—then Charrington's voice again, this time warm and friendly. "Oh it's you, Toby. Splendid. Give me that bag."

A minute later he was back in the saloon with his arm across the shoulders of a tall, thin, long-haired young man who blinked at the electric light.

"Introductions," Charrington said. "Dr. Boyd, Jack Yeoman, Marcus Harding—Toby Carlyle."

"I have seen you before," Boyd said, shaking hands. "Did you not lunch in the restaurant car of the 12:50 from Paddington?"

"Yes," Carlyle answered.

Then he turned, it seemed angrily, to Charrington. "Why didn't you tell me the name of your yacht?"

"Of course I did."

"No."

"Are you certain?"

"Yes."

"How stupid. I'm sorry. But I've caused so much trouble on the waterfront lately my name must be a household curse. Did you have all that difficulty finding out?"

"None." Toby remained staring at the lamp as if it hypnotized him. "The first fish porter I met told me her name was *Heather Mary.*"

"You look like a man who needs something good and strong to drink," Charrington said, and poured out a small glass of sherry.

Boyd, leaning back in his corner, had noticed that Toby Carlyle was drunk and that Charrington knew this although he hid it tactfully. That was good of him, but why had he not told the boy the name of the yacht? It was a strange omission for an essentially competent man.

The *moules marinieres* was very good indeed. When it was finished Charrington jumped up, gesturing his crew back into their seats.

"No, no. This is my night. The next course is cold, I'm afraid." He brought in a roast goose and carved it swiftly and skilfully.

"Well I'm damned," Toby said.

"Why are you damned?" Charrington asked, his eyes glittering.

"I expected death or glory and storms and seasickness but not whatever it was and then roast goose."

They all laughed.

"Why not?" Charrington asked. "There's no reason why a little yacht shouldn't look after her creature comforts as well as the *Queen Mary.* It's just a matter of adaptability and efficiency."

"Efficiency. I've something to say about that—" Marcus began.

Charrington stopped him with a hand. He got to his feet.

"I'm wondering how efficient the Customs Officers really are. They sealed my drink locker, but since we'll be away with the tide at three o'clock—"

He went to his cabin and returned with a bottle in each hand.

"Chambertin. It would have been a much worse crime to let the sea shake it like a cocktail."

After that the evening went as it was bound to go, with growing fellowship, brave statements and good stories. Boyd did not say much but was attentive in his sleepy way. Toby on the other hand became more mellow and talkative. Jack's handsome face became redder and redder and he laughed at every joke. Harding told most of the stories, many of them about soldiering. Charrington was the host, bringing out each man, filling their glasses. Meanwhile *Heather Mary* lay peacefully at anchor though moving just enough to show she was alive and ready to take them on an adventure for which their mood was becoming more and more appropriately keyed.

"I don't suppose this trip is going to be anything to you, Richard," Marcus said. "You've been sailing all your life. You're an expert. Old Jack there and I suppose Carlyle come near to you, but Boyd and I know nothing. How are we going to manage when we get out in the middle of it?"

"As well as I've managed since—the war," Charrington said. Everybody was silent, and he went on. "I've been sailing almost continuously since then—and always alone. I've been to the Lofoten Islands and Spain, and the west coast of Scotland and God knows where. I could cross to Bermuda alone just as easily. But I want to enjoy this trip in good company."

"That's damn good of you," Harding murmured. "We're only anxious not to let you down."

"You won't let me down—however little you know about sailing. Listen, every special occupation builds a wall of mystery around itself—law, medicine, mending watches, anything you like. As far as small boat passages are concerned the writer fellows have set up great ramparts of the death and glory and hardship Toby mentioned. But I'll make a Jericho of it. It's as simple as this: a yacht is a physical body—a strong, thoroughbred, highly efficient body. She lacks nothing except a brain. That is provided by her skipper. On a yacht this size he can, if he wants, translate his wishes into action without help. A crew—extra nerves and muscles and interesting bits of character—are a luxury. Certainly they need no special knowledge. They merely pull the rope the skipper tells them to pull or steer a certain course, like mechanical aids. Sorry to put it so bluntly but some of you appear worried and I mean to scotch that from the start. What I hope you will get out of this trip is the freedom from responsibility of passengers mixed with the pleasure of knowing you are doing the job, in fact that you are part of the yacht. As for me, I'll be able to take things easy and—and I won't be as lonely as I've been before."

Charrington had spoken briskly until he came to the last phrase. Then he had checked, and ended on a minor key.

His crew were silent, moved with sympathy.

"Now you'd better turn in," Charrington said, his voice suddenly aggressive. "We sail with the tide at three o'clock and I'll want all hands on deck. You have no responsibilities, but as volunteer muscles you can't complain at finding yourselves being jerked till it hurts when there's work to do."

He went quickly to his cabin and closed the door.

The four members of the crew remained for some minutes smoking and finishing their wine. Then, before clearing up or undressing, they went on deck.

It was still and clear. The stars were brilliant. Lights twinkled from the harbor and from the houses which rose in layers up the hill. Other people something like themselves were drowsing by firesides or going upstairs to bed. That was another world. Their own world was this lovely vehicle of adventure which lay resting but ready with her head pointing out to sea.

Toby lit a cigarette with a lighter which looked new.

They smoked in silence for a few minutes. Then all except Boyd went below.

CHAPTER 4

LEFT alone, Boyd experienced a feeling of relief. He had much enjoyed the company in which he found himself but he wanted a few minutes to himself. He moved slowly to the stern, leaned his forearms on the mizzen boom and stared down into the water oilily flowing past with the tide.

He drew on his cigarette and let his mind wander. Strange though his surroundings were he had the feeling of doing something he had done before. . . . He had leaned over the rail of a liner beside Heather Charrington, listening to her and watching the water flow endlessly past into the darkness astern.

He had known her for less than three days. He had met her when returning from America towards the end of the war. It had been a remarkable friendship, full of confidences yet almost impersonal—until the sudden end.

She had described it. "You are the easiest person to talk to I ever met. You're a stranger for one thing and we'll never meet again. You don't love me or despise me. You aren't jealous. I am just a pathetic person from another world. You're not sympathetic or anything tiresome like that. I don't suppose you are interested really. But you are calm and wise and patient and you look kind. You are never surprised by anything and you never interrupt."

It wasn't true, Boyd had thought. He wasn't wise and patient. But it was nice of her to say it. Glancing sideways at that pale, intent face, fine in detail as a miniature painted on ivory, he was not impersonal either. But he said nothing. He looked back at the water which held her attention and listened to her talking, late into the night, leaning over the rail of the blacked-out ship.

It was as if she were talking to herself, remembering aloud. She never explained what he might not have understood. But while she talked his imagination had projected a moving picture on the water.

He saw it again now.

Babies, when they begin to walk, are generally constricted—in a pen or a sandpit or a fenced garden—to prevent them from getting into trouble. Heather was not. There was no need for it. In front of the house was a wide strip of sand dunes covered like a carpet with short grass. The Jersey herd grazed there and rabbits burrowed. She could crawl or walk until she was exhausted and yet remain in view from the drawing-room windows.

Beyond the dunes was the sea. There was a melon slice of yellow sand with a crescent of dry seaweed and driftwood drawn round it at the high tide level. Then a shallow bay of green water sheltered by a cluster of little islands, all rocks and seaweed and rank grass where the gulls nested in spring. Beyond was a much wider stretch of sea, dark blue, and often stormy. Beyond again were the big islands, the Hebrides, the last land before America.

She was taken to the sea—the innermost sheltered sea—as a very small child. But she rode there on a Shetland pony (an adventure in itself) and so did not connect it with the house. Her explorations of the four zones—the dunes, the shore water, the sea and the Atlantic Ocean—were phases in the story.

She was the child of old parents. Her father from the first moment she remembered him was suffering from the rheumatic disease which caused his death; and her mother, physically, never quite recovered from the confinement. But they put no direct restraint upon her.

When she began to toddle outside their field of vision from the drawing-room window her father sent Lingha the sheep dog after her. General Morrison said, "Stop her, Lingha." And Lingha flew over the dunes like a furry arrow.

Lingha stood on the seaward side of Heather and barked furiously until she stopped. Then he lay down and wagged his tail.

Very soon, of course, it was Heather, not General Morrison, whom Lingha worshiped and obeyed. He followed the little girl everywhere, "looking after her." For all his discipline and wisdom he was young enough to prefer her adventurous, confiding company to that of a man who walked with two sticks. But by the time Heather was twelve years old, Lingha was senile and decrepit. She was forbidden to kiss him. His death, mysterious and hushed up, was the first tragedy in her life. She went down to a hidden place by the sea and wept bitterly.

Then the estate people inherited her. The shepherd took her to the sheep dipping, and later "on the hill"—into the mountains— to help him with the lambing in the bitter days and nights of early spring. He told everybody that the little yellow-haired lass— "straight as a stick except for the tip of her nose"—had the ears of a wild creature for finding a newborn lamb and more wisdom than the vet man for all his booklearning in caring for a sick ewe.

The gardener gave her the freedom of the walled garden—let her take the pick of the fruit before he carried it to the House, or crawl under the netting to forage for herself. Also he gave her the

best plot, deep dug with compost and manure, in which to culti-
vate whatever she liked. She tried to grow wild flowers there.

The stalker, a man of unknown age in self-spun tweeds, weathered and bent as a wind blasted tree, taught her the mysteries of
trout and deer, grouse and waterfowl. He was a blunt-spoken
misanthrope who had once called General Morrison "a pluddy
fool" to his face. But he became a poet when he talked of Heather.
He said she walked as finely as a stag, not caring if her long bare
legs were scratched, yet was as gentle as a baby rabbit. He called
her "my White Heather."

So she grew into her teens, queen of five thousand acres and a
hundred human hearts, counting wives and children. But to tell
the truth the loyalty of the womenfolk was not absolute. They half
suspected her of being a witch.

Amulree was an independent kingdom which had its own moods
—of weather as well as of human beings. In winter it was wild and
dark, with tireless rain slanting down and the sun dropping into
the stormy sea after lunch. In early spring it was still wild, but
bright. In late spring it was placid and glowed with loveliness.
Nowhere else in the world were the colors so varied and brilliant—snow still on the summits, last year's bracken, heather and
green grass below; then yellow ocher seaweed and the dazzling
many colored sea. In summer there was the heather in purple
flower, the bog myrtle heavy with scent and the grass of par-
nassus. But chiefly there were the sunsets, all the colors melted
into the sky and draining infinitely slowly down into the Atlantic
behind the Hebrides. It was said that one could read a newspaper
out-of-doors at midnight. But nobody ever did. They were not
much interested in newspapers.

The house, the nucleus of this world, was made of local stone.
It was rambling and of no known architectural style but it fitted
in with its surroundings. Heather loved it and the whole of Amulree—the people, the wild animals, the sea, even individual trees
and plants and rocks. She loved them all.

Now and then she pondered what she would do when her
parents died. She had always thought of them as old, and although
she was devoted to them, embracing them in her infinite, intense
capacity for love, she accepted the idea of being left in charge
while she was still quite young. She knew what this would mean.

She had been an apprentice in every branch of farming and estate management. She had learned from her father and the lawyers that the balance between upkeep and private income plus revenue could no longer be maintained unless the estate could be made to produce far more than formerly. "And that just can't be done— short of magic," the General said from his chair.

The thought that Amulree and its people's lives should deteriorate was as impossible for Heather to accept as that the estate could ever be sold. Somehow or other she must find a way out. It was her habit to take her problems to the sea and hear what the waves had to say about them.

Ideas she had in plenty. The one she liked best was that she should leave the mountains as they were. (There could be no question of butcher-marketing the deer and grouse as the lawyers had suggested.) But she would plant all the low ground with daffodil bulbs. In the springtime it would become an ocean of gold.

Heather thought by herself, her idealistic mind dodging and veering away from the lawyers' "sound advice." Always at the back of her mind was the comfortable conviction that her own man would solve her problems for her.

Her man was a creature firm in outline and vague in detail. He had varied a good deal throughout the years—largely with the books she had been reading. But there was never any doubt that he would materialize, that she would recognize him instantly and that thereafter she need not worry any more.

She waited without impatience or anxiety. She brushed her hair for a long time every day because she found pleasure in brushing it, but she consciously practiced no other form of vanity. She preferred men's shirts to silk blouses. (Perhaps, Boyd guessed, she knew instinctively that rough clothes accentuated the extraordinary fineness of her limbs and features.) She was calmly certain that her man would love her as frankly and unhesitatingly as she would love him directly he appeared.

He came from the sea. One day—it was her eighteenth birthday—the wind was strong although the sun was bright, and she had walked out to Clach Alasdair to watch the waves climbing the rocks. To her surprise and alarm she saw a little yacht to windward of the reef. It was in great danger. But she was enough of a sailor to recognize how skillfully it was being handled by the man at the helm. He rounded the point and raced inland with the white waves chasing him, dodged between the little islands, nosed into the sheltered crescent bay and dropped anchor on the sand. Meanwhile Heather had been walking rapidly along the shore to meet the yachtsman and offer the highland hospitality he deserved and surely needed. From a hundred yards away she saw him furling the sails and making everything shipshape. Then, without a glance at the land, he went below. Not until next morning did he row ashore in his dinghy to ask if he could buy eggs and bread.

When he met Heather, almost the first thing he said was that she must come aboard and see his yacht. His name was Richard Charrington. He gave her tea in the cabin which delighted her by its toy-like neatness. He told her that he was a yacht designer, working near Southampton but spending much of his time cruising to test and demonstrate his yachts. He always sailed alone. To Heather this life sounded brave, fascinating and free.

Charrington remained a long time at Amulree after the weather had moderated. General Morrison and his wife took to him at once, so did the Lowreys who lived at Salen, ten miles off, and whose daughter, Meg, had been Heather's life-long friend. But— and this was a bitter disappointment to Heather—Richard Charrington could make no impression on the estate people. They were always cautious with a stranger, of course, but it was more than that. They were dour and silent in his presence and their wives would not sell him eggs and vegetables.

But this hostility only made Heather love him more. The next summer—it was 1935 and she was nineteen years old—she married Richard Charrington in the kirk at Amulree. Very few of the estate people came to the ceremony or to the wedding breakfast. They went about their everyday tasks with dark faces, and there was a sense of tension as there is before a thunderstorm. Heather and Richard escaped onto their yacht, pulled up her anchor and sailed away, beyond the islands, out into the ocean. . . .

The cigarette butt singed Boyd's fingers. He flicked it over the side and watched it drift away until the white spot was lost in the darkness. There had been a lot more of Heather's story and he would be interested to see another side of it—his own view of Charrington's character. She had said that she would like him to get to know her husband after the war. He was taking her literally. What was his first impression of the man as skipper of *Heather Mary?* Boyd was too sleepy to decide. There would be plenty of time to get to know him thoroughly.

Meanwhile he must get some rest.

CHAPTER 5

THROUGH his closed lids Marcus was conscious that the light was burning. Sleepily he wondered if Boyd had come to bed. But that had happened long ago. . . . He opened his eyes. Charrington was standing between the two bunks, with his back to him. Beyond Charrington he could see the upper half of Boyd's body, wrapped to the neck in blankets, his paper-pale face crumpled in sleep. Charrington was staring down at him, intent and motionless.

For the sake even of a few seconds more of rest Marcus closed his eyes again. . . . Soon he had the feeling that Charrington had turned and was looking at him. It was an uncomfortable feeling. Defensively he kept his eyes tight shut. At last he heard the sound of a door opening—and saw the skipper passing through the galley towards the forward cabin. . . . A funny way to rouse a crew, he thought, puzzled but still more sleepy.

For at least a couple of minutes longer there was silence. Then suddenly Charrington's voice broke out loud and hard:

"On deck, everybody! Up anchor in five minutes."

The crew below, dressing silently while they woke up, heard him moving about over their heads.

They came on deck into a dark night with black clouds splashed like ink stains on a gray blotting-paper sky. There were no stars. Only a few street lamps were burning in the town. In the harbor was the cluster of yachts' riding lights swaying drunkenly, and the steady red beacon close to windward at the end of the mole. The four men shivered. An impatient wind hustled them while they stood awkward and idle in its way. Last night's mood was inconceivable.

"Toby, Jack," Charrington called. "Get the anchor in when I tell you. You manage the slack hand over hand. When the chain's up and down, sing out. Then use the winch. . . . Marcus, stand by to break out the roller jib. . . . Boyd, I'll need you in the cockpit. Right. Up anchor!"

The rattle of the chain began. The yacht creaked and stirred, moving up on her anchor as on the starting line of a race.

"Just coming out, I think—" from Toby, breathlessly.

"Marcus, jib! Sheet it home. Make fast to that cleat," Charrington's voice was hard and sharp as a dog barking.

The yacht began to move down wind, slowly at first but rapidly gaining speed, the smooth water rustling from her bows with a noise like dry leaves. Charrington brought her round.

"Take her, Boyd. Hold her as she is."

"Up mainsail! Jack, that's your halliard. Toby, here you are. Heave—oh, Heave—oh!"

Charrington gave the orders but from the start he had done everything himself.

Almost simultaneously with the setting of the mainsail the yacht swept clear of the sheltering mole and charged into the crowd of waves. She plunged and leaped among them, throwing her crew off balance, forcing them to hold on. The noise had changed from a rustle to that of banging doors.

"Ready about. Lee-oh! Jib sheet, Marcus. Jump to it!"

The sails flapped angrily. Then the yacht leaned her shoulder on the water and began to surge ahead. The sense of noise and struggle and speed increased. The skipper seemed everywhere at once, at the tiller or forward, guiding his crew's hands, instructing them, driving them with his tongue.

The men did their small duties with breathless over-energy. The yacht settled down upon her course. . . . And then a black squall rushed upon them from the night with the force of a fire hose.

"I'll take her. Go and get yourselves properly dressed," Charrington shouted at them through the wind.

They hurried down the companionway, and struggled into their oilskins, losing their balance, grabbing for support, for the yacht was wild with movement. Toby, Jack and Boyd scrambled on deck again. Marcus was about to follow but at that moment and

without warning he felt himself gripped by nausea. For a second
or two he fought to control himself, and then utterly and shame-
lessly he surrendered.

When it was over at last he joined the others on deck as casually
as possible. They were all in the cockpit, with Charrington at the
tiller and the log line trailing astern. The squall was over and
patches of stars had appeared here and there about the sky. But to
Colonel Harding the world still seemed hostile and undisciplined.
He looked at the dark line of the land to starboard and the flashing
lighthouse on the headland which they were leaving astern.

"Lucky to start with a breeze like this," Charrington said. "Can't
waste it. We'll get the staysail and mizzen on her."

There followed ten minutes of activity, part expert, part clumsily amateur. When the sails were hoisted and trimmed Charrington took his hand off the tiller for a moment.

"Perfectly balanced—and doing a good five knots. We deserve
breakfast. Who volunteers?"

"I can't sail so I'll cook," Toby said briefly and climbed out of
the cockpit towards the hatch.

They talked in the cockpit. The hour before dawn is not a time
for conversation. Marcus was weighing the attractiveness of a cup
of coffee against the airlessness below, the smell of oilskins and
now no doubt of cooking fumes besides. He could not risk making
a fool of himself again.

Toby's voice rose up above the straining, creaking noises of
the yacht and surging sigh of water, "Come and get it!"

"Go and eat," Charrington said. "She would sail herself, but
near land and with fishermen about I'd better watch her."

"I suppose—" Yeoman began and stopped.

"What, Jack?"

"I suppose you wouldn't let me take her."

"But of course. Thank you. We'll leave you to it."

"I'll stay and help Yeoman," Marcus said.

Charrington was already on his feet, swaying to the movements
of the yacht. He turned upon Harding with twinkling eyes, then
said, "That's bloody good of you, Marcus. Come on, Boyd. We're
the only greedy ones."

When the others came on deck again after their breakfast, dawn
was breaking with a searchlight dazzle. Only a few untidy clouds

still hung about like rags left behind after polishing the sky. One of these near the horizon was squeezing out rain. The sea grew more and more rich in color, the white crests adding their contrast yet scarcely affecting the yacht which rode steady and confident.

The sun climbed up and took the wet sparkle out of the sky, solidifying it. The land, a mile or two to starboard, was no longer a mere silhouette but clear as a neatly painted picture—shore and fields with rocky manly moors above. They were approaching a headland where a lighthouse stood, definite as an exclamation mark.

It was Toby who, in his own mind, gave it this comparison while he sat with the others in the box-like cockpit. As they approached the lighthouse, keeping as close as they dared to swing round it to the westward, he wondered why this white pillar should impress his thoughts so much. Then it occurred to him that it marked the last land he was likely to see until Bermuda. He looked at Charrington, then once more at the land. . . . As they swept close to Start Point, bearing away, he saw the waves charging the rocks and leaping upwards in a furious column of spray.

"A penny for them," Charrington said.

"What?"

"For your thoughts, Toby."

"Nothing. Damn silly."

"But what?"

"Oh well—I've started enjoying being on the sea. But over there it seems to be fighting the land to the death. Whose side are we on?"

"The land's," Charrington answered at once. "Our boat is a bit of the land. We'll be fighting the sea as an enemy till we reach the other side. It will be after our bones every hour whatever its mood seems to be. Don't let it bluff you."

"We'd better arrange some details," he said some minutes later. "Watches. Most convenient to divide up as you're sleeping—Marcus and Boyd, starboard watch; Toby and Jack, port watch. I'll keep myself free as navigator and skipper."

"You'll have to explain, Richard," Marcus said. "You seem to forget most of us are entirely new to this business."

"No, I don't, Marcus. But you're all far better than I could have hoped. However, about these watches. We'll have four-hour spells, I think. Midnight to four A.M., four to eight, eight to noon, noon to four P.M.: then the two dog watches to change things round—four to six and six to eight: then four hours again—eight till midnight and so on."

"Who is on watch now?" Boyd asked.

"What's the time? Five to twelve. Let's say Boyd and Marcus stand watch from noon. Meanwhile—it's not often we'll be all together and awake, you know—are there any points that concern us as a whole?"

Yeoman looked as if he had an important question on his mind.

"Yes, Jack?" Charrington asked.

Yeoman swallowed. "Well, Skipper, if it's not impertinent, could we know the theory of the voyage. I mean, of course you don't just draw a straight line from here to Bermuda—there's the curvature of the Earth and the winds and currents. I've read what I could and realized it's complicated. But I wondered if you could explain quite simply the course we're going to steer."

Charrington looked at him and nodded. "Glad you're interested. Briefly it's like this. In these latitudes the prevailing winds are from the west. One can get across but it's the hell of a flog. But if you go south and much further in distance as opposed to time you can swing like a man on a trapeze—the Portuguese Trades to Madeira, then the real Northeast Trades across the waist of the Atlantic. Then all we have to do is find Bermuda."

"I was wondering if we could see a chart," Yeoman said diffidently.

"Of course. I'll bring one up—or into the saloon. Only trouble is, there's several charts involved and not much space to lay them out."

"I—I saw into your cabin when the door was open," Yeoman said. "You've got a wonderful chart table there—"

He stopped, dropping his eyes from Charrington's

"There's a minute to noon—before we all break up," Charrington said. "Jack has reminded me of something I must tell you. This is the first time I've had a crew aboard *Heather Mary*. I won't burden you with standing orders. But the Skipper's cabin is out of bounds to the crew."

He spoke vigorously but telegraphically, without expression.

"I hope you don't feel I'm exceeding the bargain," Charrington said to Boyd when the others had gone below. He was facing the weather and the driving spray as indifferently as a figurehead, but his hands upon the tiller moved continually with the action of a rough caress.

Boyd, sitting hunched in the cockpit with his back to the wind, raised his eyes and looked at him enquiringly but did not speak. He had been pondering Charrington's order about his cabin.

"You told me you needed a rest cure," Charrington went on. "I can believe it. That professorship plus technical papers and advice to the production people. . . . A scientist can't shut himself away from the world these days. He has to be a man of business, even a politician too—"

Boyd continued to watch him with mildly interested eyes.

"It's very kind of you to be concerned about me," he said in his quiet voice, scarcely audible above the wind. "But you needn't, you know. I'm doing what I wanted to do."

"Good. I was afraid I might be overworking you."

"No, no. It's only my brain that I'm supposed to be resting. It will be interesting to discover if my muscles still work."

"You were an athlete? I thought so," Charrington said.

"I used to run."

"What did you run for?" Charrington asked.

"You mean for what purpose?"

"I mean for what team or club."

"As an undergraduate I was a three miler. Then I joined one or two cross-country clubs in the North. But I never won anything."

"How was that?"

Boyd's light blue eyes sparkled for a moment with the light of laughter—it was more than of a smile—although the rest of his face remained still and thoughtful.

"I seem to lack the competitive spirit." he said. "I just like jogging along at my own speed."

"So do I. That's why we aren't going to buffet straight across the Atlantic but jog along round the old Trade Wind route. Now we're clear of Start Point I'm going to run her off—bring the wind aft. That will make the steering a trifle more difficult, but you might take her none the less."

"It can still only be a question of dynamics," Boyd said.

"Try it," Charrington smiled. "There you are, Southwest by South."

They changed places. Lightly as Charrington seemed to have done, Boyd put his hands upon the tiller.

It pulled away from him and the yacht went gaily racing up into the wind. He pulled it towards him—*Heather Mary* rocked and leaped irresponsibly to leeward, jumping from wave to wave, splashing the blue water into blossom trees of foam. Boyd struggled with her, dogged and silent, his eyes glued upon the compass card which was swinging through forty-five degrees. Charrington sat back, filling his pipe and looking amused.

"Until now," Boyd said at last, "it has appeared to me pure foolishness to call a boat 'she' instead of 'it.' But—but this yacht of yours is not as inanimate as it ought to be. She—yes she—appears to have a will of her own."

He turned his eyes to Charrington.

Charrington held them. Then suddenly and enthusiastically he exclaimed, 'My God, you're near the truth. Seamanship is more than half human understanding. But ships, like women, respect strength. I don't care how you do it, but keep her on the course I give you."

Marcus Harding had spent this while sitting on the bunk in his cabin—since it was day time this was now a settee in the saloon—in a mood between annoyance and anxiety. He was annoyed with himself for being seasick below and not much help on deck, for temporarily losing the sense of humor which nobody could say he lacked and for making excuses which were not strictly honest. But there was another side to it as well. He was annoyed with Richard for hustling him and not giving him a fair chance.

He stared straight in front of him, feeling discouraged. At his knees the swivel table swung slightly and continually. Opposite to him—about five feet away—Toby sat with an open book in front of him, tilting slowly forward and back as if in a rocking chair. Above, the lamp swung like an irregular pendulum. From the galley seven feet away came an occasional clatter of crockery and the smell of food. Clumsy old Jack Yeoman was cooking lunch. He said it was the first time he had ever tried to cook. How spoiled the lower classes were by their womenfolk.

Boyd came down the companionway and into the saloon.

"Your turn, Colonel. I've done mine. The Skipper is waiting to initiate you."

Marcus went unhappily on deck. He settled in the cockpit beside Charrington and for five minutes struggled in silence with the lively yacht.

Then Charrington said, "You're a horseman, aren't you?"

"Yes."

"Have you noticed how similar steering a yacht is to riding a horse?"

"I can't say—"

"I'm sure you have. A clumsy rider tries to use the reins like handle bars. A good man treats them as a means of communication —a nerve cord. He thinks for the horse or guides it by impulses rather than tugs. And he doesn't send the beast straight through every obstacle. He weaves through them. Waves are like obstacles on land."

After a while Marcus said, "I see what you mean but it's damned difficult."

"Running before the wind always is. But we're unlikely to do much of that before we reach the Trades, by which time you'll be a real sailor."

"Do you honestly think so?"

"I know it. You're not a fool and you've got hands at the end of your arms. Look here, there's something I want to talk to you about."

"Yes?"

"Food and water for a passage of this sort make quite a problem. One can't estimate within several weeks how long it will take. On the other hand space is limited so you can't carry much of a margin. I'm sure I've got enough but I've been so busy lately that I've forgotten just what we have got and where it's stowed. Will you take over the commissariat?"

"Delighted. That's something I have got experience of."

Marcus sat thinking, stroking his mustache with his left hand.

"I'll make a complete list and work out a ration based on the longest anticipated time—what, three months?"

"I leave it to you. But I don't think you'll have to ration us severely. I calculated on five appetites and you don't seem to have brought yours with you."

Marcus burst out laughing. "Richard, you are a leg-pulling old devil—"

"Just one other thing," Charrington went on. "There ought to be an official second-in-command. You are the obvious man. I'll tell the others."

Marcus sat silent, happy at last. What a leader Richard was! He would back him up. And in spite of his competence he needed backing up. Meg had been right. He was not hard through and through. The way he had delayed calling them, for instance— standing looking at each of them as they lay asleep—extraordinary. It was almost pathetic, too, that he still worshiped Heather so much that he could not bear anybody else even entering the cabin he had shared with her.

CHAPTER 6

YEOMAN put the food in front of Charrington, Toby and Boyd and then sat down himself. He tasted a couple of spoonfuls, and shook his head.

"It's not good," he said sadly.

The others were silent.

"It's what I was saying to the Colonel," Yeoman went on. "I've had no experience of cooking. My dear wife spoiled me. And my girl's just as bad."

He looked at his plate, dreamily stirring the stew with his spoon. "Sunday. It would have been a slap up dinner if I'd been home. Me being away I don't suppose Tilly bothered with more than a cup of tea and bit of toast. But you ought to see what she can do when there's company. . . . I wish she could have come along to look after us."

"So do I, Jack," Charrington said. "But I'm afraid we'll have to manage without the ladies for quite a long time. . . . Now let's chuck this stuff away and get out the goose. . . . Don't be discouraged about your cooking, though. There are plenty of other jobs on board a yacht and I'll have to give you each a special duty. What are you particularly good at?"

"Well I don't know," Yeoman said.

"You've had experience maintaining yachts, haven't you?"

"Well, in a way—" Jack began doubtfully.

"How would you like to take on bosun, look after the sails and cordage? Knots and lashings. You can manage that."

Yeoman's face lit up. "Knots and lashings are just about my favorite hobby. Is there anything you want doing at once?"

"Not much until the chafing starts. But you can begin by lashing down the anchor."

"Certainly, Skipper. I'll attend to it directly I've washed up."

"I'll help you with the washing up," Boyd said.

He stood at the end of the saloon, took the plates as Yeoman passed them through to him from the galley, dried them and put them carefully away in their locker.

Some two hours later, when Yeoman had made the anchor so secure that nothing less than an axe could have freed it, he took his turn at the helm for the second hour of the first dog watch. The wind had dropped to a gentle breeze. The waves had become smooth as rumpled velvet, silvered by the low sun. *Heather Mary* sighed and shook her head as she went wearily through them. England was still visible to starboard, a dim bluish outline. The sea horizon was dotted here and there by the smoke of steamers, but they did not appear likely to pass close. Jack let his mind wander to his home and his daughter. He wouldn't mind betting that Tilly was giving the old place a real spit and polish now he was safely out of the way. Women were practical and knew men were not whatever age they might be. He remembered his mother saying to him as a kid, "You run along, Jackie, and play with your boats. I'm busy." Weren't they still kids?—playing with boats, playing with things they didn't understand, and night coming on. But that was romance, he supposed.

He yawned, he could do with forty winks like the others were having.

Suddenly from below him, clear and loud and friendly, he heard a woman say, "*Good* night, children."

He started violently. Before he had collected his wits a man's voice announced, "This is the B. B. C. Home Service. Here is the shipping forecast. . . ."

So there was a radio aboard, in the skipper's cabin by the sound. Such a little ship and so much one didn't know about her yet. He must listen. He tried to, but became puzzled by the areas—Sole, Fastnet, Dogger, Finisterre—and was always behind in attention when the expected weather was announced. It was going to blow in some parts and in others it was going to rain with bright intervals—the usual sort of thing but so much more important now. Pity he had not followed it exactly.

Charrington came on deck with a half-full bottle of gin in his hand. Yeoman smiled. He could do with a spot.

Charrington went to the compass, tilted it within the binnacle and studied it closely. Yeoman became nervous, wondering if he had got off the course. He'd rather forgotten about that.

"Damned bubble," Charrington said under his breath. He put down the bottle, took a screw driver from his pocket and began working on the compass.

While he was doing this Boyd and Marcus came on deck.

"Gin. Good show," Marcus said.

"Damned air bubble in the compass fluid," Charrington muttered. "Might upset the card. Got to fill up with spirit." He removed the metal cap and tilted the bottle over the opening.

Marcus looked shocked.

Charrington screwed the cap into place again, tilted the compass on its gimbals and studied it closely. Then he stood up, recorked the bottle and threw it over the side.

They watched it drift away astern, lurching over the waves.

Boyd said quietly, "Somebody's lucky."

"What's that?" Charrington asked.

"I was always told by my nurse that when you pick up a bottle on the shore there's probably a message in it. But the fellow who finds this one will get three fingers of gin."

"It was no use to us. We don't drink at sea—except on special occasions. Then we'll open a new one."

"What, if I may ask, constitutes a special occasion?" Boyd asked.

"You will recognize it when you meet it," Charrington said. "Six o'clock. Who's taking the next trick?"

"We've tossed up. It's Boyd."

"Good." Charrington, standing on the deck, turned slowly in a complete circle, studying the sea and the horizon. Then he raised his eyes to the sails and looked at them for a full minute. He went forward and made some adjustments to the sheets and halliards. Those watching did not understand what he did but Yeoman at the helm felt the yacht sailing more contentedly, better balanced.

Charrington came back to the companionway.

"If you're doubtful about anything at all, thump on the deck and I'll come up," he said, and went below.

Boyd took over the helm and Yeoman went to examine the lashings of the anchor.

Marcus finished a cigarette in the cockpit and then said briskly, "I must go and start my duty listing the stores."

"Tomorrow will do for that. Why not prepare supper. Otherwise Jack Yeoman will do it—and the cold goose is finished."

"Goose. How much did he waste before that? I emptied the swill bucket—half full of M. and V.," Marcus said. "All right, I'll take the hint."

When he had gone, Boyd chuckled to himself. He had attempted an innocent deception and had failed. There could be no secrets on a yacht.

At the end of the hour Marcus came up and said, "Supper's ready. I've snatched mine."

"Good?" Boyd asked.

"I funked the issue. Tinned ham. And there's still plenty of bread. What's the course?"

"West-south-west. She steers it without you having to bother much. But I doubt if we'll get through the night without rain."

The rain came quickly. Twenty minutes later Marcus shouted for his oilskins. Boyd took them up and returned at once to the saloon where they were smoking and talking over the cup of tea which had followed their meal.

"How long? Nine years," Charrington was saying. "I saw her at Hamble and fell in love with her at first sight. But I couldn't afford her."

"What happened?" Toby asked.

"My wife gave her to me. What are you clicking your tongue about, Jack?"

"I was thinking that was just like Miss Heather," Yeoman answered. "She was always impulsive with her money."

"You were giving her good advice even then, were you? Never mind. That was the best investment Mary ever made. The lead ballast alone is now worth more than she paid for her."

It was hard to tell from Charrington's expression if he were amused or annoyed.

"Have you sailed in her every year?" Toby asked.

"Yes—except for the war, of course. I spent one cruising season in a gunboat and four behind barbed wire."

There was a pause, then Boyd said, "Tell me if you will—after being imprisoned so long didn't you want to be somewhere freer, less constricting than on a yacht?"

"Good God, what is freer or less constricting than being able to sail to anywhere you damn well please, answerable to no man? The only thing that kept me sane those four years was planning cruises and imagining us doing them."

Each of his hearers noticed the word "us." Charrington lapsed into silence, drawing strongly at his pipe so that the small saloon was blue with smoke.

Toby said, "You planned, and did, a good many escapes too, didn't you?"

"One couldn't just sit there," Charrington said.

Marcus Harding's voice broke in upon them. "Richard, come on deck please." His tone was unemotional, a little too calm.

Charrington was out of the saloon and up the companionway in a moment. The others followed.

It was twilight. The rain squall was still striking them, puckering the smooth surface of the swell, surrounding them with a curtain of gray threads.

From ahead and slightly to one side an enormous ship was approaching. It was hard to judge her distance but she was coming at what seemed the speed of a train, ploughing up a bow wave as high as the yacht.

"Keep her as she is, Marcus," Charrington said.

Marcus stood by the tiller as if he were on parade.

The liner was converging upon the yacht's course at an obtuse angle and very fast. As she approached they could hear the noise she made cutting through the water. It was the noise, magnified in proportion, of a knife slashing through calico.

Then they all realized that the liner would pass ahead. She was in fact over fifty yards away when she crossed their bows. But from that distance she looked immense—long row upon row of lighted portholes, superstructures, funnels, with more lights above. And not a human being visible anywhere. The most alarming effect was that this huge, rapidly moving mass was blind as a comet.

"Sorry, Richard. I should not have called you up," Marcus said.

"Don't be an ass, of course you should. You can't judge angles and relative speeds without experience. We don't want to pass any nearer than that. Hold on!"

The wash of the liner struck them and for a moment *Heather Mary* tossed about like an empty bottle.

"The reason why a skipper doesn't stand watches is so he can be called up for anything at any moment," Charrington said. "You must not feel that you have to take any decision yourselves. . . . O. K., Marcus? Can you fix the navigation lights, Boyd?"

When they were all below again, finishing their tea, Yeoman asked, "Do you think they saw us? Nobody seemed to be about."

"It's a nasty evening and dinner time. They might have seen us from the bridge about as soon as we saw them," Charrington answered.

"But steam has to give way to sail."

"You can't alter the speed and direction of forty thousand tons all in a moment."

"Then they had no business to be blinding along at that rate in thick weather," Yeoman said angrily. He had been the last on deck and until now had shown no reaction at all. "They might run someone down."

"They have a schedule to keep. Also they no doubt have radar. But I don't suppose it would pick up a small wooden craft like this—eh, Boyd?"

"No," Boyd said.

Charrington scraped out his pipe bowl into an empty cigarette tin and immediately began to fill it again.

He said. "The ocean is large. Once we are out of the Channel we'll be off the shipping lanes. Steam and sail don't go the same way. . . . You're very silent, Toby. What's on your mind?"

Toby gave an embarrassed laugh. "Only a silly thought."

"What is it?"

"Well, you know how you remember things from ages ago— never anything important but just some isolated incident?"

"Yes."

"When I was extremely small I used to go to America and back fairly often because my father worked there. I was about seven. We'd just left—I can't remember which English port. We were well out to sea. And we passed a toy yacht—damn nearly ran her down. I was the only person who noticed her at first. She was a lovely little thing, fighting with waves which were huge for her. I ran shouting for the Captain to stop and pick her up. But of course people only smiled. I suppose we were keeping to a schedule. But I've always wondered what happened to her—"

Yeoman interrupted him, breaking in with extraordinary excitement. "I'm sure she'd be all right. If they're well made and don't have an exaggerated sail plan a model will ride anything. Why I— Look here, Skipper, I'm glad of a chance to tell you this before everyone. I said I'd had sailing experience. I've sailed all my life— but I've never been on board a yacht. It's all been with models like the one you've just heard about. That's all I could afford. So I deceived you and I'm sorry but it was only because I was so keen to come. You can put me ashore if you like—but if you don't I'll do my very best to make up for it, I really will."

All this poured out in a stream while Yeoman sat looking miserably into his empty teacup.

Charrington put a hand on his shoulder. "My dear Jack, you didn't deceive me."

"You knew?"

"One doesn't choose a crew for a trip like this without making certain enquiries. I know more about you all than you think. But don't be worried. I wouldn't exchange a man of you for the best yachtsman in England. You are exactly the crew I wanted."

CHAPTER 7

"TO be alone at night and responsible for the lives of others—that's not an experience many people have."

Jack Yeoman had been alone on deck for an hour since he had relieved Toby at ten o'clock. He had settled himself in the cockpit with the tiller in the crook of his arm. The yacht had ambled along over the swell—there were no more squalls—and already he felt himself sufficiently competent not to be worried except about the lights of other shipping. Through these spots of light, which might have been any distance away, he guided *Heather Mary*. He had almost imagined that the tiller was the arm of a girl he was conducting across a dangerous moor. . . .

He had thought of Miss Heather. It was she who had used that phrase to him a fortnight after the death of his wife when he still brooded continually and could not rouse himself to take interest in the office or even his war work as Senior Warden of which he had formerly been so proud. How miserably, angrily helpless he had felt when the doctor told him that the red things in Norah's blood were turning white, that they knew what the disease was but could not cure it. And when she had gone how utterly lonely he had been, Tilly away in Devonshire with her evacuated school and the house eerily quiet. . . . Then Miss Heather had appeared like a good fairy. In her impulsive, gentle way she had taken charge of him and healed his spirit with her magic. Afterwards he had tried to express his gratitude to her in letters. He had not done it adequately, of course, but to tell the truth he had been surprised by the poetry he had discovered in himself.

The yacht was heading towards two great anvil shaped clouds. He remembered that at sunset they had been almost the same shape but soft and pink as the cushions in the parlor. Now they were black and hard as iron against a slate-gray sky. The sea was dark—he couldn't say what color. The sky was full of stars. And he, Jack Yeoman, was alone steering a yacht at night.

Staring in front of him, he saw the light go on below and Charrington's head rise through the suddenly illuminated square of the opened hatch. His features looked strange with their shadows thrown upwards.

Charrington came and sat down companionably by the tiller. For some time he smoked in silence, then he said, "Jack, I'm damned glad to have you on board. I've heard so much about you."

"From Miss Heather? Skipper, there's so much to tell you. . . ."

Charrington waited but Yeoman could say no more. He wanted to show his gratitude to Miss Heather by helping in every way in his power the proud and lonely man whom she had left behind. But Colonel Harding had warned him against talking to the Skipper about his wife. . . .

At midnight Boyd came up to take the helm. They greeted him in silence, and for a few minutes sat quietly together in the cockpit while the yacht moved with a silk-rustling sound over the dark water. Then Charrington and Yeoman went below, leaving Boyd alone with the tiller under his arm—with the sound and the association to bring Heather's story back into his mind.

The honeymoon was to be spent in a cruise round the west coast of Ireland and so to Southhampton Water where Charrington's work was and their home would be. Therefore, on the day after her marriage, Heather sailed for the first time into what she had looked upon as the outermost zone. As a baby she had explored the dunes, as a child the sheltered sandy beaches and the little islands, as a girl in her teens the sea—fishing mackerel, going on picnics or visit to the neighbors. Now she was sailing beyond the Hebrides, beyond even the outposts of the land which contained Amulree. Everything she had known was dropping down below the horizon.

In her mood of romantic excitement she was thrilled by this. Everything she had known would rise again above the horizon still lovelier and happier when they sailed back again. She wanted to share this idea with her husband, who sat at the tiller with his back to the drowning land. They were alone as newly married people rarely are. (This, too, delighted Heather.) It was a scene for perfect confidence.

When she had described what she felt, he looked at her indulgently and answered that there were other beautiful places besides Amulree and other seas than those which lapped her islands. The world was theirs. They were bound to no single part of it.

The sunset while they were speaking was hanging in front of them like a molten rainbow, and the land astern was every now and then coming up faintly to wave good-by. But he would not allow her to stay and watch it. He hove-to the yacht, put his strong arm around her slim body and took her below.

Early next morning she came on deck and looked eastward. But there was no land to be seen.

For some time she was uncertain whether she was drowning in overpowering happiness or in something entirely different which justified the stab of terror which now and then she felt. Richard and she visited a dozen harbors on the west coast of Ireland. Heather remembered nothing of any of them. She only remembered sitting throughout the evenings under the oil lamp in the tiny saloon, hoping that somebody from the little town they had visited for shopping during the day would row out and call on them before bedtime.

But she loved Richard. He was—as she had known from the first moment of meeting him—her man. He dominated her. That was entirely right. Only, after the freedom she had scarcely appreciated, it was difficult to adjust herself to the state of being dominated.

Although she was a competent sailor she was not allowed to steer except under his close supervision. If she made any technical suggestion he answered kindly enough but as a man talks to a child. When once she persisted he became impatient. So she left the whole management of the yacht to him and did what she was told, silently and anxiously. She longed to please and was used to being praised.

She tried to talk interestingly. Of course she talked of Amulree, for that was the most interesting subject she knew. Again he answered kindly but she was sensitive enough to realize at once that he did not want her even to think of Amulree or of anything connected with it. Alone among the people she knew, he called her by her second name, Mary. He never called her Heather. She began to understand why.

He was blindly jealous. The realization of this was not at first wholly displeasing. When he insisted on accompanying her, at great inconvenience to himself, on some trivial errand in a tiny fishing village, she was amused and flattered. Similar instances were common. Still determined to be happy, she decided that such foibles were lovable. It was a sign that Richard worshiped her.

But soon she realized that she was not the only subject of his jealousy. He was also jealous of the yacht, *Helen,* which he had himself designed. That was why she, Heather, was not allowed to take any responsible part in sailing her.

So, instead of the free and open companionship she had envisaged, their days were spent in order and obedience, and—on her part—in anxiously rehearsed conversation. For when she remained silent he insisted on knowing what she was thinking. And after each day there came the night and the enclosing walls of the cabin and the callous murmur of water. In spite of herself she began to dread the sunset.

Still she was hopeful and determined. When the cruise—the honeymoon—was over she would reach his house and make it into a home. There she would have her own sphere. She would find new roots.

It was a red brick building in a row of others, with a tiny, tidy garden protected from the road by a privet hedge. Richard said he liked it because it was near the sea. But the sea was a ship yard, with mud at low tide; and you could not even see it from the house because of the other houses. The furniture was nothing in particular. Richard said that sort of thing did not matter when you were ashore. The house though small had plenty of labor-saving gadgets. He was not interested in the "trivialities" of chintzes, pictures, wallpapers and flower vases.

Quite soon he told her they were going to sea again—to try out a new yacht. Her courage failed her for a moment. In his enthusiasm he quipped her for telling him at their first meeting that she loved the sea. Of course she loved it, caressing the shore at Amulree, looked at from the land. But the gray untidy thing on which Richard liked to sail, with scarcely a glimpse of the shore, was different altogether. It was impossible to explain that sort of thing to him.

Again, with nobody else near them, she experienced the pain and silly worry of a triangular existence. Richard loved her, masterfully. He also loved the yacht. He was jealous of both of them.

Heather could do nothing to the yacht. If the yacht behaved badly in rough weather and upset his wife, he was furious.

When they returned, Heather found a letter from Meg Lowrey, suggesting a visit. She was delighted. A third, real person would relieve the tension. She was not at all disturbed although she knew Meg admired Richard enormously and might even have married him if he had asked her.

Meg spent an observant week with them—then criticized Heather severely. (She had always criticized her since they were children together.) Now she told her that she was driving Richard crazy by her obstinacy.

Heather did not try to defend herself. She never had, although criticisms had rarely changed her own opinions. But longing for comfort and advice she described some of her difficulties. Meg cut her short. Stuff and nonsense! She had seen them together and it was plain as the nose on your face how much Richard adored her. However many people were about he never took his eyes off her. Richard was perfectly charming—everybody said so. Meg herself was going to become engaged to a soldier named Marcus Harding who had come up to Salen for the fishing, and she gave Heather a lecture on the perfect marriage. Heather listened, thinking her own thoughts.

One evening during the first summer after their marriage Richard came home in a state of unusual excitement. He had seen the perfect yacht. Walking up and down the room, unable to sit down, he described her in detail. She was called *Guillimot*. She was a yawl of twenty-two tons, with an overall length of fifty feet and a draught of just over six. She was built of oak and teak, had nine and a half tons of outside lead ballast—and so on with a host of technical details. But the thing which had most struck him, Richard said, was that she was a racing yacht with the strength of an ocean cruiser. She had the delicate lines of a six-meter but was as strong as any vessel he had ever surveyed, and possessed storage space for food and water enough to carry one half round the world. She was for sale as a bargain—because she had no auxiliary engine to drive her, only a little thing that charged the light batteries. The damn shame was that he could not afford her even at that knock down price.

Heather listened, pleased by her husband's enthusiasm. Next

day she went to see the yacht. *Guillimot* was a most unsuitable name for the tall, white graceful creature, poised on the blue water. Heather, who loved beauty, fell in love with her, just as her husband had done. And while she looked at the yacht an idea came into her head. She could not afford the purchase price—without digging deep into the capital which belonged to Amulree. Yet she would buy the yacht. She would change the name to *Heather Mary* and give her to Richard. That would be the end of his tiresome dualism. The yacht he loved would be identified with the wife he loved.

When Heather finally made up her mind nothing could divert her. Very soon afterwards, Richard was the owner of *Heather Mary*.

They went on a trial cruise together. The yacht behaved perfectly but the human relationship was not a success. The absurd jealousy, although subdued, occasionally came out in an enigmatic and more bitter form. Charrington, as the Skipper of *Heather Mary*, was less sure of his authority over his wife, and in that state he could be most imperiously cruel.

Hurt almost to breaking point but still determined to succeed in her marriage, Heather began to work upon another plan.

Next summer—it was 1939—she persuaded Richard to make a cruise to Amulree. They had not been back there during the three years of their marriage. She had been homesick. But Richard had made it evident that he did not want to go to Amulree; and she, unselfishly as she believed, had given in. Now she blamed herself for not insisting. If she could teach him to know and to love the place as she did—and surely she could do that—it would be the perfect bond. They would have that safe and inexhaustible subject of conversation. Besides, since her marriage, her father had made over the estate to her; so there was a material reason why Richard should be interested.

He agreed to the cruise. In *Heather Mary*, the perfect yacht, they rounded Land's End, sailed northwards through the Irish sea, and so past Islay, Mull, Tiree and Coll. They were both excited and gay. Charrington was pleased by the swift, unchecked passage; and for once Heather wholeheartedly approved that they should put in nowhere, even for a night. Never since they were married had they been so unconstrained.

For a whole day Heather sat in the bow waiting for her own islands to appear above the horizon. . . . It happened at last as she had always imagined it. There was just sufficient breeze to fill the sails and make the water chatter at the bow, but not enough to break the rippled surface which glowed with all the shot-silk colors of a cloudless sunset. And from this—dim at first, then solid as a dream come true—her islands and the hills of Amulree came up and floated on the water.

When the leisurely northern night closed in on them, Charrington hove-to the yacht and went below to prepare one of his special dinners. How charming and interesting he could be. That was what everybody said of him. Tonight Heather scarcely remembered, and then only as a contrast, how hard and egocentric he generally was when they were alone together. Even a glimpse of Amulree had begun to work a cure.

They sailed in next morning. A dozen telescopes had spotted them, half a dozen boats escorted them to harbor and there was a crowd of people waiting on the shore. Even in the flood of greetings Heather noticed that Richard was behaving in the most simple, likable and cordial way that anybody could desire. She was utterly happy.

During the first two days of the visit she remained, almost deliriously, in the same mood. Every waking moment was spent with her parents or in visits to the crofters, seeing the new babies, recognizing the old animals, revisiting favorite places. She felt herself revived, felt the old strength and courage. Richard went out with a gun or a rifle and she saw little of him.

On the second night, when she went up to her room—the room which had been hers all her life—she threw the window wide and stood looking out through the opal moonlight, across the dark folds of the dunes and the silver sea to the black silhouettes of the islands with the ghost of sunset hanging beyond them like a curtain lighted dimly from behind. Nearer at hand, to the left, was the outline of the gardener's croft with a candle burning in a window. From the right, where the fir wood lay black, came the witch-wild cry of an owl, a prick of fear in the gentle magic of the night.

The soft and lazy air was heavy with memories of the day— the grass cut during the morning, the seaweed stirred by the full

moon tide, the fir tree felled, the ground dug by the gardener. . . .
Heather knelt down and leaned her breast against the window
sill, breathing all this in and in until it began to hurt.

It hurt because she wanted to share it. It was too beautiful for
one person alone.

She heard Richard come through the door, walk across the
room and stop behind her. . . . She waited.

He put his hands under her elbows, lifted her up and turned her
round. She looked eagerly into his face . . . And her heart shrank
into a tight, hard ball.

He drew the curtains.

"Time for bed," he told her.

She remained for some moments with her back to the window.
But it was no longer her own room at Amulree. It was the room
in the suburban villa. She had a violent longing to run out of the
house into the night.

She stayed where she was and asked calmly, "Don't you like
being here?"

He answered with an aggressive joviality, "Not as much as you
do, obviously. Everybody treats you like a princess."

"Doesn't that please you?"

"Princess is the wrong word. They pet you and patronize you.
You are their mascot—and you adore it. You ought to have more
dignity."

"What do you mean?" she asked. She was in a thin nightdress
and felt as helpless as a little girl. He never took his eyes from
her.

"Today for instance," he said, "I had a damn good day. I killed
two stags. The old stalker grumbled because the second wasn't
the beast he had told me to shoot. Told me to shoot! I put him in
his place. That's what they need, these clansmen. They have been
spoiled by your charming but invalid father and, if I may say
so, by their toy princess. Come to bed."

She stared at him, shivering in her nightdress, her fists clenched,
her eyes cold and hard.

In the morning she saw clearly. She saw Richard projected
against Amulree. He was out of place as a pylon, and as un-
appreciative. She heard him talking to the people. It was they
with their soft voices and instinctive good manners who had the

dignity. And it was they who were her loyal and devoted friends.

In a mood of desperation she walked to Clach Alasdair, the point from which she had first seen him fighting the storm in the little yacht.

The sea was calm and no vessel was in sight. There was only a big white solan goose flying majestically up and down. Watching the bird, she tried to analyze why she had accepted Richard as her man. The method of his coming had caught her imagination. She had built a picture of him before they met, and the rest had confirmed it. She liked his walk, thrusting forward as if he were forcing his way through water. She was fascinated by his dark, deep-set eyes, and by his voice which made everything he said exciting. She admired a man who did exactly what he wanted and who accepted the challenge of the elements. Finally, the sullen and unexplained antagonism of the estate people had drawn her towards him.

Was her love built only on these elements? What did that matter—she had given it. . . . She compared it with her feelings for Amulree. It was impossible to analyze these, but if she should be banished for ever from Amulree she would not want to live, for no other country could take its place . . . For three years, without resting, blaming only her inexperience of life when she failed, she had struggled to preserve the Richard to whom she had given her love. It had been hard and she was tired. Bringing him back to the place where she had met him was the climax. At the result she felt no anger with him, but. . . .

The white bird closed its wings and fell like a stone into the sea.

Heather got up and began slowly to walk home. She had arrived at a realization, and this gave her a feeling of relief. She knew without question what was best to do. But instinct and experience told her it would not be simple to convince Richard of her reasoning. She could not bear the idea of a quarrel at Amulree. She decided to postpone the explanation until they sailed, but she dreaded the time between.

Fortune, in a twisted way, now seemed to favor her. The news of the outside world was bad. When the newspapers arrived next afternoon Richard said that they must return at once.

After her wedding only her parents and two or three of the estate people had seen her off. This time there was a crowd of men and women on the shore, with a piper among them. And while, with Richard, she sailed slowly out of the bay the notes of a Jacobean lament followed her across the water and echoed in her heart so that she could not have said when her ears ceased to hear them.

> *Better lo'ed ye canna' be.*
> *Will ye no come back again?*

Then, swallowing her tears, she resolutely set about the explanation with her husband.

It was a hard passage, stormy all the way. They put into no harbor and sailed fast, carrying as much canvas as *Heather Mary* would stand. But the struggle between personalities was harder still. Richard would not take her seriously at first. The toy princess was petulant at being taken away from her kingdom, but even a lieutenant in the R.N.V.R. had his duties.

Tense as a watch spring, Heather kept exactly to her argument. Whether or not a war were coming they must settle their own lives. They had both been in love, passionately and wholeheartedly, with ideals of their own imaginations. She took the blame for seeing him differently from what he was and for failing to live up to his ideal of her. But it was so. And, rather than destroy the dream, surely it was preferable to live where each preferred. He was only happy in his work at Southampton and in his cruises as Skipper of *Heather Mary*. She, the woman, had given her love to both the man and the yacht but only felt her true self at Amulree. So they must live apart.

Richard's anger came slowly as a thunderstorm—the feeling of heaviness, then a few flashes, then the tempest . . . He was ready to give her anything she asked. Had he not, solely to please her, taken his holiday at Amulree instead of in the Norwegian Fjords as he had planned? If she did not get what she wanted from their marriage it was her own fault for not asking it. But in any case they had vowed to love each other for better or worse. What was this suggestion about separating? Was that marriage before God or man? If she did not love him—then she loved someone else. Who was it? She would not tell him? He would discover for himself and settle with the man. But he would never let her go. Only death could part them.

He terrified her, shouting with such fury. It went on, like a succession of storms throughout most of the passage. All this time the yacht was driving southwards through half a gale, often with the tiller lashed while they sat in their own storm below. Oh, she was tired of it all!

When they rounded the Lizard the wind dropped to a breeze. Quiet from exhaustion they sailed up Channel, still with nothing arranged between them. They picked up their mooring and went ashore to their house, meaning to settle it there, after a rest.

On the mat in the hall was a telegram. Richard was ordered to report for duty. He changed into uniform while she packed his things.

She had already realized that her own life did not matter. She, with Richard and fifty million others, was caught up like iron dust by the same magnet.

The declaration of war came in Mr. Chamberlain's heartbroken voice out of the varnished box in the lonely characterless parlor.

For most of her local acquaintances it was like a starter's pistol. They were off at once on duties long ago prepared for. Many of the men had gone away. The women put on trousers and were self-assured and busy. But Heather did not know what to do. Richard had not allowed her to volunteer for A.R.P. or any of the "ridiculous" women's service. Her place was in the home, he said. So now she was unprepared for anything, living in an empty house which was certainly not a home. There was nothing to prevent her from returning to Amulree. But it seemed like running away. Surely there was something useful she could do.

Richard was stationed on the Norfolk coast. After a month he wrote and told her to join him. She hesitated—then decided that she had no right to think of herself while the war lasted. He was doing something useful and she believed that she might help him as a fellow combatant.

Until the next summer she lived in little comfortless hotels in the small ports where he was based. She shared a sitting room with other wives. None of them knew at any moment whether her husband was fighting a battle in the North Sea or drinking gin in the mess before coming on a night of shore leave. They used to sit and knit. Whenever the door opened they all looked up. Generally it was only another wife or a servant to collect the tea or coffee cups or to draw the blackout curtains. When it was a husband, he and the wife sat and talked, generally in whispers, before going out or to their room. Then the knitting needles began again.

When it was Richard . . . He had magnanimously forgotten their "quarrel." A hideous wallpaper, a cheap china washstand and an iron bedstead made up as good a cabin as any ashore. He only wanted to be alone with his wife.

Living in such strange surroundings, feeling impersonal, she lacked confidence to insist that she should do active war work. But more and more every day there grew in her the longing for Amulree. If only she could find a sufficient reason for going there, she would become a real person again.

Heather, when she reached this stage of her story—although she had not been telling it in these words—suddenly stopped and looked enquiringly at Boyd as he leaned beside her over the rail of the liner.

"Do you think Fate has a sense of humor?" she asked.

He did not answer. His imagination was fully occupied in discerning the pictures which her voice projected on the phosphorescent water which slipped by continually like an unwinding film. He waited for her to say something more.

"I believe it has a cruel, beastly sense of humor. I didn't use to, but I do now," she said.

He turned his head and looked at her.

She went on. "The thing I had been longing and praying for was a good reason for going to Amulree. I got it all right. My father died."

The water writhing up and then subsiding and flowing away with extinguishing color into the blackness astern made Boyd think of the impersonal finality of death. He moved, just touching Heather with his arm.

She described the Highland burial, the coffin on a farm cart and the piper playing a lament—the slow, high-pitched, wavering music.

There was a lot of solicitor's business to be attended to. In the absence of the junior partners on military service the senior clerk was sent to Amulree. He was a kind uncle-like man who had won her heart fifteen years ago when, on a visit to strange London, he had brought her a flower pot of white heather. With child-like frankness she had said that it was not proper heather, and he had answered that of course it was not because the only real heather grew at Amulree, the name of all the place names in his dusty files which had inspired him with a wish to visit it. Mountains and sea were the two things he dreamed of. She reminded him of this now and he went red with pleasure. They became great friends.

A fortnight later Heather's mother fell downstairs and broke her arm. She had been sturdily brave and competent since her husband's death, carrying on the tradition. Now she had done this stupid thing. The dear old lady was so disgusted with herself that she turned her face to the wall and died within a week.

Heather remained at Amulree for a month longer. Then—not only because Richard was beginning to write impatiently—she felt bound to return. The factor could manage very well without her. But she could not go back to the East Coast lodgings. She wrote to Meg for advice.

Meg answered her by return of post. Of course Heather ought to remain near her husband while she could. But there was no reason why she should sit and mope while he was away. There was work for girls of her education in the cypher department at the Foreign Office where she herself was in charge of the female personnel. Heather could share her flat in Hampstead and entertain Richard there whenever he had leave. Meg's husband was overseas and her children were in the country so there was plenty of room.

That is what Heather did. She found the work more exacting than she had expected, but it was a relief that the intimacy of Richard's visits was diluted by Meg's presence. Meg was one of the very few people—perhaps the only one—whose opinions influenced Richard. He tried to please her. More than once when he came on leave he brought a fellow officer, Patrick Canning, so that they made a square party. All Patrick's stories were of Richard's achievements.

Although the war was now fully joined this might have been almost a pleasant period. But Heather found it increasingly exhausting. This was not primarily due to the bombing, although that nagged at her nerves, nor to the long office hours which were more and more tiring as she was promoted to responsible work.

There were plenty of gunboat battles in the North Sea now, and Richard thrust himself into more than his share of them. His periods of leave were rare. But he came whenever he could, invariably unannounced; perhaps only for a few hours. And when he came he expected Heather to leave the office—which Meg could generally arrange—or to be waiting for him in the flat. He demanded a hero's welcome. He was always in a high state of excitement. He was even excited in his sleep. Sometimes he shouted orders. Once he seemed to fight a whole savage battle at her side. "Kill the swine! Drown them! Blow them to bits!" Heather had no love for her country's enemies but she felt that she was being mistaken for them. It was pitch dark, there was an air raid in progress, and bombs were dropping close at the time.

Once, on a Sunday, she went to tea with Jack Yeoman and his wife. When she was about to leave, a heavy raid started and they persuaded her to remain with them for the night. She returned early next morning and found that Richard had come and gone in her absence. Meg told her that he had been terribly upset. Heather wondered what he would write to her. But she got no letter. Instead she received a telegram which said he was missing, believed captured

Before it was officially confirmed that Richard was a prisoner, Patrick came up to London "to put her mind at rest." That was typically kind of him. He had been in the same action, "a nasty rough one—much too many E boats." Richard had led them into the attack and fought like a tiger. They had sunk one of the supply ships which the E boats were escorting and damaged the other. Good enough. "But it was one of those parties it's so difficult to get away from." Patrick had last seen Richard standing on the deck of his crippled gunboat before he himself had "run like a rabbit."

Later Heather learned that Patrick had been given a D.S.C. Richard had not. But she thought little about this. Her overwhelming feeling then, as at the moment she had first heard of his capture, was relief. The self-justifying part of her mind tried to tell her this was because he was safe. But she knew it was because she was safe from him.

Now her whole heart was in the work that she had undertaken. She was good at it. Her Celtic imagination saw the messages which she coded or decoded at the start or end of their long, swift, vitally important journeys as living things. She took the utmost care of them and worked for longer hours than her strength allowed. She lived on her nerves. She felt herself at the very heart of the war. She knew what Prime Minister said to President and Foreign Minister to Ambassador. For any woman complete secrecy is a strain. But she had found something that she could do better than most and she worked on without rest.

Every now and then came letters or postcards from Richard. They were almost as exacting and exhausting as his visits used to be. Prisoners were only allowed to send one letter and three postcards a month, and their length was strictly limited. (If one wrote too small the censor rejected them.) It was evident that Richard spent much of his time composing these communications so as to condense as much into them as possible. The telegraphic style made them imperative, but did not hide the passion. He asked all she had done and whom she had seen. He told her of their intimate life together when he "got out." (He never mentioned their differences.) He sketched the cruises they would make alone on *Heather Mary*. While she read she could see his eyes and even feel his breath.

She could not hurt a prisoner but she tried gently to show him that the old life was finished. In his replies this part of her letters was ignored.

Heather took no real holiday until the spring of 1944 when, for her health, she was directly ordered to go away for three weeks. She went to Amulree.

Meg's husband, Marcus, was on leave at Salen, ten miles along the coast, and came over every day for the fishing. Heather liked him. He was an unexacting companion, quietly content even when untangling a cast. He made little jokes which were not very funny but which she laughed at because she needed to laugh. But chiefly she liked him because he was so appreciative of everything concerned with Amulree, its weather, wild or calm, its scenery, animals and people. Showing it off to him, being warmed by his praise, gave her something she had lacked.

When she returned to the Foreign Office everybody said how

well she looked. She felt it for a day or two; and then the press
and bustle of London which she had always disliked weighed
on her heavier than ever in contrast to the last three weeks. Meg,
in her capacity as chief of the women's personnel branch, had
already told her there would soon be a vacancy in Washington
which she could fill if she liked. Heather found herself thinking
about it a good deal.

Then she received a letter from Richard which puzzled and
startled her. She was used by now to his strong, highly concen-
trated style—"like a glass of neat rum." But this letter was all
about a jersey which he had knitted for her. He gave such details
as "vertical tucks and buttoned band cuffs." He hoped the breast
measurement was correct. Heather was alarmed. His letters, she
thought, had become increasingly strange lately but now apparently he had gone quite mad.

Patrick came on leave a couple of days later. He had always
visited her whenever he was free in London, and she was always
cheered by his visits. He had known Richard since schooldays and
admired him enormously. He had the knack of recreating the
man whom Heather had loved, but he was tolerantly conscious of
this man's faults as well. Heather had become very fond of Patrick
indeed, as of a wise elder brother. He was so sane. She showed
him the letter.

He burst out laughing, "The cunning old fox!"

"What do you mean? What does the letter mean?"

Patrick looked at her with a smile in his eyes.

"Didn't you know that Richard has been trying to get out every
moment since they put him behind barbed wire? Of course he
couldn't say it in his letters but—you must have realized. You're
his wife."

Heather stared back into the brown interested eyes. Phrases she
had not understood began to make sense. Without at first knowing why she began to feel afraid.

"How do you know this?"

"He has made at least half a dozen damn clever attempts at
escape. Three times to my knowledge he has got clear of the camp
and been caught only by bad luck. You have very nearly had
him home."

"How do you know this?"

"Other people have got out of the camp at the same time as he has, and a few have got right away. Two officers reached home via Sweden last month. That was Richard's doing. I've met them. I didn't tell you because—well, I knew he'd get out himself sooner or later and I didn't want to spoil his surprise."

Heather got up and moved slowly round the room looking for a cigarette. She had taken it for granted that she would have time to prepare herself for the moment of meeting Richard again.

"But that doesn't explain about the knitting," she said.

Patrick swung out of his chair and took her by the hands. He shook them slowly up and down while he spoke.

"I learned a bit about prison mentality from these two lucky fellows. They talked—how they talked! They'd had to keep quiet so long. With every German indoctrinated and trained from babyhood escape is about ten times as difficult as it was in the last war. It's the devil of a mental strain. And prisoners themselves find it hard not to talk. Organizing, which is Richard's strongest suit, is about as difficult as running some vast business concern without letting anybody's right hand into the secret of what his left hand is doing. No ordinary person can keep it up for long. If they don't get out themselves one of two things happen. They go mad or else they take up religion or knitting. The German security guards know that is the choice, and without doubt Richard is a marked man by now. So he has taken up knitting."

"You mean he is really interested in knitting. That doesn't make sense," Heather said.

"Of course not—to us who know him. Unraveling old socks and construing some damn silly booklet a welfare organization has sent out. Richard can do it. He can go to endless pains to get what he wants. But it's all a blind. That letter was for the benefit of the German censor. I bet he is still planning to get out. He might walk in on you this very moment. . . . Heather, dear, there is no need to look so worried. Richard can look after himself. What you want is to forget your troubles in a good party. And I've got the very thing all arranged. If you won't be a gay grass widow you shall come as chaperon."

••

CHAPTER 8

••

AT four o'clock Toby was called by Marcus who had relieved Boyd two hours before. Toby blinked at the light, dazed and resentful. He had, he thought, been awake all night, but he found himself at the bottom of a black pit of sleep into which he must have fallen a few moments before.

He dressed—put on rubber boots and a few extra clothes—slowly and clumsily. He felt cold. The skin of his face was loose and heavy with sleep. He put out the light, went through the galley, through the saloon, up the companionway and across the four feet of deck which separated it from the cockpit.

Marcus had returned to the helm after waking him. He told Toby the course, pointed out the two or three shipping lights, and went below.

Toby looked at his watch. Five minutes past four. An hour and fifty-five minutes until he could call Yeoman. He blinked because the salt breeze made his sleepy eyes water. But his skin no longer felt loose and heavy. It was tight and hard.

He took his hand off the tiller. It scarcely moved. The yacht could steer herself. There was nothing for him to do. How the devil did one spend an hour and fifty minutes of idleness in the middle of the night? The light went out below. Marcus was in his bunk. He, Toby, was the only one who had to keep awake.

He looked idly round the circle of the horizon. In four directions there were spots of light. Charrington had said that stationary lights were fishing boats, nothing to worry about. Then he noticed that one of the lights was moving. He looked away and back again. Yes, it was coming towards the yacht—gradually it became two lights, one over the other. They approached. How far off was the ship? Should he call the Skipper? He didn't want to do that. He went carefully forward along the deck and examined the yacht's navigation lights. They were still burning—

but how dim they were! He went back to the cockpit, took an electric torch from the locker and flashed it on the sail to make sure of being seen. The two lights were surely on the same vessel but they seemed to be moving slowly apart. What did that mean? Then he saw a green light, then porthole lights. The invisible ship went slowly by, the green vanished and there was only the stern light receding into the darkness.

Toby's mind was entirely occupied for twenty minutes by what has been described in a paragraph.

Then he relaxed and looked at his watch. An hour and a half until he could call Yeoman. In that time he must get things straight. . . . He loved Elaine. He had met her when, having taken part in the last phases of the war in Europe, he had come home feeling dissatisfied and unsettled. She was small and very pretty. She was restful and unexacting. She understood without his having to explain. Seeing her every day, the delirious memory of July, 1944, had faded into a romantic dream and he had begun to picture with contentment his future with Elaine. He had felt justified in leaving her for a few months on the principle of "I could not love thee, dear, so much loved I not honor more." It would give him something original to write about, he had told her. And now he found that the yacht was called *Heather Mary*. It brought the dream to life again. Her name in the log, her name on the life belt in front of him—everywhere. It hurt like hell and it was going to be damned difficult to think about Elaine.

The breeze had died away until it only just filled the sails. There was no longer any impression that the yacht was moving forward through the dark water. There was only the rise and fall—a movement like breathing—as the swell passed under her. In the silence Toby's watch ticked busily, but the luminous hands appeared motionless.

He waited for the dawn. He made his neck stiff swiveling round his head to look eastward. The light grew in the sky and his mind became keyed to an extraordinary pitch of exhilaration. He had a feeling not of loneliness but of intimacy.

He took a cigarette and lit it with Elaine's lighter. Dear, faithful Elaine. But here upon the endless water where he might have been floating in space Time was swept away like the smoke of his cigarette. . . . He was in the uniform of a subaltern. He parked his car in Soho Square and walked through narrow streets to the Ninety Nine. He was thinking, "Something special, something to remember, has got to happen tonight."

He went into the club, hesitated then approached a table in the corner where a dozen people were sitting. All the men seemed to be covered with medals and he had none at all. Patrick was the only one he knew. Toby apologized for being late.

Patrick jumped to his feet, tall and striking in his naval uniform, his frank clear-skinned face beaming with pleasure.

"Never too late, Toby! You are only two drinks behind so you'll soon catch up. This is a classic party. We've even got a chaperon. Sit down there beside Jonquil."

Toby asked Jonquil to dance. When they had shuffled halfway round the crowded floor, her face which he had been studying with a sort of eager anxiety crinkled at him and she said, "You're a bad type."

Not knowing what to answer he shuffled on in silence. Their bodies rubbed against each other like dry sticks. At last he said, "Are you the chaperon?"

"Do I look like a chaperon?" she asked, pouting.

They moved very slowly with people bumping into them. Jonquil's face had disappeared behind her make-up. But Toby's heart was swelling and he longed to confide. "This is my last night out," he said.

"You don't seem to be enjoying it much," Jonquil answered.

The music stopped and they went back to the table. Everybody seemed to be talking at the top of his voice. Toby felt sober and depressed. He had wanted a party very much indeed but he was out of tune with this one. He took a drink but it didn't do any good. Jonquil had turned away, so had the girl on the other side of him. He tried to think of an excuse for going home. Nobody here could share his mood.

"Aren't you going to take any notice of me, Cousin Toby?"

It was spoken not loudly but in so clear and unusual a voice that it came to him through all the laughter and shouted conversation.

She was leaning forward across the round table and he knew immediately that she was entirely different from every other woman in the room.

He stared at her—eyes like the sky after rain and parted lips.

"Don't you remember?" she asked. "We used to bathe together with nothing on."

"Yes of course," Toby said suddenly and enthusiastically, remembering nothing at all.

"Toby," Patrick said. "You must not flirt with the chaperon in public. Take her into the jungle."

They danced together. She talked all through the first dance, eagerly like a person who has lived long among strangers. Her voice was like a small stream moving rapidly over stones, not particularly beautiful but excited and full of changing expression.

She was Heather Mary. Her father and his mother had been second cousins. A dozen years before he had been taken for a summer holiday to Amulree. But after that, with his home in Kent, and his father's job in America, he had never returned to the Highlands. She had rarely left Scotland until she married eight years ago. Eight years married—was it possible, Toby wondered. Patrick had been in the same Flotilla as Richard at the beginning of the war. She had met him when she went down to Harwich, and Richard had brought him to their London flat. After Richard had been taken prisoner she had given up going to parties. She would not have come to this one except that Patrick had begged her to.

"I asked him who was coming and recognized your name," Heather said. "I wanted to talk to you about Amulree. But you have forgotten all about Amulree—and me."

Her nose, which he had been thinking was as delicate as porcelain, suddenly wrinkled and she made a face at him, like a small girl.

He protested that he did remember Amulree and her. He asked her to go on talking about Amulree. He wanted to hear her say the word again . . . And all this time they were dancing.

When the music stopped they walked very slowly back towards the table. Patrick stood waiting for them at the edge of the floor.

He said, "Heather, are you happy or will you dance with me?"

"I'm happy and I'm grateful and I *will* dance with you," she answered.

Toby sat down next to Jonquil. He felt lost. As well as he could he watched Heather. When she and the others were back at the table again, he tried calmly to analyze why she had attracted him so strongly. She was pretty of course, very pretty. The way she held her head. But it wasn't just that. In some indefinable way she was another species of woman. She was out of place here and therefore striking, like a flower in a ruin. And then he noticed something else. Although she was talking as vivaciously as anybody there was something almost desperate in her gaiety. She was trying hard to fit in, but it was difficult—just as it was for him.

He caught her eyes. They beckoned to him through the haze of cigarette smoke like will-o'-the-wisps. He knew that they must dance once more and that they must share their private feelings.

She came to him quickly on the floor, smiling, and fitted into his arms. She was wearing a blue dress of some silky stuff. The drummer was shaking gourds with shot inside them and the music was wild. The rhythm was too quick to let them talk but he watched the color growing in her face and the way her hair moved like seaweed when the rising tide begins to lift it. He held her closer until even through his stiff uniform he could feel her breasts against him.

Suddenly it came to an end. She stood in front of him, panting and laughing, "Oh, it's wonderful—" she said.

"What's wonderful?"

"To be happy and dance and—" she met his eyes.

"This is my last night," he said. "Tomorrow I'll be cooped up until—"

"I understand."

They began to dance again, slowly and silently, not looking at each other. They moved like that until they were opposite the door. Then he halted and took her by both hands and said, "Come."

"Where?"

"Outside."

"Why?"

"You said you understood."

She studied his face.

"You will have other nights, Toby. I don't think I shall. Please don't spoil it."

"I promise not to spoil it. You are not really happy here. Please come—just for a little."

"But Toby—Why?" She looked at him tenderly but full of doubt.

"Because I want to see what color your eyes are in the dark."

"Like cats'," she hissed, suddenly gay again and pressed her nails into the palms of his hands.

It was black dark outside except for the dim lights of traffic and here and there the oval glow of a pedestrian's torch zigzagging along the pavement. She held tightly on to his arm and asked, "Where are we going?"

"I've got a car. We'll sit in that."

They found the car and got into it in silence. Although they were alone together he did not dare to touch her.

At last he said: "I wanted something like this so much. I wanted something I could take with me and be happy and proud about and not ashamed at all. I don't want to be killed. I don't even want to kill anybody. But I've got to try. And I need something like this—you alone, not in a crowd—that I can take out of my memory to help me when everything else is foul."

She put up a hand and touched his face. His own hands he had been resting against the seat on either side of her. He could see her eyes now. They glistened like pools of water in the dark. His hands touched her sides. He could feel her heart beating very fast.

But he felt her stiffen. For a moment he was puzzled, hurt. Then his own body grew rigid and he listened.

It wasn't a car. It wasn't an airplane—quite. He had never heard a buzz-bomb but he knew immediately that this was one.

Neither of them spoke. They remained exactly as they had been while the sound approached. It came nearer and nearer until it seemed almost directly above them. Then it stopped.

There was absolute silence. They remained in the dark together, the pools of her eyes looking into his. They waited.

The explosion came with such shattering noise and blast that for some moments they were stunned. Then the things which had been hurled into the air began thudding down with an appalling clatter. It was as if the sky were raining houses. Something struck the hood of the car, making it rock.

They got out. She gripped his hand and they began to run. It did not take long to reach the place. Half a dozen houses had been destroyed. The street was full of smoking rubble and broken glass. The air was so thick with dust that one could scarcely breathe. The bomb had fallen exactly on the little club and it had vanished. There was no question that anybody who had been inside was still alive.

Heather collapsed in Toby's arms. Her face was terrified and her sobs stabbed agonizingly up and down her throat. Yet nothing he could do would make her go until she had seen. And then it was some time before she was calm enough to tell him her address so that he could take her home. But surely that had been a sign, surely—for if she had not come out with him they would both have been dead too. So why had she gone away to America without answering his letters? Toby sat in the gray light, wondering.

Charrington came on deck. For several minutes he stood absorbed. Then he loosed the staysail sheet from its cleat and let it run out a foot or two. He adjusted the jib sheet and the mizzen. The mainsail after long consideration he left alone. The tiller pressed against Toby's arm and the rhythmic swish and sigh of water at the bow increased in volume.

Charrington sat down in the cockpit and filled his pipe. All this time he had not spoken. He lit his pipe and sat smoking.

Suddenly he asked: "How long have we been at sea?"

Toby started and stared, fumbling at arithmetic. "About twenty-seven hours," he said at last.

"You took a long time to work that out."

"I know. It seems so much more than a day. You can't measure it in hours."

After a pause Charrington said, "Sorry I was so damn stupid as not to tell you the name of the yacht."

Toby did not answer. He sat waiting defensively while the dawn light grew. He could feel Charrington's eyes on him, but he was determined not to be drawn into that sort of conversation.

"You're a bit of a writer, aren't you?" Charrington said at last.

"Hardly. I'm very interested in it but I've not published anything worth mentioning."

"That will come. You've got feeling and perception. All you need is experience—something to write about at first hand. You look surprised."

"Only that you should say that. It's the main reason why I wanted to come on this voyage."

"You want to write a book about it?"

"Nothing I'd like better than to try to—if you don't mind."

"I'm delighted. Shall I give you a tip?"

"Please."

"Yachting books are generally dull because the authors spend too much time describing the yacht and the weather instead of the reactions of the crew. Subordinate the inanimate and concentrate on the human and personal. Yachts are always much the same but people can behave strangely on a long passage. You never know, you might produce a best seller."

"I see," Toby murmured thoughtfully.

"But to do that you must keep a complete and intimate diary of all that's said and how you feel. It's surprising how quickly you forget that sort of thing otherwise."

"Yes," Toby said. "Yes, I see." He thought with growing enthusiasm about the project. And "subordinate the yacht"—that was the double answer. The yacht was a yacht like every other. He would concentrate all his energies on writing about the five men aboard her. He would write for Elaine. The dream could remain a dream.

While he thought about this, the near side of every wave in front of him suddenly glowed with bright color, and looking over his shoulder he saw the sun floating on the water.

CHAPTER 9

Toby's diary. 22nd August. Last night Jack and I sat up late talking about the necessity for organized rest. We are all a bit sleepy— except the Skipper. There is plenty to do in the daytime—housework, sailing and maintenance—and at night we are still unused to getting rest in four hour shifts. As soon as I climb into my bunk I start telling myself that I must go to sleep at once. Consequently I lie awake for two or three hours.

Another cause of weariness is the unceasing motion. I suppose we have been lucky so far. We have been three days at sea (it seems much longer owing to the number of times one has gone to bed and got up in that period). It has not been calm since the first night but the wind has been no stronger than Force 5 on the Beaufort Scale, a "fresh breeze." All the same the yacht has never been still. Swerves, rolls, seesawings and worst of all the bump and shiver that happens when a wave slaps her from an unexpected angle.

Jack and I get the full benefit of this motion in our forward cabin which is the polite name for the chain locker. The egg basket which is slung from the ceiling swings madly all the time. We have to wedge ourselves into our bunks and learn to hold on while we're asleep. Our dreams always have violent ends. I wonder why our unconscious minds can never bring themselves to face the truth. They are supposed to be the things that show us up as we really are. In fact they are chronic liars. What has actually happened is that we have been bumped against the side or been shaken half out of bed. So why not admit it? But in that split second our unconscious minds make up some long and complicated story about skating on thin ice or running down a marble staircase in nailed boots or being drunk on a dance floor.

This endless and irregular motion is tiring in the daytime too. If you stand on one leg to pull on a boot of course you dive straight on to something sharp and hard. But even if you sit down to it and a sudden roll comes you pitch headfirst across the cabin and hurt yourself. In a moderate breeze you have to hold on with one hand whatever you are doing with the other, and that is hard work for both hands.

It is our hands and arms and shoulders that we use. Our upper halves are stiff and aching from unaccustomed jobs or merely from keeping ourselves upright or pulling ourselves along. Also we are bruised as if we had been in a rugger match. But the absurd thing is that in spite of this exhausting exercise our conservative insides maintain we are living a sedentary existence because we don't walk more than a hundred yards a day. Therefore we are costive.

This led to an incident yesterday evening which shows that virtue is sometimes rewarded. I was reading in the saloon during the dog watch. The other four were on deck and I could hear them talking. You can always hear people talking unless the wind is strong. I heard the Skipper say, "Here you are, Marcus."

Then Marcus: "Steady, I can't drink all that."

Skipper: "Of course you can. Do you good . . . That's for you, Jack."

Jack: "Not a whole mugful!"

Skipper: "Of course. You try it, Boyd."

And so on with a lot of laughter.

Since the tragedy of the gin and the compass I'd made myself forget about drinks. Now I didn't know if the Skipper's mysterious "special occasion" had arrived. But I did know I wanted a drink. However I'd decided that I would spend an hour reading Gibbon, and since I have undertaken this voyage for the improvement of my soul, character and mind I managed to decide that I would go on reading for an hour.

The moment that hour was over I scuttled on deck and asked, "Is there any left?"

They roared with laughter and said, "Yes, plenty."

The Skipper had been making them drink sea water as an aperient.

I feel extraordinarily lucky to have tumbled into a crowd like this. We pull each other's legs unmercifully—and there is plenty of scope for it since nobody knows the first thing about sailing except the Skipper. But everybody takes it in good part. And they are all well worth knowing. D.S.O.'s don't grow on trees but Marcus Harding has got one. As he puts it he went Cook's touring everywhere between Norway and the Far East during the war. Boyd, I think, was in on most of the top level scientific secrets and traveled to and fro between England and America on V.I.P. missions. Jack Yeoman was an Air Raid Warden who went through everything from the blitz to the V2's without either glory or reward. The Skipper seems particularly interested in him. He has long talks with him during his night watches. Once or twice Jack has looked worried when he came below. But I haven't a guess what it's all about. There's not much chance for private conversation—except possibly in the middle of the night when one is either asleep or busy.

The Skipper had about eighteen months in gunboats. He had the reputation for being one of the most aggressive commanders in Coastal Forces. Then his boat was knocked out and he was captured. He spent the rest of the war organizing and doing escapes. I was told this by Marcus and in part by Patrick during that leave when he got killed. I haven't made up my mind about the Skipper. He can be charming. But when there is work to be done he doesn't care a damn what he says and can be abominably rude. "You bloody fool" is a form of endearment in comparison. But I am certain he is not merely a tough sailor. He is contradictory, hard to define. He might even prove disappointing. At this stage I'll describe him as an interesting character—as Heather's husband ought to be.

23 August. Last night the shipping forecast which we get at five minutes to six, our only link with England, promised us dirty weather—a fresh wind with low visibility in BBC language. It kept its promise. Jack and I had the midnight to 4 A.M. watch. Since things were difficult we were both on deck, and the Skipper who doesn't seem to need sleep was with us most of the time. The wind was gusty and changeable. We had to tack twice for by our dead reckoning we were near the coast of Brittany. (Because of cloudy weather we have not been able to take an observation.) Also we had to look out for shipping and the Ushant light. All the time it simply poured with rain which stung our eyes as we peered into it and trickled down the back of my neck because I couldn't get the collar of my new oilskins buttoned up.

Suddenly Jack shouted, "There's a light." The Skipper asked, "What's the interval?" We both counted and got different answers. The Skipper went to his cabin for a stop watch and settled it. Two flashes in ten seconds—Ushant. We were heading almost straight for it. We saw only the blearily winking light but knew it meant rocks. So we had to tack out into the Atlantic again. This is all waste of time for what we want to do—as we saw from the wind chart the Skipper brought on deck yesterday—is sweep southward passing within a hundred miles of Cape Finisterre and the Coast of Portugal to catch the Trade Winds beyond Madeira.

By the time we called the other watch—with the greatest possible satisfaction, they looked so warm and comfortable—I was soaked to the skin and shivering. So for the first time on the voyage I got out of all my clothes and into pajamas. Jack said that I was tempting providence. Damn him for being so sensible! Two hours later the Skipper called all hands on deck. The wind had risen and we had to reduce sail. It was still pouring. Pajamas are off the ration until the sun shines—until these famous Trade Winds I suppose.

At eight o'clock I was called by Marcus who made one of his morale raising jokes through chattering teeth. I put on my damp clothes and went on deck. I found the Skipper there who said it was only half a gale. It was the wet half of a gale and it was blowing straight in our teeth. It was daylight but one couldn't see anything except gray water—rain coming down and waves jumping up and smacking us. The Skipper told me to call Yeoman and set the No. 2 jib. Yeoman was quite pleased. He is an extraordinary fellow. He seems to have lived fifty years for this chance to be uncomfortable.

Afterwards I sat shivering in the saloon. Marcus was rolled up in blankets like a chrysalis on the other settee, but Boyd was in the galley trying to make breakfast. Suddenly he put his head out, looking like a professor whose experiment has gone wrong, and said. "Toby, you know more than I do about the etiquette of the sea."

I said "Umph" if I said anything.

"What do you suppose would be the right procedure if the egg basket carried away?"

"Why?" I asked.

The northern lights came into his eyes and he answered. "Because it has."

He reached behind him and held out the basket which was weeping white of egg.

"Call the Skipper," I said.

Boyd went and hammered on the cabin door.

The Skipper came out of his holy of holies looking about as friendly as a rain squall. He couldn't have had much sleep last night. Boyd who when he does speak is abashed by nothing told him what had happened. The Skipper listened with his head down, scowling. Then he went on deck and we heard him giving instruction to Jack about heaving to.

He came below again, Jack following, and shut himself into the galley alone. We sat and shivered, I with mutinous thoughts for I believed he was counting up the damage like a miser. But twenty minutes later he produced the most fabulous dish of scrambled yolks of egg, dozens and dozens of them, and strong black coffee to wash it down.

He has the gift which I suppose makes the great admirals and generals of driving and bullying and then suddenly producing a delightful surprise which puts everybody in good spirits.

Evening. By noon the wind had gone down but the swell remained —steep and awkward dunes of water. *Heather Mary* climbed them with difficulty, skidded down the other side and buried her nose in the next dune. The boom kept swinging aft and banging out again. Every rope complained and every block kept slapping against something else. Under these conditions one can well believe the Skipper's statement that in the old sailing ship days the worst enemy was not the French or Spaniards but chafe. Ropes which get foul of each other or of something hard get chafed away in no time. The Skipper is always on the lookout for trouble of this sort and sets the bosun to right it. Jack loves these tiresome little jobs. But I wonder if he will be able to keep up with them. He's keen and thorough but about as quick as a tortoise with lumbago.

At midday the sun appeared. The Skipper wedged himself against the dinghy which is lashed upside down over the saloon skylights and did a sextant observation. One measures the angle of the sun above the horizon, but with everything going up and down it must be difficult to know what is the true horizon. He says the little blow we had doesn't account for this swell. There must have been a big storm out in the Atlantic—where we are going!

24th August. Instead of growing used to this life most of us get increasingly sleepy, more and more stiff in the arms and shoulders and sore in the hands.

All last night we were bowling along with a good beam wind. Steering was exciting and hard work. Towards the end of the watch—I suppose I was getting tired—I had the impression that I was holding the handle of a huge black frying pan with the horizon as its rim. As I moved the handle the frying pan tipped from side to side while waves of boiling fat hissed up white and spread and subsided into the pan again. That sounds nonsense but it's easy to lose one's sense of the relative size of things.

Just before I called Boyd the Skipper came on deck. I made cocoa and then remained for half an hour listening to them talking about the stars. Boyd has taken a vow not to read any books but he is interested in everything—everything that is except the management of our voyage, for he still insists as far as possible on being a passenger. He generally spends his time at the helm in trying to calculate the speed of the waves and the distance between their crests—that sort of thing. Of course he knows a lot about the stars but he could not identify them as the Skipper can. I learned that the two bright ones which chase each other over the western horizon in the first night watch are Venus—a naked pink and white —and Mars who gets very hot and red following but never catching up. Then Orion hitches his belt obliquely up the southeastern sky. Sirius comes out barking at his heels and Cassiopeia looks on from her uncomfortable chair.

Watching the stars for hours together one appreciates how they move in unison in a great unhurried procession. One thinks of the vast distances—but it doesn't bring Bermuda any nearer.

One trusts the Skipper because he knows his job, but he is not a comfortable companion. I say this because of a remark he made just before I came below. We had seen a shooting star flash across the sky and vanish. He said, "That shows how little our fate matters."

"It matters to me," Boyd said.

"It is too late to worry about that now," the Skipper answered.

"Why?" Boyd asked.

At that moment I had a sudden empty feeling as if the Skipper were going to tell us that the yacht was sinking. Actually he said something about the fate of that star having been decided by things which had happened thousands of years ago. There was nothing particularly original in his argument but I came below feeling depressed. I suddenly appreciated how completely we are in his hands and how little I know about him. Now I realize how difficult the voyage is going to be, I can't help wondering why he invited four men who can't sail.

Evening. All day long the bows of the yacht have been rising and falling, cutting through the endless Bay of Biscay like a tailor's scissors through blue cloth. It's been a bright day without too much wind, but anything except an idle one. The Skipper caught me writing after breakfast and told me there must be no more author-ing. There was work to do.

The work consisted principally in changing sail. Staysail to bal-loon staysail—No. 2 Jib to No. 1 Jib—Hoist topsail—Down topsail—Down mainsail because gaff jaws were wrong and a crack had formed in the gaff. Hoist trysail—Down trysail and hoist again because the Skipper wasn't satisfied the first time—No. 1 Jib to No. 2 Jib—Balloon staysail to staysail.

This took most of the day and we ended up almost exactly as we started. Long before we had finished my hands were as dry and rough as sandpaper and my temper much the same. One has to admire the Skipper but he's a bit of a sadist. (I hope he doesn't read this diary.) I began to grumble. Marcus, ever the second-in-command, whispered back, "He's training us. Damned necessary."

I knew there was something wrong with that answer but un-fortunately couldn't think what it was until now, and now—as usual—there is no chance for private conversation. We are being trained all right, but it has a horrid similarity to my period as a conscript on the barrack square. Then we were drilled because such discipline helps men to obey orders automatically under fire. But no one suggested it taught us how to run the war. And that—from the point of view of this voyage—is what I feel we ought to learn. We are drilled in hoisting an alternative bit of canvas which we pull out of the sail locker, but we aren't told why this change is being made. We are instructed how to set it, but why it should be thus set is not explained. We are, as the Skipper said on the first day, muscles only. That is all very well but none of us would have the faintest idea how to get to harbor if the Skipper went sick or fell overboard.

Marcus asked him at lunch what the drill was (Marcus likes the word drill) if somebody fell overboard. The Skipper answered, "Throw the life belt after him." (The life belt lies like a wreath round the binnacle.) "Or anything else to mark his position if a sea is running. If it's night, throw the flare overboard—it lights itself. Jibe round—try not to carry everything away doing it—and then sail up on to him like picking up a buoy. . . . But people don't often get picked up, you know, if they fall overboard. It's best to hold on."

Hold on! As if we ever did anything else—particularly when

we are alone at night. I know that when I decide that I must make sure that our green and red navigation lights are still burning, I move along the deck most cautiously and holding on to everything available unnecessarily tight—however calm it is. It's like the concentration you put into walking across a plank twenty feet in the air when if it were on the ground you wouldn't hesitate. It's the disproportionate fear of going overboard without being noticed. It's the fear of falling off the world.

We passed several other worlds today. Most of them were steamships. We saw a smudge of smoke on the horizon. Then masts appeared above the surface, then the funnel and hull. The ship approached, passed by, and gradually sank below the opposite side of the horizon.

The first time this happened Jack became quite pink with excitement. The Skipper said, "You eternal child, didn't you know the world is round?" Jack answered, "Yes, but it's wonderful actually to *see* it."

Only one vessel passed us close, a Breton tunny fisher. She was on an exactly opposite course, making for harbor, and went by within twenty yards. She was a strange craft with boom-like fishing rods sticking out from her sides, trailing long lines. Two of her crew held up a fish almost as large as themselves.

One man shouted, "*Où allez-vous?*"

"Bermuda," we shouted back.

They shrugged their shoulders.

CHAPTER 10

YEOMAN was writing to his daughter.

Darling Tilly,

Six days we've been at sea and it's been lovely. I can't post this till we reach Bermuda but I'd better start writing now or I never will. The trouble is there's so much to tell I hardly know where to begin. It's August 25th and we started on the 19th.

I've been splicing the gaff until the Skipper told me to go below and take things easy. You remember that time I dropped *Firefly* getting on to a bus and you scolded me for turning the kitchen into a shipyard, you said, because I was so long putting her to rights? I thought about that, working on the deck of a real yacht.

But *Heather Mary* is not so big either. The galley—what you'd call the kitchenette—would make you die. You can touch all four walls at once—in fact that's what you generally do—and there's the mast in the middle of it. Cooking you have to be a bit of a juggler, hold everything on the stove with one hand and stir with the other. Then perhaps the kettle and the saucepan start boiling over at the same moment and the yacht gives a violent roll. Too much broth spoils the cook, as the Colonel says. And washing up! The fuss you women make, when you've got a big kitchen with a floor that stays level and corners that don't sneak out and hit you and crockery that doesn't jump on to the floor! You'll never be able to work that grumble on me again. But I do see what you mean about directly one meal's over it's time to start the next.

There's nothing wrong with the grub. We've got special Board of Trade rations—tins and tins of butter and ham and all sorts and enough sugar and tea to take us round the world. The Colonel is making a list and he hasn't got through the half of it yet. Only trouble is water. We can't afford to use fresh except for cooking. We wash our faces and the plates in buckets from the sea. The Colonel is the only one that manages to shave. But salt water's useful. I drink a little every day and I've never been so regular. Also I put my teeth in it at night and they're fresh as daisies next morning.

My cabin mate and the one I share the watch with is Toby Carlyle. He's the lanky sort. You'd say he was good looking. He wears a canary sweater somebody must have knitted him. I'm sure he's very clever. At any rate he has long hair and is nearly always writing or reading. But sometimes he's charming. Sometimes, too, he gets impatient with your Dad who's twice his age because I like to do things slow and thorough. Never mind, he'll get calmer and wiser as he grows up. He's got the right stuff in him and will make some nice girl very happy, that I'm sure.

By the way, don't you go marrying anybody behind my back!

Dr. Boyd is just the opposite of Toby. I like him and you would too but he's the one I seem to know least so far. He's a scientist but he's not vague a bit. Whenever he does speak he's sharp as a needle. If there's a joke made he sees it at once, but his eyes don't share it with the rest of his face. He pretends to be lazy but isn't. He's all there but not altogether on *Heather Mary* yet. Here's an example. In the yacht's log there's a column headed "Remark and Notes." The sort of thing that gets put in it as a rule is "Head wind again," "Rain and low cloud," "Crossed shipping route." This evening the Doctor wrote "Distinct halo of 22° radius round the sun. Colored, with the red inside. The cirro-nebula gradually increased in density until whole sky became grayish white with cirro-stratus. Part of advancing cyclonic fringe?"

He's not trying to be funny. That's what he's interested in—whatever it means.

Colonel Harding—we all call him Marcus—is the one I know best. He's a real gentleman. He always hides his feelings and you can see exactly what they are. He's got a wife and two little girls he's going to join in Bermuda and have a real holiday with, so we'll meet them. He'll enjoy this trip after it's over. He's always making jokes with a face as if he was swearing. I think he feels responsible to jolly things along, although he isn't in the mood himself.

He's invented several extra members of the crew. (Isn't your old Dad being witty? It's the responsibilty of writing to a well educated person like Miss Tilly of the County School. Also I suppose it's from living with people much cleverer than myself.) We don't have a motor for driving *Heather Mary*, only a tiny thing to work the lights and pump. This motor is Dr. Boyd's special responsibility, and the Colonel calls it Little Tich. When Tich goes on strike which does happen even under a socialist government (Boo to you!) we have to use a sort of piston with a T-handle you work up and down in a hole in the deck. The Colonel says it's a Chinese hand named Pump Ship Dri. I worked him too hard this afternoon, standing legs apart over the hole, and got wet as I haven't been since I was six months old.

And there's another member of the crew. When we're beating up wind and can lash the helm and hold the course (just like with a model) the Colonel says that Jo is at the helm. I don't believe he really thinks of this person as Jo. He was the first to talk about Miss Heather and to warn us against mentioning her because of the Skipper. But I think the Colonel is wrong and the Skipper wants us to talk about her. I know I'd want that. So I talk about her freely when he joins me on the night watch, and he always stays a long time. I've said I believe it's her, not Jo, that steers the ship when no one's at the helm.

But here's a thing I don't quite understand. I wouldn't mention it except I want to get it clear in my own mind at once. You didn't see Miss Heather when she arrived with just a bag the day of Mother's death. But you did soon after. I've tried to give him a picture of her then. What a lovely picture it is! I can see her clear as anything when I'm steering at night. She was a bit tired. That generally makes women ugly but it didn't Miss Heather because even the bones of her face were lovely, the bones and the eyes. That's what your mother said a week before she was taken ill and Miss Heather came to tea. And her skin was so bright and clear although it was so pale, as if it was lighted from inside, like a lamp with a nice shade. And her clothes so simple and straight as if she was a girl, yet smart as a princess. I've tried to give all that to the Skipper but he isn't satisfied. He seems more interested in times and dates which I don't remember so well.

Tilly girl, I'm worried about the Skipper. That is a terribly impertinent thing to say except you realize how much I admire him. We couldn't sail across a pond without him aboard. But he was four years in prisons and two years sailing alone and it must have all been a great strain. I wish I could talk to the Colonel or Dr. Boyd about him but there never is a chance and I wouldn't know how to begin.

Anyway, it will be over and settled before you get this letter.

CHAPTER 11

THE waves had changed character. They had scarcely increased in size but there was an aggressive sting in them. They put their heads down and charged the yacht. Some vaulted aboard and washed along her whole length, hissing excitedly. Others struck the bow, exploded into the air and came down not like rain but in bucket-loads and bathfuls on to the deck. But most impressive was the sense of strain. The sails bulged outwards, trembling at their edges. The mast strained audibly against the weather stays. And the tiller strained in Boyd's arms as he sat with Marcus in the cockpit. The wind was cold, and the mottled purple sky showed that the sun was setting.

"When you are in a battle, are you frightened?" Boyd asked.

"Always," Marcus answered between his teeth.

"One can be frightened in such different ways—stultifyingly before speaking in public, shiveringly before a cold bath or worriedly about money or a disease. Can you be more precise?"

"Like the cold bath, I suppose. I shiver all right. But my mind is clear enough—more so than usual. Why do you ask?"

"It would be interesting if one were in a fit state to make some observations. . . . Here's the Skipper."

Charrington stood with head and shoulders out of the companionway, studying the horizon, the sea and the sails with more than his usual intentness.

"Call the other watch, Marcus," he said at last.

When Toby and Jack came on deck they furled the mizzen and the staysail, set the small jib and the trysail instead of the mainsail. *Heather Mary* became more docile and the waves minded her less.

"Best to get most of it off her before dark," Charrington said, and sent Toby and Jack below again to prepare supper.

"Give me a hand with the hatch covers, Boyd. We'll make her snug as we can. Quite a bit must have gone down the forehatch already."

As they pulled the covers out of the sail locker, Marcus asked, "You're expecting a bad storm?"

"Are they ever good?"

For twenty minutes they were busily engaged securing everything on deck. Then Charrington asked, "Can you get Little Tich working on the pump, Boyd, if Marcus takes the helm?"

"I'll try."

Moving slowly and methodically Boyd uncovered the engine. It sighed, coughed and stuttered, then settled to a steady purr and dirty water began squirting through a rubber pipe over the side.

"Now we'll rig life lines between the mast and the cockpit. Then supper ought to be ready," Charrington said. "We'll lash the helm and have a damn good meal."

It was the first meal they had taken all together since the night before they sailed. It was simple yet abundant. And although the swinging table held the plates at head level for those on one settee and waist level for those upon the other, and although the lamp hung at an angle which seemed against the laws of gravity, Marcus found that his appetite was as good as it had ever been on shore. But the precautions which the Skipper had ordered while on deck and the feeling now of surging faster and faster into the growing night kept him silent until the meal was almost done.

Then he said, "Tell me frankly, Richard—it's better we all know what we are in for—what do you expect?"

"The wind will go on freshening all night," Charrington answered. "When it veers a few points we'll be able to go about and still hold a course that will take us clear of Finisterre—our proper course in fact."

"And tomorrow?"

"Whether it is then blowing stronger or going down depends on the size and type of the depression and how fast it's traveling over us."

"Is there any way of calculating that?" Boyd asked.

"I've only the shipping report to go on—which you all heard. The wind force gives us a hint of the gradient between the isobars—it's not steep yet. And the time the wind takes to veer will give a rough idea of the size of the depression. The wind will have to go round into the north before it drops."

"It's Shakespeare to me," Harding murmured.

Charrington turned to him. "You started by asking if it would be a bad storm. All storms are bad. They are filthy things. I hate them like hell. The man who says he likes a storm at sea is a landlubber who's only seen waves breaking from the promenade. But the consolation is that natural laws can't be broken. The sea has to keep the rules. So if you prepare for the worst and you and your ship are sound it's only a case of toughing it out until the damned storm has spiraled its way past you."

"A good many ships have been lost without trace, haven't they, Skipper?" Yeoman asked. "How does that come about?"

"For a man sailing alone illness or falling overboard can finish the yacht. For a crew this size it's restricted to all the water tanks springing leaks when one is in mid-ocean, or fire, collision with a wreck, lightning or what is called a freak wave. A freak wave is the product of a freak storm, meaning a storm which that particular mariner did not understand. I have always taken pains to study the weather."

"Study the intentions of the enemy," Marcus said.

"Exactly. Hence the precautions just now."

"And as a result we can sip coffee at our ease while Jo steers and Tich pumps the bilges dry."

"It was worth the risk for the sake of a good meal all round," Charrington said. "I don't know when you'll get another. But it's time you were on deck again, Marcus. I'm going to get some sleep. Call me when the wind has veered to west."

Marcus buttoned his oilskin up to the neck, pulled a sou'wester over his ears and tied the ribbon under his chin with a jerk. He felt taut, half excited and half nervous, just as he used to be when riding to the start of a point to point. Until now he had frankly disliked standing a night watch, done it with grumbling jokes as a soldier does a fatigue. But then he had always been feeling more or less ill. Now—Lord knew why—he was fit as a fiddle. And Richard had given them a clear, confident picture of the situation. There was a storm to ride and they would ride it.

He climbed the few steps of the companionway, slid open the hatch, got himself on deck and closed the hatch again, shutting off the light from the saloon where the other three of the crew were talking and laughing. . . . All of a sudden he felt lonely. It was dark and the cold wind pressed against him with the strength of a river. He shivered.

Then, taking hold of the life line, he crawled the two paces aft into the cockpit and sat down beside the tiller. The sea, a black mass dotted with momentary explosions of white, heaved all around him. In his ears was the noise of traveling at speed, punctuated by the thud, splash and disappointed hiss of waves. There was nothing definite to see beyond the white triangle of the reefed staysail and the thin wedge of jib which reflected a greenish blur from the starboard light. The yacht was ploughing out towards the middle of the dark Atlantic, and there was nothing one could do about it.

Nothing? One might at least be responsible for what was happening. He unlashed the tiller and took it under his arm. It snuggled there, nudging him strongly. He had the sense of doing something he had done before. A wave broke over the bow and swept aft in horizontally flying cupfuls of water. It struck him, stinging his eyes and pattering against his oilskin. He rubbed a hand over his face and looked at the glowing disc of the compass. West by North—forty-five degrees off the course to Bermuda, but the best he could do. Steer more to the left, to port, and the jib began to crackle like a bren gun. Up helm, and the yacht heeled over with water seething and hissing along her deck.

In snatches, as what he had to do came more easily, he thought of other things. His family. The brats would be in bed, and Meg reading a book or out at a lecture—doing something definite in any case: she was a great one for filling every minute. He wondered what it would be like in Bermuda, and about his life afterwards in England, trying to be a farmer, fitting in with the County. These thoughts should have been enthralling but they could not stand up to his surroundings. . . .

The tiller pulled at his arm and the wet salt wind pressed against his face. With extraordinary clarity he remembered an incident during that leave in 1944. He no longer felt lonely.

It was a wild April day. In one of those sunny intervals which in the West Highlands can be startlingly bright Heather and he had scrambled up on to a little hill by the river mouth. Below them, beyond the tawny fringe of seaweed lay the sea, bluer than any other blue. And in it the islands were floating—they really seemed to be floating. The air was so clear that one could distinguish the white houses twelve miles away.

"One can damn nearly see America," he said.

"I don't want to see America," Heather answered, like a child.

He looked down at her. Her oilskin coat was thrown open showing the thick navy jersey with her white neck sprouting out of it. Her face was pointed directly into the wind like—like some particularly delicate kind of weather cock, with her hair flowing behind.

"Meg thinks you ought to go to America," he told her. "Richard will be back as soon as the war is over. Meanwhile you ought to break the old associations. London is bad for your nerves. Meg is half sorry she got you into the Foreign Office now. But she thinks she could fix it for you to go to Washington as a cypherette."

"Is this you talking or Meg?" Heather asked.

"Well, they are her ideas I suppose. I scarcely knew you—did I? —until a week ago. But I can't help seeing her point."

"She sent you up here to persuade me?"

"She didn't send me. I had a fortnight's leave, before going overseas. Meg couldn't get away and she knows I hate London. She's a damned unselfish woman. You'd told her I could have your fishing if I came to her people's place. And of course she knew we'd meet. Ten miles isn't much up here."

He moved so that he could see more of Heather's face. She was still looking into the wind. There was something definite and yet elusive about her eyes, like blue stones at the bottom of a clear swift river.

"Meg always wants to arrange my life," she said. "And she generally believes she has."

He did not understand that, so he laughed and changed the subject.

"I hope we are going to get better weather for our last week. This leave is so darned precious for both of us."

"What do you mean by better weather?" she asked.

"Not quite so much wind and rain."

"I like wind and rain," she said. "When it's calm it's like when you wake up in the night and it's a long time till dawn and you can't help thinking."

As if it were answering her wishes a squall broke over them. Heather buttoned her oilskin coat, and the big yellow fisherman's hat which had hung behind her shoulders she pulled on to her head. But she did not move except to put her arm through his. And so they stood side by side thrusting themselves against the pressure of the wind until the islands which had vanished came gradually into view again and the gray smoky sea became once more vividly blue.

Now, sitting at the tiller, Marcus rubbed one hand over the oilskin of his other arm. That was the feeling, hard and wet and slightly sticky when you pressed. It was a strange association for one's most romantic memory. But he had often thought about her—

incased like that and inside soft and warm and gentle and impulsive.

Boyd came on deck. He was wearing a hooded cape which made him look more than ever like a monk.

"A quarter past the hour. I thought you must have gone overboard. You don't generally overstay your watch."

"You ought to be grateful, having longer below."

"No, it's worse waiting to be called."

"What's the glass doing?"

"Still going down. Has the wind changed?"

"It's getting stronger all the time. And I think it's working round. I can't steer much better than west-north-west. Do you think we ought to call Richard?"

"He said not until it veered west. It's what—south-west now? You go below. I boiled a kettle."

"I say, Boyd," Marcus said.

Boyd waited.

"We've shared a watch for nearly a week and I hardly know a damned thing about you, or what you think."

"You haven't asked," Boyd said.

"Of course not, but—well, leading this sort of existence one is supposed to get to know the other fellow intimately."

"You know I don't often want a second helping, particularly of my own cooking. You know I'm average competent with an internal combustion engine. You know if I snore, which is more than I know myself. And you'll soon discover how I behave in a storm. Those are the essentials of this sort of life."

"Yes. But one would like to talk of other things. I had some rather strange thoughts just now—"

"I don't think we had better talk—or rather shout—or we'll wake the Skipper," Boyd said.

"Oh very well," Marcus said, and went below.

Boyd was always careful to make himself comfortable but it was difficult now. The kapok-filled cushion was hard with water and the hatch covers were being used for their proper purposes. He sighed and looked with disapproval at the black and white splashed heavings of the ocean. "But there is only half an hour to wait," he thought. "A very short watch thanks to Jo. Jo—why Jo? It is natural enough to personify the lashed helm. But if Heather

Mary is sailing her yacht, why not say so—or at least think it? I
wonder how many of us have thought it. Marcus was right that we
don't know each other. We never get a chance to discuss anything.
I wonder if it was that he wanted to talk about."

Boyd's ears caught a slightly different note in the panting of the
engine. He pulled in the slack of rubber tubing and saw that no
more bilge water was draining from it. So he turned off Little Tich
and closed the hatch on him. Then he returned to his thinking.

"Little Tich, Jo, Pump Ship Dri, Skipper Richard, Marcus, Toby,
Jack—the things and people aboard all have nicknames or Christian names—except me. I'm the only one that gets called by his surname. But it's always been like that since I ceased to have a family.
I've always been Boyd. Peter is a perfectly good name but—except
Heather that last night—nobody ever calls me by it. But they confide in me—Marcus would have if I'd given him a chance. They
ask advice. And I'm always being asked the way by strangers. So
it can't be I've an unsympathetic face. It would be an interesting
study, the surname class and the Christian name class. Somebody
ought to write a thesis on it. . . ."

The noise of the waves and the bustle of the sea—which had at
least something to do with Boyd's state of mind—now broke full
into his consciousness as a wave leaped into the cockpit and soaked
him. He stood up and shook himself like a dog, disgustedly. He sat
down again and began to steer with care, peering into the darkness
ahead and bearing away whenever he saw anything particularly
white and fierce charging the weather bow.

At midnight Boyd lashed the helm, got himself to the companionway with the help of the life line and went through the saloon to
the forward cabin. Passing through the door from the galley he
had to stop and hold on tight for half a minute while the bows of
the yacht rose, quivered and slapped down with the action and
something like the noise of a hammer breaking coal. How the
devil could anybody sleep up here he wondered. He switched on
the light.

The two figures lay, one on its back and the other on its side,
sleeping like corpses. Boyd wondered what was going on behind
these closed faces which had shut out the growing storm. Jack Yeoman's face had a calm, proud almost leonine expression.

He turned to Toby. As usual—as Boyd by now knew well—the
sleeping face was puckered and disapproving. He put a hand on

the boy's shoulder and rocked him up and down. He did it gently and reluctantly, remembering the cold and the unfriendly wind on deck.

Toby's arm moved petulantly, "No, darling, no," he murmured, and turned over on the other side.

At two o'clock, when it was Toby's turn to call his relief, he did it more violently and less sympathetically than Boyd had done.

Yeoman sat up at once and swung his legs out of the bunk.

"Listen," Toby said. "I don't know if this famous storm has arrived yet but there's a pretty bloody wind. I'm soaked. The Skipper's snoring in his private room and said he wasn't to be called until the wind veered west. Why it should go anywhere in particular I don't know, but it is about west as far as I can judge. Anyway we've been pushed north on this tack until we're heading for Ireland which is just damn silly. We'll have to go about any minute and it's more sensible to do it now than after I've undressed. So I'm going to call him. You get your things on quick."

He went out of the cabin. Yeoman who had been listening tight-lipped and silent made his toilet and put on his outer clothes. When he came on deck he found Charrington with Toby in the cockpit. He could not distinguish them at first because of the darkness and he could not hear what they were saying. Charrington was beside the binnacle, pointing his finger into the wind and bringing it down across the compass. He took his time about this. Then he shouted, "Lee-oh, Toby. Jib sheet, Jack."

Toby pushed the helm down and *Heather Mary* came up into the wind in a hiss of effervescent water. There was a moment of wildly flapping sails. Then she was lying over on the other tack. She settled down as if she liked it.

"Southwest without forcing her. That will clear Finisterre nicely. Toby, off to bed."

A few minutes later Charrington lashed the helm and settled down with his hunched back to the wind.

"Shove up, Jack. We'll sit close together so we can keep each other warm and talk without shouting."

"Wind's a bit strong," Yeoman said, conscious of a disturbing sense of intimacy while they were silent, with the noisy darkness all around.

"This is only a strong breeze."

"But you said there was going to be a storm."

"There will be. Are you worried?"

"No, I'm excited. It will be something to remember and talk about. . . Skipper, you can't be worried by storms either. You know what to do. But you said you hated them. How's that?"

"I hate my enemies."

They sat pressed against each other while the wind blew by like a solid thing invisible in the darkness. The Skipper's last remark seemed a strange one to Yeoman, but he had to make some reply.

"This isn't an ordinary conversation," he said. "You couldn't have an ordinary conversation now."

"Why do you say that?" Charrington asked, studying the earnest face dimly lighted by the glow of his pipe.

"Well, you couldn't tell a lie—no more than if the parson was there with the Bible and you just going to pop off."

"Do you want to tell a lie?"

"I don't mean that. It's just I don't want to say anything ordinary."

The sails made a continuous noise, the sea growled and hissed, driven by the wind, water seethed intermittently along the weather side of the deck, whitish and bubbling, as *Heather Mary* raced into the darkness.

"Jack, you never say anything ordinary. You are the only one I have been able to talk to on the subject I want to talk about. Perhaps that is because you have lost a wife too."

The wind was getting stronger every moment. There was a crescendo of excitement and strain.

"I wonder if you felt the same," Charrington spoke on thoughtfully. "While Mary was alive she filled my world. I accepted my happiness as one does the sunshine. I was smug I suppose. Certainly I didn't try to analyze it. Then the light went out. I groped desperately. That was horrible. But as I grew calmer I thought that at least I might see her again in imagination. I couldn't though. In the old days she used to hold that tiller. While I was sailing alone last year I often thought that I could see her. I could for a moment—but she had no expression. She was only a shadow. I had taken too much for granted while she was alive, not noticed and appreciated. . . . That's why I could not see her clearly when she was dead, when I wanted it most of all. Can you understand that sort of wish?"

"Yes," Yeoman said.

The sense of tension between the yacht and the wind and the sea was like a bow drawn to the full extent with the wood and cord creaking at breaking point and the muscles of the archer trembling.

"You call her Heather," Charrington said. "I don't because it reminds me of a side of her she kept to herself. Never mind. You knew her before I even met her. You are privileged."

"I know I am," Jack murmured, disturbed but fascinated.

"I've been particularly interested to hear of how she came to your house after your wife died. That was while I was a prisoner. She came and looked after you, you said. Didn't your daughter help you at all?"

"As much as she could, of course. She was in charge of an evacuated school so she couldn't come at once or for long."

"How long did Mary look after you?" Charrington asked.

"A week or so—it was at first. But then she used to pop in after for quite a while after that."

Yeoman wanted to stop the conversation. There was something wrong which he was not clever enough to put right.

"Hadn't I better unlash the tiller and steer?" he asked.

"Let her steer herself. I have something I want your comments on."

Charrington reached for the electric torch which was always kept in the cockpit locker. Then he took a folded sheet of paper from an inside pocket. He smoothed it out, holding it down against his knees so that the wind could not get hold of it. It was a letter.

"I'll read this to you," he said. "You can explain it."

Yeoman glanced at the letter—then shouted, "Look out!" *Heather Mary* had surged up into the wind, straight towards a great mass of white growling water. The wave fell upon her deck like an avalanche. It poured into the cockpit and knocked the two men anyhow. They were on their knees, up to their necks in the brimming cockpit, clutching at the life line.

As the water began to drain away, Charrington plunged over to the tiller and began furiously to unlash it.

CHAPTER 12

The Log: (Written by Charrington.) 4 A.M. Violent squall from W.N.W. Force 9. Gusts of Force 10 with hail. Skipper washed into scuppers. Jib carried away. Set spitfire jib and fully reefed trysail. Forereaching on course S.W. by S. Seas still coming on board but vessel now under control.

The crew had suffered for what felt much too long from the senseless bustle of the wind and the sullen flogging of the waves. They were exasperated as one is by a headache. Some of them had wondered how they would recognize a real storm from this.

Now—the three who were below jumped from their troubled dreams into their oilskins and scrambled on deck.

There the breath was knocked out of them in the dark. There was only one man in the cockpit—Yeoman. He shouted and pointed forward. From that direction came a stutter of crackling noises—like dry sticks on fire, only much louder.

Marcus, Boyd and Toby made their way along the deck. They found Charrington in the bow, working with a furious energy. One corner of the jib had torn free. It was streaming out into the night, cracking itself to pieces. They almost succeeded in getting it in, but it broke free of their hands, banged a dozen times and vanished into the night. They moved aft and took the last reef in the trysail. The canvas flapped about stiff as plywood and Toby was slapped in the face. Then they set the spitfire jib. Meanwhile the hail pattered against them in a horizontal deluge and the bow of *Heather Mary* parried, stabbed and slashed like the sword of an outlaw.

Toby's diary: "Yacht went mad. Thrown on deck to shorten sail. Hell of a job. Feeling of being caught in other people's fight. Believe Skipper hadn't expected gale before morning. Never seen him so worked up. But he calmed down when he got the yacht under control again and became, as usual, confident as God. He sent me and Yeoman below. No chance of sleep, though. Bunk soaked. Galley like tinker's cart galloping on cobbles. Waves being delivered like a ton of coal on deck every half minute. Water sloshing about on deck. Everything wet and squalid below. Front of my jersey sticky with blood from what feels like a broken nose, hair and face with salt. Eyes so gummed up they'll scarcely open. But must make these notes—on damp paper. Two hours till dawn. Lord how I look forward to it—"

At that moment Yeoman, coming into the saloon to look at the barograph, was struck on the head by the swinging lamp. There was a shattering of glass and inky darkness.

"You bloody fool!" Toby shouted.

Yeoman did not answer, but he could be heard trying to sweep up the mess with his sou'wester. This made a splashing as well as a tinkling noise for the bilges were overflowing. Kneeling in the darkness, Yeoman listened to the water—below them, on each side and on the deck above. He thought that the noise, with the wind added to it, was like a football crowd; all the emotions—hope, anger, despair, triumph—following each other so close that you could hardly distinguish them. Toby, feeling his tender nose, was remembering that he had been dreaming about a girl when the squall had shaken him out of his bunk. The odd thing was he didn't remember who it was so he did not know if there were anything significant in his being slapped in the face.

And then he remembered the Skipper's remark on the first day of the voyage, that the sea would be after their bones every minute.

"Jack."

"Yes, Toby."

"Sorry I was cross. I know you couldn't help it."

"That's all right."

"Jack, why don't we turn down wind? Why do we go on butting through this?"

"We might be driven too close to land. Finisterre juts out."

"What's wrong with land? Nobody wants rocks but surely we could get into some harbor when it's light. Think of being still. How wonderful it would be."

"The Skipper doesn't want to go anywhere near land. He said that the other night. He said we'd seen the last of it. Toby, there's something odd about the Skipper. He—"

Odd! I should damn well think there is. We've known for days there was a storm coming. We saw that tunny boat running for shelter. Why didn't we run too? We could have put into St. Nazaire or Bordeaux or somewhere. It would have made a good break and there's no hurry. Or he might at least aim at a Spanish port if he's such a good navigator. Not a bit of it. We go blinding out into the middle of the Atlantic where the storms come from and there's no shelter before America."

The hatch slid open, letting in the roar and whistle of the wind, and a voice shouted, "Jack, Toby—on deck!"

It was still dark outside—black dark in the hollows but with a dim view of white breakers when the yacht was on a crest. There was little sense of moving forwards. It felt as if they were rising and falling with violent jerks as an airplane does in a cloud.

Charrington had decided they must heave-to, facing into the storm which was now blowing from the northwestward.

When this had been done *Heather Mary* rode more easily again —as she had for a while after shortening sail. But the wind was still rising.

The dinghy, in its place above the cabin skylight, had worked loose. They relashed it. Everything conceivably movable had to be made fast. Then they pumped out the bilges. There was no question of running Little Tich. They put a rope round their waists, like climbers on a rock face, and took turns at the piston pump. Each spell could be no longer than a boxing round. Every action was exhausting in the constant motion and the harassment of wind and water. It was even an effort to breathe the rushing air. And all this was in the dark.

When Toby and Jack were sent below again at last—after an hour—they went straight to their bunks. They climbed into them with their boots and oilskins on. The mattresses squelched under them as they snuggled down, pulling the sticky wet blankets right over their heads. They sighed with relief because they were shut away from intimate contact with the storm. Perhaps it would have eased before they had to go on deck again.

Log. 8 A.M. *N.W. Force 9. Heavy sea. Barometer still falling. Hove-to on port tack.*

When Toby opened the hatch to see the daylight the wet wind struck him on the back of the head, pushing his sou'wester over his eyes. He scrambled out quickly and closed the hatch. Then he looked about him—and his heart prodded his ribs.

The waves may not have been much bigger than they had been during the last hours of the night. But he could see them now—see the nearest at least. It was as big as a row of houses. It swept forward while the yacht sank down into the gutter. And then the yacht began to nose its way up the side of the wave. It reached the crest and stood there trembling for a moment, giving a view of an infinite number of great waves all galloping along, all gray except for the white splashes, under a low gray moving sky . . . Then the yacht began to sink down into the next hollow where there was no view—only the walls of boiling water in front and behind.

Marcus and Boyd were in the cockpit with Charrington a few feet away. Toby could see their mouths opening wide and closing slowly as if they were shouting. But he heard nothing except the wind.

There was an endless succession of necessary tasks. But the greatest achievement of the morning was that Marcus made a bowl of hot soup. He handed it to each man as he came below for it would have gone on to the floor if he had put it down.

He finished the dish with Boyd. Boyd was a remarkable sight with tangles of gray hair pulled out like overstrained springs by the wind and his wrinkled face powdered with salt. Marcus, by his own standards, was disheveled: for the first time on the voyage he had been two days without shaving, and his tired face was smudged with soot from the stove. But he tried to be jovial.

"Well, Doctor, how do you feel?"

"Anxious but interested sums it up," Boyd answered, and lapsed into thoughtful silence.

Marcus tried again. "A penny for them—as Richard would say."

"I was thinking about him, as it happens. He has a nice calculation to make."

"What do you mean?" Marcus asked.

"If we keep the sails on her, they'll blow away soon—and maybe the mast as well. If we take them off her we'll drift with the wind. Blowing as it is at present that means we'll drift on to the Spanish rocks."

"They are still a long way off."

"Yes, but what will she do without sails. I've been trying to calculate it, but I'm not sure. We won't be able to steer her and if she gets beam on—will she roll over, I wonder."

"It's like the Russian on a sledge who has thrown everything to the wolves except his wife and the horses," Marcus said. "I see what you mean that it's a nice calculation."

Boyd nodded, looked thoughtfully at Marcus, then asked, "Do you believe in God?"

"Of course. Don't you?"

"At home I got on very well without bothering God. But here—in those black pits during the night—"

"What do you feel here?"

"It would be very comfortable to believe. But I keep mixing up God and the Skipper."

Not knowing what to answer, Marcus got up and reached for the cigarette tin which was kept behind the barograph.

At that moment the yacht made a particularly violent movement. Marcus was thrown backwards against the table, which carried away, tearing out the screws which held it to the floorboards. It and he fell together against Boyd, knocking the soup saucepan out of his hands. They rolled together in a heap.

The hatch opened, letting in the storm. Then Charrington appeared in the doorway. While they were clearing up the mess he stood refilling his pipe.

"I'm going to get the sails off her," he said.

"What do you expect will happen then? I have been trying to calculate—" Boyd began.

"There's only one way to find out. Come on deck."

On deck the elements seemed mad, tearing and screaming along, wind and water together. The strain upon sails and rigging was painful as the drawing of a tooth. Toby's hat went overboard and his long hair streamed out like black smoke.

It was exhausting work getting the sails down. When the men were kneeling on them, lashing them to the deck, they looked up to see what would happen to the yacht now that there was no means of steering her.

The valleys were deeper and wider than they had been before. A wave higher than the mast was sweeping towards them.

She used to face the waves, plough into them and fight her way up and over. Now as the thing grew in height and swelled towards her, she began to swing away from it as if afraid. She was almost beam on when she was at the bottom of the valley with the wave towering over her, its top curled by the wind. She was helpless.

But the wave did not drown her. It heaved her up to its crest. There she remained for a moment, wavering like a toy. Then she sank down into the next deep valley.

She was not fighting any longer. She was passive. She took the shock of wave crests which dropped on to her deck. The wind made a different noise in the empty rigging—a continuous boo-oo.

Log. Noon. N.W. 10. Off sails. Set weather cloths and streamed hawser. Lying seven points off wind. Rolling heavily. Occasional water coming aboard.

When they had done the tasks listed in the log, four of them went below, leaving one man at a time to watch on deck. It was lonely there. He felt so small in the immensity and clamor of the storm, shut off from his fellows by the closed hatch. Now and then, protecting his salt-gummed eyes with his hand, he looked across the compass into the wind. The wind must veer before it dropped. But it still blew from the northwest, driving them sideways towards the rocks of Spain. The yacht swayed and dipped unresistingly. The waves for the most part ignored her, but now and then one of them would leap away in a slightly different direction from the the rest, rush towards *Heather Mary* hissing like a great snake and leap on board. There was nothing for the man in the cockpit to do except endure. He was tied with a rope. For a minute or so the cockpit would be frothing full, up to his waist. But this was not sufficient reason to call the others. The sky was the color of cobwebs. Every half hour or so a darker line appeared above the horizon to windward and swept towards the yacht to batter her and her watchman with rain or hail. There was the hope that the next squall would bring a change of wind. But it still blew from the northwest and the barometer continued to drop.

It went on like this all afternoon. Each man took his turn on deck and suffered it. Below they sat, shivering and fully dressed. Charrington was with them, silently smoking. They talked about the storm among themselves, hoping that Charrington would tell them what he expected. For a long time he appeared neither to see nor to hear them. But suddenly he said: "This is a copy book storm. The wind will go round before night."

"Suppose it doesn't," Marcus said. "Suppose it backs and pushes us into the Bay."

"It won't. It has to keep the rules. We'll be drying out in the Spanish sun tomorrow."

They all felt hopeful after that.

Toby who had just handed over the cockpit to Yeoman was making his notes.

"No clear division between air and sea. Surface does not seem made of water—all seething eddies, storms within storms. Yacht flounders in the troughs. On the crests she shakes herself like a wet dog. Wind booing continually. Hardness of water. Feeling of dependence and difficult patience, like a bombardment. Tried to think what I could give up in exchange for calm. I can understand the idea of sacrifice."

There was a crash upon the deck above. The yacht shivered, creaked and heeled over. Everything in the galley clattered together. Something fell to the floor in the Skipper's cabin. Then, just audible above the sloshing of water in the scuppers could be heard Yeoman's voice shouting for help.

Buttoning their oilskins they went hurriedly on deck.

Log. 16 hours. N.N.W. 10. Violent squall and shift of wind. Stay-sail washed overboard and lost. Radio carried away and destroyed. Glass rising.

Glass rising—that was the thing which mattered! The smudged line on the damp barograph chart was definitely curling upwards. The wind still seemed as strong as ever, but since the storm's center had passed over them it must soon die. There was a limit to it. It was a pity about the staysail. It had been furled on deck but one of them had failed to lash it down properly or stow it in the sail locker. Surprisingly, Charrington asked no questions. He gave each of them a tot of rum. They felt it scald their empty stomachs and the fumes rise dizzily into their heads.

Marcus said, "If this is a special occasion, Richard, I hope we don't get many more."

Charrington smiled. "What about some food, Marcus? Bully beef will do."

Marcus tried each of the lockers under the settees in turn. But the wood was swollen and he could not open them. Then he found a tin of biscuits and some chocolate in the galley. They ate these sitting with shoulders drooping, staring straight in front of them as tired men do.

"You look worried, Boyd?"

"No, Skipper. I was only thinking. The wind has gone round a lot, but not enough. We would still hit the land, drifting like this."

Charrington had filled his pipe and was trying to strike a match to light it. But the damp heads only rubbed off. Toby handed him his lighter.

"Thank you. I know what I'm doing. The wind will veer another point very soon. That will take us clear. Then we'll be finished with this waste of time and can start traveling again."

It happened as he said. Although the sea remained high, the wind veered another point and eased perceptibly before sunset. At midnight the Log read: *North 9. Pumped bilges. Unlashed tiller and bore away. Vessel scuddling down wind.*

Heather Mary had come alive again. With one man at her tiller while the others slept she raced through the darkness under bare poles.

CHAPTER 13

"LAND—OH!"

Yeoman had been hoping during half the dawn watch that he might be the one to give that romantic cry. But until the light strengthened he could not be sure that the dark line in front was anything more solid than a cloud.

Marcus, Boyd and Toby came on deck and studied it with shining eyes. It was land all right, but it was difficult to be certain whether its western extremity lay directly down wind or whether they would drift clear of it.

During the latter half of the night the clouds had slipped down the dome of the sky, letting through the stars one by one. Now it was the soft blue of a fine early morning. The wind had veered another point and dropped to Force 7—"Whole trees in motion," according to the Beaufort Equivalent. The whole sea was very much in motion too. The waves were subsiding more slowly than the wind. Lacking control, they tumbled about anyhow. *Heather Mary* was still running under bare poles. Her rigging and the canvas lashed upon her deck were jumbled together anyhow. If it were necessary to sail clear of the land it would take some time to hoist sail.

"Better call the Skipper," Marcus said.

When nobody volunteered to do this he went below himself. They could hear nothing of what passed because the skylight was battened down and the hatch closed against the wave crests which still jumped on board.

Marcus came on deck again looking impressed. "Richard won't even get up. He says of course we'll clear the land. We're to leave her as she is."

"How does he know we'll clear the land?" Toby asked.

"I don't know. I suppose he has been charting our course."

"We'll see for ourselves in an hour," Boyd said. "That land can't be many miles away."

They waited, watching the land. They knew that there were plenty of jobs to be done, but they were in the convalescent mood which follows a period of strain and none of them had the energy to start work without orders. There were half a dozen small birds on the deck. They sat with hunched wings, tired and indifferent as the men. They took no notice of the biscuit crumbs which were offered them.

Meanwhile the land loomed nearer. It was an iron-bound coast, sheer cliffs and barren hills. When they were still a mile or two away they could see the spray rising high into the air like white smoke. But by that time they knew they would drift clear.

"If Richard had miscalculated—if we had that in the night—!" Marcus said.

Toby rubbed his thigh. "I hit something pretty hard. I think it was the anchor."

Marcus laughed. "I'm covered with bruises too, but Lord knows how I got them."

"Preoccupation is a good anaesthetic," Boyd said.

"Preoccupation! I don't mind admitting I was scared. One felt so outnumbered. Look here, I don't know about you others, but I had begun to think I knew how to sail. That storm made me realize we'd be helpless without the Skipper. What do you think, Toby?"

"No doubt," Toby answered. "I'll see if I can cook some breakfast."

"And I'll try to fix a table to eat it off," Boyd said.

"How do you feel, Jack?" Marcus asked when they were alone together.

"I—I'm all right, Colonel."

"You sound a bit strange. What's on your mind?"

Yeoman looked unhappy. Then in a low voice he said, "The Skipper."

"The Skipper?" Marcus repeated, puzzled.

"Colonel, I wouldn't say this to anybody else. But you are second-in-command and I think you ought. . . . There's something odd about the Skipper."

"What do you mean?" Marcus asked, his face turning a dark red under the powdering of salt.

Yeoman swallowed, then continued with difficulty. "It's about why he invited us. I'm sure it wasn't just for company or to help him to Bermuda. He's talked to me a lot and just before that squall he had a letter I'd written. He's asked me some funny questions and said some very funny things—"

"What the devil are you talking about?"

"It's about his wife—Miss Heather," Yeoman said.

Marcus looked angrily at him. "Oh. You have been talking to him about his wife. Didn't I specifically warn you not to as soon as we came on board? Don't you realize that he has never recovered from that tragedy? Do you wonder he was upset? And you have the impertinence to call him odd—after he brought us safely through that storm. You ought to be bloody well ashamed of yourself."

"Yes, Colonel," Yeoman said, miserably.

After breakfast, at which Charrington joined them—a wonderful breakfast it seemed—they all came on deck, and Yeoman went below to eat by himself. Charrington was in boisterous spirits.

"What did I tell you? You'll be able to dry out your things this afternoon when the swell goes down."

"There are two swells," Boyd said. "One from the southwest and the other from the north."

"Slapping each other in the face. That's why it's so bumpy," Charrington laughed. "We'll get the jib on her. Then she'll run easier."

When Yeoman came on deck again they had set the spitfire jib. He was full of apologies for not helping them. The others began to talk and he lapsed into silence. Boyd watched him with interest.

"Where is Oporto?" Toby asked, looking at the coast.

"Why are you interested?"

"I thought we might be putting in for a night or two. It would be so much easier to straighten up in harbor."

Charrington laughed. "It won't work, Toby. No port wine, no señoritas. We've wasted enough time already with that storm. But I promise we will hurry into the next land we see."

The mountains were receding and the land looked less barren. There were little white houses on the shore, and fishing boats were putting out. The birds flew away and the men followed them with their eyes. But as the dropping wind still veered the yacht drew further from the shore until it was characterless as a low cloud. A liner went by, taking no notice of the little yacht. It vanished to the northward, leaving a smudge of smoke. By afternoon they were alone in a tumbling sea which no doubt held more storms. Bermuda seemed a very, very long way off. The day which had begun with such high hopes began to fade in a mood of depression and anticlimax.

They tidied the deck and patched the sails. Boyd and Toby unshipped the little engine and carried it below to dry it out on the galley stove.

"We'll be able to set the mainsail very soon," Charrington said. "Jack, see if the halliards are clear."

Yeoman looked still more grateful than usual for being given a task. He went to the mast and tugged and flicked at the cordage. But it hung tangled as spaghetti on a fork. He began to climb the weather shrouds.

Marcus, sitting at the helm beside Charrington, was glad that he himself had not been given the job, for the mast was waving like a signal flag. But he had no sympathy for Yeoman.

Jack got a knee over the cross trees and began work on the tangle. But the necessity of holding on always with one hand and often with two made him intolerably slow.

Charrington left the cockpit and climbed up to join him. It was not long after that before the halliards were clear. But the two men remained standing on the crosstrees, apparently doing some small repair to the burgee.

Marcus watched, feeling sick and worried. The Skipper should not risk his life like that. But Charrington seemed quite at ease even in that precarious position. Marcus could see his lips moving in conversation.

By a roll of the ship no more violent than the others Yeoman was peeled off the mast. He fell like a starfish and splashed into the water. He came to the surface level with the cockpit and clawed at the yacht's side. Marcus reached out to him; but the wash covered him. When next his face appeared, gaping and frightened, he was several yards astern.

Marcus, shouting at the top of his voice, jumped to the binnacle and threw the life belt overboard, leaving the helm while the yacht surged forward with the wind. Yeoman's face appeared once more, then vanished behind a wave—a long way off. They were racing away from him.

Charrington jumped into the cockpit, pushed Marcus out of the way and heaved the helm right over. Meanwhile the other two had come on deck. Charrington ordered them to hoist the mainsail.

Then began a straining, anxious race, zigzagging up against the wind along the course they had been following so easily. The waves had suddenly become aggressive again. They threw themselves against the bow. Worse, they prevented any long or continuous view. There was no mark to show whether they had reached or passed the place where Jack had gone overboard. They had been tacking for a long time: surely they had reached the place.

Charrington was at the helm, the others at the shrouds or in the bow, darting their eyes in every direction. The disordered sea rose and dropped, the two swells colliding, spurting upwards with the collision, then falling apart again, leaving deep hollows.

How long could a man remain alive in such water? Oh God, how miserable and horrible it was!

Suddenly Marcus shouted. Their hopes leaped up. He had glimpsed something white on top of a wave. It took several minutes to reach it. It was the life belt. They could read the words *Heather Mary H.Y.C.* as it rode light upon the water, drifting with the wind. But there was no sign of Yeoman.

They went on staring at the useless life belt with that disemboweled sensation of tragedy which comes before thought.

Charrington was making the yacht race up and down in violent zigzags, driving her as she had never been driven before. But they could see nothing except the senseless and disordered waves.

He shouted, "Get to the masthead, somebody."

They all moved together but Toby was the fastest. He was halfway up the rigging before he began to think. Then he became nauseatingly conscious that the mast was flicking like a fly rod. He imagined what had happened to Yeoman. He remembered that the Skipper had said people were rarely picked up when they fell overboard. But he went on climbing, desperately, burning up his strength by the excess of muscular effort with which he held on to the wire ladder and pulled himself up. He reached the crosstrees, got his legs over them and embraced the mast with both arms.

The first thing he did, foolishly, was to look down at the deck where three faces stared up at him from far below, swaying from side to side as if they were suspended on pendulums. The bile rose in his throat and the water into his eyes and nose, and for a moment he buried his face in his arms, dizzy and sick. Then he remembered that he had called Jack a bloody fool. He had to find him.

From the deck he had only been able to see waves. Now he could still see only waves—but he could see infinitely more of them. And he could look down into the nearer hollows. His eyes raced up and down over the endless ploughed field of water; then began to search with care.

He saw something. He was not sure what. But immediately and instinctively he shouted and let go with one arm to point. Charrington swung the helm over.

Twenty seconds later those on deck had a glimpse of Jack Yeo-

man, on the crest of a wave. Next moment he had sunk into the
trough and they scarcely believed in what they had seen. He had
been swimming a conventional breast stroke, an intent and worried expression on his face—just like a bather at Clacton or South-
end who has gone a little too far out of his depth.

They saw him again and it was true. Dear, sturdy old Jack!
They would have him aboard in a minute. They glanced at Charrington. He looked troubled. This puzzled them—Jack was so
close. . . . And then they understood.

Jack was a-beam of them to windward. It was necessary to sail
on and then beat up to him on the other tack. By the time they
had come about he had vanished.

One of the most difficult things in the world—in fact it is probably impossible—is to select visually a point in the changing sea
and hold it from a moving vessel. Each of them kept his eyes on
the spot where they thought Yeoman had disappeared. They
stared at it with the strain of holding their breaths. Then they
began to lose confidence and glanced elsewhere. Then they did
not know where to look and were in a St. Vitus' dance of anxious
searching.

After an intolerable pause Toby shouted again. Marcus and
Boyd, who without realizing what they were doing had climbed
halfway up the rigging, saw Yeoman a moment later.

He was paddling desperately with his hands and going under
every other second, swamped by the waves.

Toby, Marcus and Boyd shouted and pointed. The yacht
swung into the right direction. All three men slid down the rigging, lay flat in the bow or climbed down on to the bobstay to get
hold of Yeoman as soon as they should reach him. They may
have heard but were much too excited to understand what Charrington was bellowing from the helm.

By the time they had got into position to grab and pull him up,
Yeoman was only about ten yards in front. He was making feeble
movements with his hands and his eyes were goggling. His mouth
kept gasping wide—more often taking in water than air. His
rescuers worked themselves down and forward, precariously
reaching out towards him while the bow of the yacht rose and
fell, ploughing through the disturbed water and half blinding
them with foam and spray.

Then they realized that the yacht was not heading directly for Yeoman but would pass a yard or more away. They shouted but could not signal—and next moment were abreast of him.

Toby leaned out, touched Yeoman's shoulder, and lost his balance. He would have gone too if Marcus had not grabbed his long hair. Then Boyd got hold of an arm and Marcus on the bobstay improved his grip. With a great effort they got Toby out of the stream of water which was already sucking at his legs and pulled him sufficiently far on to the deck for him to save himself. Meanwhile Yeoman had passed out of their sight along the side of the yacht.

Marcus, Boyd and Toby scrambled to their feet, panting and turned aft—towards Charrington.

Charrington was not there.

The cockpit was empty and the tiller swinging. The stern at that moment was sliding down the steep side of a swell. The unguided yacht had veered up into the wind and slowed almost to a standstill. The sail flapped, helpless as they were.

Then the yacht was in the middle of the bowl formed by the double swell. There were banks all round but the surface was as smooth as the grass in a chalk hollow—except directly astern. Astern there was a commotion as if a shark were fighting on a hook. It was a moment or two before they saw what was really causing it.

Since the yacht had been beating up wind, close hauled, the bulk of the main sheet had been on the deck. Now it was trailing taut astern. Charrington was at the end of it with Yeoman in his arms.

They got them on to the deck—none of them could describe what they did better than that. Yeoman lay dripping and motionless. Charrington was on his feet at once. He hove-to the yacht, then knelt astride the body. Salt water came pumping from the open mouth, trickled across the deck and dripped over the side where it belonged.

The flow ceased. The body grunted, groaned and moved. Charrington and Toby picked Yeoman up and carried him below to the saloon. There Boyd stripped him and wrapped him in the driest blankets they could find while Toby furiously pumped the pressure stove to make a hot drink quickly.

Charrington, who had retired to his cabin, came back in a towel dressing gown and with a bottle in his hand. Toby gave him a cupful of boiling water which he laced golden with whiskey. He took Yeoman's head in the crook of his arm and poured the toddy into his mouth. Yeoman spluttered and blinked. He said in a weak voice, "Tell Tilly I'm all right." Then he slipped slowly down on to the settee and went to sleep like a child.

Charrington passed the bottle round. When it came back to him it was half empty. They had needed a drink. They sat down side by side on the other settee and relaxed with the glow of whiskey spreading through them like a fireside yawn.

"Tell us what happened, Richard," Marcus said.

"You bloody fools! When he got close I couldn't see him from the tiller—and not one of you signaled. I saw him alongside. So I hitched the main sheet round me and jumped."

Charrington went to his cabin.

"Where would we be without him?" Marcus murmured.

It was on the tip of Toby's tongue to answer, "On shore." But his annoyance at not putting into port seemed out of proportion now.

<hr />

CHAPTER 14

ACCORDING to the Pilot Book they should now have picked up the Portuguese Trades and be running comfortably southward to the latitude of Madeira.

But it did not happen like that. Marcus said that the Portuguese Trades were all black market. There were winds from every direction, a half gale, an occasional calm and an endless swell—much the same conditions as they had experienced in the Channel and the Bay of Biscay. Unexpected repetition of discomfort is always harder to bear than the first discomfort was. It resulted in several quarrels about nothing in particular, and a general sense of strain and impatience. An extract from Toby's diary gives one point of view of their surroundings.

"People talk about the majesty of the sea. Majesty my foot. The most striking thing about the sea when you get to know it is its weakness of character. It is like the dull gray mass of the proletariat on which the agitators work so easily.

"It is lying calm and passive, the whole world at peace. Then the wind starts a whispering campaign. Within a few hours it has organized a procession. Soon the waves are marching along with banners. The *agents provocateurs* fan them and they lose their heads entirely. They run amok, trying to destroy everything . . . The wind stops and goes elsewhere. But for two or three days the sea continues to bang and heave about, although it has lost any real incentive it may have had . . . Then, before it has calmed completely, another whisper has begun. And within a few hours the sea is on another hooligan rampage—from another direction but with the same slogan, 'The Ocean for the Waves! Down with everything that isn't water!' "

Life on the yacht, ordered by the watches, followed a set pattern whatever anybody might be thinking. Only two or three incidents are worth describing. The first happened within an hour or two of Yeoman's rescue.

Boyd was alone in the saloon with Yeoman when he woke up. Jack opened his eyes and stared in a puzzled way at his surroundings. Then he sucked his lips in and spoke awkwardly.

"I fell overboard, I'm sorry."

"It might happen to anybody at the top of a swaying mast," Boyd said.

"Yes, I was at the top of the mast with the Skipper."

They were silent for a while.

Like a candle lighted in a cottage window, a thought appeared in Yeoman's sleepy eyes. He looked at the two closed doors, then asked in a low voice, "Where's the Colonel?"

"Making his inventory in your forward cabin. Do you want him?"

"No! He said I shouldn't have talked to the Skipper about Miss Heather."

"Did you?" Boyd asked.

"Not till he started. Then I just said what was natural. She was very good to me, you know, after my own wife passed away."

Boyd waited.

"It's not his talking about her that's odd though. It's the things he says and the questions he asks. He wants to know every little thing about when she came to look after me when I was left alone—what we talked about, how we got on, even what room she slept in. You'd think he was jealous if that wasn't absurd."

"Wishing to hear of the kind acts of a lost wife isn't necessarily jealousy," Boyd said.

"No—but, Doctor, he had a letter I'd written to her. He was going to ask me about it, I think. But it was washed overboard at the beginning of the storm."

"You are sure it was your letter?"

"I think so. I didn't get a clear view of it but I thought I recognized my handwriting."

Boyd looked thoughtfully at the honest, worried and tired face. "Listen, Jack," he said. "Let us stick to what we know for certain. The Skipper suffered a great shock at the death of his wife and hasn't got over it even yet. We have that from Marcus. Mrs. Harding, who knows the Skipper well, wanted Marcus to come on this trip to look after him. From what I happen to know of their marriage, Charrington and his wife were in love but didn't hit it off somehow. They talked on different wave lengths. It seems to me perfectly natural that he should want to hear about her from us. There is nothing to be disturbed about in it."

"But I am disturbed," Yeoman said.

"Why, Jack? Don't forget he has just taken a big risk to save your life."

Yeoman looked again at the closed doors of the saloon, then whispered, "You don't know what he said when he got hold of me in the water."

"Nor do you. You were unconscious."

"Perhaps I was. But he gripped on to me so it hurt and I'd swear said, 'You can't escape like that.' "

The door suddenly opened and Charrington was in the saloon.

"Hello, Jack. You're awake. Why are you looking so bothered?"

Yeoman stared up at him with tight closed lips and bulging eyes.

"He's lost his teeth," Boyd said. "And they were such a lovely set."

"He doesn't look so handsome, does he?" Charrington laughed.

Another incident which, to a certain extent, bore on the same subject, happened two days later.

Marcus, in the cockpit with Charrington, apologized for taking so long over his inventory of the stores.

"You must blame my queasy stomach," he said. "Until recently I could only work below when it was calm."

"That's all right," Charrington answered. "No hurry. How far have you got?"

"I've listed the food in the saloon lockers and the galley and forward cabin. And I've checked the two water tanks with a dip stick. One is still full but the other's nearly empty. I was wondering—"

"What?"

"We are running just about parallel to the shore. Wouldn't it be a good plan to put in and fill up with water before we start across the Atlantic?"

"No."

"But why not?"

"We've wasted enough time already, and there's no need. That full tank under the galley holds seventy-five gallons—nearly a quart a day per man for three months. And there's half as much again in the spare tank in my cabin. Good God, there's almost enough fresh water to wash in."

"It would be nice to have a wash in fresh water," Marcus said. "We're all sticky as fly papers. And a night or two ashore would push up morale no end."

"Marcus, if you don't like salt water you shouldn't have come to sea. I made you second-in-command to back me up, not to criticize my plans."

"The last thing I want to do is to criticize you, Richard, but—"

"If you don't want to criticize, don't talk like that. I know how to run a yacht—and a crew."

Marcus was silent, feeling hurt and angry. Richard was being damned unfair. He looked at him as he sat hunched over the tiller, brooding like a hawk. His beard had begun to grow, his Captain Kettle beard. Unimaginative though he was, Marcus suddenly saw Charrington as a gunboat Commander, ruthlessly driving both men and vessel. He had made a great reputation by his aggressive leadership. His last action, heavily outnumbered, had been the best of the lot. He had gone on fighting until his engines were stopped and his ammunition done. But they hadn't given him a medal. Marcus remembered how indignant Meg had been at this. Most of all she had been angered by what was said to be the reason for this lack of recognition—that he had allowed his ship to fall into the enemy's hands. "Did they expect him to blow himself up, or bore a hole in the bottom, or what?" Meg had asked. . . . But, as Marcus realized, the fact remained that Richard had failed in his final duty, so he had no reason to be so damned aggressive now.

"Marcus, you haven't yet checked the stores in my cabin. Come down there—will you?—when you've finished your watch," Charrington said and went below.

Half an hour later Yeoman relieved Marcus at the tiller. They scarcely exchanged a word. Relations had been strained since Marcus had condemned him for his criticism of the Skipper. Strangely, Yeoman's rescue had not cured this state of affairs. Things were better, but—now Marcus felt awkward.

"Damn it," Marcus thought as he went below. "This is no state in which to launch off across the Atlantic—four thousand miles and no company except our own. God knows what I'm in for now in Richard's holy of holies."

He knocked on the cabin door and a warm, friendly voice told him come in. On the instant his spirits rose at this.

Charrington was lying on his bunk with a book in his hands. He put it down and sat up—careful not to bump his head.

"Come in, Marcus. I can't ask you to sit down because there isn't a seat. By the way, I must apologize for biting your head off just now, but you and I can snap at each other when we're tired without bearing any ill feeling. What do you think of my cabin?"

Marcus stood in the small floor space, swaying slightly as he had learned to do to keep his balance. The water sighed and hissed outside the walls as the yacht drove forward. He looked round. On the starboard side was the bunk on which Charrington sat with his legs dangling. Above the bunk there was a shelf of books. Aft was a folding washstand closed against the wall. To port there seemed only to be a paneled wall. All round at ground level there were lockers. It was strictly tidy, as one would expect. Marcus wanted to respond to Richard's conciliatory tone, but he could think of nothing worth saying about the cabin and wondered why Richard had made such a mystery of it.

"It's very snug."

Charrington pushed out of the bunk and jumped to the floor. In so doing he disclosed the part of the book shelf which his body had been obscuring. On it, in a leather traveling frame, was a photograph of Heather Mary.

It was a snapshot, perfectly natural, but with the art and detail of a studio portrait. She was standing up to her ankles in water, dressed in trousers and a jersey, her hands in her pockets, leaning forward with a question in her face, her hair blowing behind.

Marcus' eyes were held by the eyes of the photograph. He remembered her looking exactly like that.

"What's interesting you?" Charrington asked.

Marcus started, and a surge of contradictory feelings and resolves passed through him in a moment.

"I was—well, I was admiring the cabin."

"Neat, isn't it," Charrington said. "It was well designed when I got her and I perfected it little by little. Plenty of unobtrusive storage space. There behind you is the chart table. It's where the other bunk used to be. It folds down like this—" He pulled down the panel, making it into a table with a chart of the Portuguese coast on it—"Here we are. Tomorrow we bear off to the westward to pass Madeira and reach the Trades. You are going to enjoy the Trades, Marcus. Flying fish jumping into the frying pan for breakfast, all the romance of tropical seas and nothing to do but sit and gossip and enjoy it."

"Yes," Marcus said. He had been trying hard to pull himself together in the barrage of Charrington's words. "But you know, Richard, I came down here to check your stores."

"You needn't bother. I find I have a list. Here it is, food and water. That's as far as I got but it completes your inventory. So you have nothing more to do now than help me to keep people cheerful on the long crossing. What shall we have for dinner tonight?"

Marcus left the cabin, half elated and half ashamed. He had a grand leader and it was his own clear duty as second-in-comamnd to pass on the Skipper's enthusiasm. He was half ashamed, though, of his sin of omission in denying notice of Heather's photograph. What else could he have done? But he had an uncomfortable feeling that he had put himself in a false position.

CHAPTER 15

IT was the dawn watch of one of these uncertain days while they still waited for the Trades. The yacht was scudding south-westward before a fresh northerly breeze and Boyd and Charrington were together in the cockpit while the others slept, when a bluish-purple hump gradually took shape on the horizon to port.

Charrington had his back to it. Boyd, sitting opposite to him, was silent until he was certain that what he saw was land, not cloud. Then he said, "That's Madeira, I suppose."

Charrington turned. "Yes," he said. "I had hoped to pass it during the night."

"Shall we put in?"

"No."

There was a pause. Then Boyd in his quiet voice said. "May I ask why not?"

"We have enough food and water. No spars went in that storm. We lost a couple of sails but we would not be able to replace them, and can do without. You have got the charging engine running again yourself. There is no justification whatever for putting into port."

Boyd had been looking thoughtfully at Charrington. Now the flicker of a smile came into his eyes.

"Then why not put in just for the pleasure of it?"

"What pleasure?" Charrington asked.

"To be able to walk more than five paces in one direction and on something solid and stationary—to see strangers and talk to them if one felt inclined—to wash in fresh water—to eat a meal cooked, served and cleared away by someone else—to get into a proper bed between sophisticated sheets instead of hairy blankets, knowing one had clean linen to put on first thing in the morning—"

"Does that sort of thing mean so much to you?" Charrington asked.

"No more than I believe it does to you. I'm not complaining. But it would only add a day or two to the voyage. Therefore I wonder why you are determined to deny it to yourself—and us."

"Did the others put you up to this?" Charrington asked.

Boyd looked blank and then his eyes opened wider. "Surely we can talk to each other like intelligent beings," he said.

Charrington put a hand on Boyd's shoulder.

"Forgive me. I'm on edge. I have not made up on my sleep since that storm."

"Isn't that another reason for putting into harbor?" Boyd asked.

Charrington shook his head.

"If one's primary object is to get across the Atlantic there is no justification for putting into harbor."

"I don't follow that. For instance—" Boyd began.

Charrington interrupted. "If we dropped anchor in Funchal the odds would be against our every reaching Bermuda. I can't explain that logically but it's a fact. And I assure you I'm now speaking as one intelligent being to another. Listen. In the ports of Madeira and the Canaries too I dare say, certainly in Gibraltar, you'd find plenty of yachts that put in to rest and refit for a few days—perhaps a year ago. They may go home but they'll never go on."

"But why?" Boyd said.

"You will have to accept my word. I am quite certain that if we rested in Funchal Marcus would cable home and hear that one of his kids was ill and he must take an airplane at once. Jack Yeoman would get homesick or discover that his vocation was to grow vines. And Toby would fall in love or decide to return to the girl he left behind him. You would stay: I'm sure of you. But any of the others might desert for one good reason or another."

"It interests me," Boyd said, "that you can be worried at the possibility of somebody leaving the yacht. I'd have thought you were the last person to depend on a pressed crew."

"Good God!" Charrington exclaimed. "I would sail her round the world without any crew at all."

"Exactly—"

"But that's not the point," Charrington said, calmly again. "We set out on this passage together and we will finish it together."

Toby's long untidy hair and his thin, bored intelligent face appeared through the hatch. He ignored the men in the cockpit but turned slowly round, examining the horizon. . . . At the top of his voice he shouted, "Land! Bloody good land."

He swung back to the cockpit. "Didn't you see it?" Without waiting for an answer he turned, ducked his head into the companionway and yelled, "Land—Madeira for a quid. Come and see it, you sleepy baskets!"

Marcus and Yeoman sprouted up beside him. They stared where he pointed, shading their eyes from the sun. They shouted with excitement.

Then for the first time they looked at the two faces in the cockpit, and were immediately sobered.

"Aren't we going to put in, Richard?" Marcus asked.

"No. It's off our course."

"But you said we'd hurry in to the next land we saw," Toby said.

"I didn't expect this visibility. I meant Bermuda. We'll hurry on to that. It would neither be good policy nor good seamanship to put in now. You must take my word for that."

"If we are in such a hurry to reach Bermuda," Toby said, "Why do we go by this roundabout route?"

"Because it is the best. You will understand that when we are fairly into the Trades. Nor is it roundabout, as you'd appreciate if you studied it on a globe. Look here, I don't often exert my authority as Skipper, but, when I do, I expect my decisions to be accepted without any damned argument."

"Of course we accept your decision," Marcus said.

But Boyd had a different reaction. He was not entirely happy about the spirit of the voyage. That was why he wanted a day or two ashore—to take stock under more normal conditions. That had been refused. So it seemed wise to put his anxieties to the test in public while it was still possible to halt the voyage.

"I don't mean to be impertinent," he said. "But before that land drops under the horizon we ought to be told frankly how we stand. You told me just now that a Skipper cannot trust a crew ashore before starting across the Atlantic. Do you really consider us a crew of that sort? In that case why did you invite four men you hardly knew? Do you regret your choice?"

"Why did I invite you? Not for your skill as sailors. None of you can navigate. You know very little about trimming the sails as I discover every time I come on deck. And although you have been through one moderate storm I doubt if you would feel competent to face another on your own."

"You never taught us anything," Toby said.

"No. This isn't a training ship. You are strong, and I thought you were willing—which was all I asked for as far as sailing was concerned."

"So you are satisfied," Boyd said.

"Perfectly. As I told you on the first day I wanted company. I never had many intimate friends of my own. Most of that few were killed in the war. None of the rest could get away for so long. So I searched among my wife's friends. Finally I discovered you four, who accepted. Personally I have never regretted it."

They were silent. Boyd glanced at Marcus who was stroking his mustache. Yeoman's round face showed an expression half doubtful, half relieved. Toby frowned.

Still no one said anything, and after a moment Charrington went on.

"I'll tell you one reason why I haven't regretted it. I had the richest, happiest married life for three years before the war. In your different ways you must each have known Mary well enough to realize the fascination there was in being the husband of such an intricate, fairy-like creature. . . . Then the damned old war came . . . We are being frank: I must admit that I enjoyed bits of it while my innings lasted. But it complicated married life. And then I was locked up, or a fugitive, for over four years. That was neither war nor peace, marriage nor hermit-like celibacy. We wrote to each other, of course. But you can't expect a spirit of the mountains and the sea to express itself in censored letters . . . I tried for over four years to escape and return to her. Finally—by the last means I could have expected—I was successful. But before we could come together she had vanished. I am glad of companions who can help me fill in the gap."

"You know, Richard, you ought to have written a book about your escapes," Marcus said.

Charrington finished lighting his pipe, then said, "If I had written a book it wouldn't have been about escaping."

"What then?" Toby asked.

"Everyday life," Charrington answered. "The really interesting side of a prison camp was how the inmates evolved their individual solutions of how best to spend their captive lives. The book that's wanted is an anthropological and sociological study."

"That's a bit deep for me," Marcus said.

Charrington went on with growing animation. "Prisoners of war are like inhabitants of an old and highly civilized world removed haphazard by a dictatorial providence to populate a brand-new world it has just created."

"Surrounded by barbed wire instead of space," Boyd said.

"Exactly. Barbed wire or walls or water."

"How did it develop?"

"Much as this world did—"

Marcus interrupted with his sudden laugh. He was glad that the talk had moved from Heather Mary to the safe field of wartime reminiscence and he wanted to encourage it. "You are damned philosophical, Richard," he said.

"That was part of the evolution. In our camp forum we would argue for days together on every subject under the sun. But that came later. I believe that right at the start—at the time of the fall of France—prisoners were little more than a semi-conscious mass only interested in food and sleep. Even after that, when I was caught, men who had been wounded or exhausted—sailors who had been in the water for instance—were in much the same state to begin with."

Boyd asked, "What happened next?"

"People began to talk. They discovered the need to boast. Since there is nothing to be proud about in being captured they described how heavily they had been outnumbered and what crippling casualties their ship or unit had suffered. This caused the first division of society, for there were some people who could not boast. There was an R.N. Commander I knew who had been a Beach Officer at Dunkirk. He went inland to make contact with the military unit he was responsible for—and got captured. He felt he had lost his ship. He put himself in the other division of society. I joined him there—for I really had lost my ship."

"Through no fault of your own," Marcus said at once.

"What difference does that make?" Charrington demanded ex-

citedly. "All we knew—those of us who were any good—was that
we had to redeem ourselves."

He was silent, drawing hard at his pipe.

"How else did the society develop?" Boyd asked quietly.

"Into those who accepted their fate more or less calmly and
those who were restless and tried to change it."

"Were those the same divisions as before?" Boyd asked.

"I don't know. Not necessarily. I had no time to study it."

"You were too busy trying to escape," Marcus said.

"Most of the time, yes. But if anybody did study the subject
he would find the acceptors of their fate the more interesting
group."

"I don't believe that," Toby said.

"It's true. What is the instinct of a wild animal when it is shut
up? It tries to get out, hurts itself on the bars, on and on incurably.
That is what the restless did, and it is not a very interesting reaction. On the other hand the acceptors built a new world in the
image of the old. They organized theaters, concerts, lectures. They
had sports, football matches with enthusiastic backing of different
teams. If the camp were large and mixed and the guards sufficiently corrupt there was a flourishing black market, and rich and
poor in the luxuries of food and drink. When books arrived people
read history, fiction, biography, learned languages or studied their
profession. I knew one man who went through the whole chartered
accountant's training, working from nine till six every week day
and giving himself a fortnight's holiday in the summer. There were
artists and artisans. Some of the roughest took to religion—one
is a monk now, fasting and sleeping in his coffin. Some went mad.
If that isn't a broadly developed human society—"

"Without women," Toby said.

"Inevitably. We lived on idealized memories."

"Tell us about the restless prisoners," Boyd said.

"Restless—that wasn't a good term really. I suppose most of us
were restless at times for one reason or another. I applied the word
to those who did something practical—not only the escapers but
also the expert helpers who forged passes and identity papers, made
German uniforms, and civilian clothes, maps and compasses, and
those who distracted the guards at critical moments, or gave food
and mackintoshes and so on to escapers."

"Surely everybody would do as much as that. After all it is the duty of every officer—"

"Everybody hasn't got your code, Marcus. There were the completely passive or self-contained, like our chartered accountant, and there were some actively opposed to escapes because they caused trouble. In one camp I was in a tin was thrown over the wire into the German compound. In it was an anonymous letter saying that under the floor boards in a certain hut there was a tunnel being dug. As it happened the tin was picked up by a British orderly and the letter given to our Man of Confidence."

"Who could have done that—not a British officer, certainly."

"Nobody else could in this case. Marcus, I don't say you would behave like that, but you would have been surprised, if you had been a prisoner for four or five years instead of raging around in search of death or glory, to discover how a sense of duty can get distorted. People who may have been fine officers in the old world did very odd things in the new. They had their reasons of course. In this case I believe it was because of the news."

"What news?"

"The B.B.C. news as opposed to the German propaganda version. You can't realize how passionately hungry prisoners grew for news, contact with the old sane world—"

"I can," Toby interrupted. "I can see war news was the same for prisoners as weather news would be for us. I've missed nothing so much as hearing that man from London giving the shipping forecast since your set was smashed."

"Exactly. Sooner or later every camp acquired a receiving set. The guards were always on the lookout for them but the radio men became amazingly cunning. The reception, the writing down and reading out of the news was, I imagine, something like the intercommunion of the early Christians in Rome. Methods of escape were always carefully concealed even after the escapers had been recaptured. This caused extra severe searches by the guards. That might result in a receiving set being found. The man who threw the tin over the wire wanted to prevent that. He thought the means justified the end. Being prisoners, we were all secretive."

There was a silence while the yacht sailed on, spreading her wake of foam behind. There was a sense of urgency in their endless motion.

"But God laughed at all prisoners," Charrington said. "They were made to feel forgotten, useless—"

"Can you explain?" Boyd asked.

"I can give examples. It was a shock to us when after three or four years younger men came in who held higher ranks than we did. And there was a Lieutenant-Commander picked out of the water in 1940 without firing a shot. He was a widower. He used to talk almost exclusively about his boy of fourteen who might get into the second XI of his school. Just before the end he received a letter saying that his son had been killed in action. . . . Other people talked a lot about their wives. A man I'm thinking of at this moment had been married only a month before the war. He was one of the law-abiding acceptors. He'd taken up needle-work and made his wife a *petit point* evening bag. He spent a couple of years over it and it really was a beauty. Somehow or other he got hold of a cardboard box for it with the name of a smart shop on it. He was going to pretend to her, as a joke, that he had somehow bought the thing in Paris. It was a tremendous con-spiracy and he talked about it to everybody. Then he received a letter from his wife saying she was in love with a Canadian. . . . Oh, I could give you dozens of examples. Right at the end, when the camps were liberated by the advancing allies, the prisoners were flown home. All the wives and sweethearts were on the air-drome waiting for a certain plane. It crashed and they watched it burn—"

Charrington let the mainsheet run out a foot or two. The wind was swinging astern and freshening as they sailed south westward.

"You must have some splendid escaping yarns, but you have been mum as an oyster about that side of things," Marcus said. "Won't you tell us, Richard?"

Charrington was silent for a full minute. Watching him, Boyd saw his face set hard. It was as if a mask had been drawn over it. But his eyes showed something. Whatever his thoughts, they were not happy.

"Under the wire, through the wire, over the wire," he said at last. "Out by the gate as a workman and a German officer, down through a hole cut in the floor of a cattle truck. They all ended the same. Most people gave up before they went mad—took to religion or handicrafts instead. But some tried to climb the wire in daylight and got shot like rats, or became melancholics and lay on their bunks staring at the ceiling."

"But you did escape," Marcus persisted.

"Do you know how?"

"No. Tell us, Richard."

"I will not."

"Well, of course not, if you don't want to. But the whole idea of escaping is so damned interesting."

"How would you define escaping?"

"Getting away—"

"From what? From the camp—and you were brought back again nine times out of ten. From Germany—and you might still be caught in occupied country and returned. Into England—one in several hundred got as far as that. And I wonder how many were content when they did. It's not enough escaping from something. You must know what you are escaping to—and find it. Marcus, since the subject interests you, who do you consider did the best escape in history?"

"Lord, I don't know. Who would you say yourself, Richard?"

"Samson."

"Samson? But he—"

Boyd said urgently, "Skipper. If your whole crew asked you as a favor to put into Madeira just for a day or two—wouldn't you do it?"

Charrington came slowly back to his surroundings. "With the best will in the world I couldn't do that now," he said. "You see those little hurrying clouds? They are Trade Wind clouds. And this wind astern is a steady Force Five that won't change much. Even I couldn't get you back against it. We are in the One Way Street."

CHAPTER 16

DARLING Tilly,

Picture your old Dad being wafted down the Trades! That's been going on a fortnight now, although the view is just the same since we lost sight of Madeira. You teach your kids there's three times as much sea as land, but when you are in the middle of it you can hardly believe there is any land at all. I'd better try to tell you what it feels like. Then I'll have a bit of good news for you.

Mostly the wind comes from the same direction, that's to say behind or over your right shoulder. But it doesn't waft, it blows real hard. There wouldn't be any more for the *Skylark* if it was like this off Brighton pier. And sometimes for good measure there's a squall that comes charging up from anywhere, and then the wind and spray fair cane you.

All these two weeks we've had big waves chasing us and washing right over often enough. Do you remember that time last summer when it was rough and we swam out just the same but coming in got wave after wave overtaking us and frothing over our heads until we were half drowned? It's felt something like that. But today for the first time it's started to calm down and I can't wait any longer to try to write to you. You will have to forgive my handwriting. The yacht isn't what you'd call steady. And forgive smudges too. It's hot as an oven with the hatches closed in case waves come aboard and I can't stop my hands perspiring.

It's all as romantic as the books say, though—more I think. It's so bright and big. And such strange things happen so naturally. Fish flying, for instance. Imagine how I felt the first time I came on deck and found one that had delivered itself for breakfast. We had it fried, just a taste each. I didn't fancy it. But they're a lovely sight skimming over the waves. It's as if someone was playing ducks and drakes with silver coins. Squids jump on board too. The Skipper says they do that when they're being chased. They're creepy things. If you don't pick them up at once they stick to the deck. We had to try them too because the Colonel's keen on what he calls supplementing the rations. I couldn't manage mine no more than it'd been a bit of cycle tire. It made the others laugh. But to see them squirt themselves along! We weren't the first to invent jet propulsion as Dr. Boyd says. And the way they spit out ink. You wonder how they make it.

If you lean out over the stern you can see two lovely colored fish. They have followed us nearly a thousand miles already. You can't help wondering why. They aren't there to be caught, that's certain, for the Colonel's tried often enough.

Then there's the birds—one in particular. It's a lovely big white bird that sort of swoops along lazy as can be and seems to like our company. I don't know how it sleeps. Although it's always with us it hardly gives us a glance. We aren't more extraordinary than anything else, I suppose. Not than a whale, for instance. We saw one this morning. It came up quite close and spouted high as a tree.

I expect you think we're idle, sitting on a boat being blown along by the wind. Listen to this, young woman. I've been wanting for three days to ask the Doctor about that bird. But it's just been a case of the four of us relieving each other at the helm. Seven hours total in twenty-four makes almost a working day as it is, and there have been all the other jobs, extra in rough weather, and snatching forty winks when we could. Him or me has always been asleep or busy.

What other jobs? You ask. You used to laugh at me for all I found to do on *Firefly* every evening when you wanted the kitchen table for something else. *Firefly* never did a passage that lasted more than five minutes, and here have we been at sea nearly six weeks and never a let-up. There's always ropes to be spliced. (The Skipper said the other day I spliced pretty well.) And sails that need a stitch or two, or gear to be cleaned and oiled, or some bit of carpentry below or aloft. Besides there's the yacht herself to be kept shipshape and Bristol fashion—the Skipper sees to it we go down on hands and knees with a scrubbing brush—and meals to be prepared and washed up, which is worse with these flying fish and squids and all the mess they make. We don't get a minute for anything like a chat.

But I'm not complaining—far from it! Everybody's well and happy and everything is going splendid. That's the good news I said I had for you. I've written before there was something odd about the Skipper. And in my last letter I told how he got excited. Who wouldn't describing that dreadful time in prison. Anyway, if there was something odd, these Trade Winds have blown it out of all our heads. In a way it's been like the war, this strong wind, making everybody pull together. Nobody could have been friendlier than the Skipper, the few times he's had a talk with me. He said he wanted to hear about Miss Heather. But since I've told him all I know already we can just sit quiet and have a smoke and think of her. You can't help thinking of her on her own yacht.

All this time we're bowling along towards Bermuda where I'll find the right job and you'll come out to look after me and we'll live happy ever after. I'm excited all day long thinking about it. But now I must close because my turn at the helm has come around again.

Yeoman folded his letter and put it carefully away in his sponge bag with the others. For a moment he thought of destroying the one which contained references to "something odd." But he decided not to. It wouldn't be quite honest—like being wise after the event. Besides, there were some good things in it. He put the sponge bag in his locker.

Then, since it was evening, he changed his shirt and trousers, being careful not to wake Toby who was sleeping on his back, stark naked, with little beads of sweat lying on his brown skin like quick-silver.

Yeoman went on deck.

Boyd was gripping the tiller with both hands, steering with the utmost concentration, looking—with his wild gray hair, his eyes screwed up against the sun, his wrinkled face and almost naked body—like some ancient witch doctor. Marcus was behind him, sitting back to back and equally naked—but brick red as opposed to Boyd's old parchment. One of Marcus' hands was on the mizzen shrouds while the other held a fishing line which streamed out parallel to the log line.

Yeoman, coming out of the companionway, felt the warm and powerful wind leap on him like an over-friendly dog. But it was not botheringly strong as it had been. While the other two men remained intent on their occupations he stood looking round him, breathing deep and happily.

It was the familiar scene, but because it was calmer you could appreciate it more. (You didn't have spray stinging your eyes, for instance, and you could look astern without feeling scared.) There was the vast circle of dazzling blue ocean, striped from horizon to horizon by the hills and valleys of the moving swell. Trade Wind rollers! Yeoman liked the word rollers: it sort of explained what happened. When they rolled too fast the waves flew from them like sparks, and even now they seemed to carry the blue and white flecked surface like a conveyor belt. Everything—sun, clouds and sea—was hurrying westwards, sweeping the little yacht along.

"A penny for them."

Charrington had been doing something by the mast and came up behind Yeoman.

"You owe me quite a lot already," Yeoman answered, greatly daring.

"I always pay my debts. Your thoughts are worth the money."

"I was just wondering if we'll ever be able to stop."

"We will. We've the Horse Latitude to cross before we reach Bermuda."

"How far is there still to go, Skipper?"

"Best part of three thousand miles. But the Trades won't help us for more than two. We've had their strongest blow already I should think, and we'll lose them altogether when we start to trend northwards. Then the wind may blow from anywhere, or not at all."

Marcus had rolled up his line. The four men sat together in the cockpit watching the last little clouds hurrying to overtake the sun and pose themselves for the climax scene.

"He'll be late," Marcus said.

"Not he—there he is," Boyd said.

Toby climbed up through the forward hatch and sat with his back against the mast. He watched the passionate expression of colors—the orgasm of beauty as he had called it on his notebook.

When the sun was gone, and sea and sky had put on their pearl gray nightdresses, he rose and joined the others in the cockpit.

It had become a habit for all of them to meet on deck during the last half hour of the dog watch, for until this evening it had been necessary to shorten sail before dark. Then all except the helmsman went below.

Already they had fallen into a Trade Winds routine, broken only by the sudden demands of rough weather. And from this evening onwards, for two weeks, there was nothing more distracting than the occasional rain squalls—which they looked forward to as the only opportunity for a fresh water wash. The wind still blew—but only with sufficient strength to make the heat bearable and to fill the sails. The tiller no longer jumped and tugged under the steerman's hand: it lay there quietly. They no longer heard the groan of blocks and grunt of hard strained rope. The surface over which the yacht moved so prettily was scarcely more than rippled. Except for the clouds, a swooping bird or the flash of a small breaking wave here and there, *Heather Mary* was the only white thing in the great circle of vivid blue. Day changed into night as smoothly as the crests into the valleys of the rollers. Time moved on, as the yacht did, without anything to measure it against.

Thus there is little to tell. But a few incidents may give detail to the picture.

First a night watch.

Since taking over at midnight, Marcus had been at the tiller for half an hour when Charrington came up and joined him. This was a custom which had developed from the stormy period. Now they could sit at ease, smoking and talking—not that they talked much. But in their silences as much as in their conversation he felt that a personal companionship—quite apart from the link which Meg made—was growing up between them; and he believed that this had a lot to do with Richard's recovered calm.

On this occasion Charrington asked, "Catch anything today?"

"No," Marcus answered.

"Lots of sailors will tell you fish don't take bait in deep water."

"I don't believe that. They must feed, and they can't know it's bait or they wouldn't take it even in shore water. That's common sense. I'll haul 'em in when I discover the local secret."

There was a long pause. Then Charrington remarked. "You are an expert fisherman, I gather."

"My dear Richard, I've never tried this sort before. And I'm a pretty average tiro with a trout rod. It's just I like the peace of it and thinking my own thoughts and that."

There was another silence.

Charrington said at last, "Meg is good, isn't she?"

"Expert—and keen as mustard. She taught me all I know up at her people's place when we were courting. . . . Good old Meg."

"Good old Meg," Charrington repeated. Then, confidentially, "You get on well together, don't you?"

"Of course. Why do you ask?"

"Only that after the war when you were so little together— even on your leaves—and then two years in the East. Well, it seems odd she should encourage you to go off on a trip like this as soon as you get back."

Marcus muttered, "She always likes me to do what I want." He felt that Richard wasn't quite convinced, but obviously he could not repeat Meg's instruction, "Look after Richard." So he said no more.

Later, when Boyd had relieved him, he went to the galley to brew coffee. While the water heated he found himself picturing their arrival in Bermuda. It was a calm blue harbor with clean white houses clustering on the shore. They would anchor among spick-and-span racing yachts and men in spotless white would hail them, asking where they were from.

"Brixham."

"Not Brixham, England?"

"Yes."

Meg and the brats would come out in a motor launch—how excited those two little ragamuffins would be, and how thrilled to be shown over the yacht! Meg would already have dug herself in to the local society. She'd have been elected a member of the club. They'd have drinks there—probably have to dine there too. A bit of a bore, but everybody would want to know about the voyage. "Storms? Oh Lord yes, but one gets used to storms. . . ."

The coffee bubbled. Marcus took a cup to Boyd in the cockpit.

"How long has Richard been below?" he asked.

"He went just after you did."

"I was wondering if I should take him a cup. Do you think he's asleep?"

"His light is still on. But coffee isn't the best thing for bad sleepers."

"How do you know he's a bad sleeper?"

"He told me so—a result of his escaping days. He got the day and night habits reversed and hasn't righted them. He hardly ever seems to turn his light out. I offered him some of my sleeping tablets—"

"You don't use sleeping tablets?"

"I haven't needed them—any more than my seasick pills. But the Skipper wouldn't have them."

"Oh well," Marcus said. "I'd better not take him any coffee."

He went below and lay on his bunk. Turning out the light he tried to recapture his imaginings.

After dinner he would walk with Meg to their bungalow, through the soft night with her thin and vital arm in his. He would ask her what had been in her mind when she told him to look after Richard. He would describe Richard's strange excitement and how he had dealt with it. She would congratulate him on being a good second-in-command.

Then, without conscious transition and certainly without surprise, Marcus was standing by a highland burn. His body was swaying forward and back as he cast a fly. He wasn't catching anything—but he wasn't much interested in that. Heather was beside him, her big oilskin hat thrown back upon her shoulders, the chin tape round her throat, her face eager and bright. She was talking to him, her voice like hurrying water. . . . What made it so satisfactory was that she would be with him all the voyage. Meg wouldn't mind—even if she knew. Richard wouldn't know either. It was perfectly innocent, but there were things one didn't talk about.

Marcus fell asleep, smiling.

During the next afternoon an excited shout from the helmsman, Yeoman, brought them all on deck. There was a tiny cloud of black smoke on the horizon. Gradually it grew larger and moved to cross their bows. During the next two hours they watched it almost continually, wondering how close it would pass. At its nearest, when it was exactly ahead, they could distinguish it as a two-funneled liner. But she was many miles away and did not appear to notice them. She moved on northwards like a bonfire going out.

"Any chance of passing one closer?" Marcus asked.

"Not much," Charrington answered. "We've probably got the Trade Winds route to ourselves. The steamer lanes cross it about at right angles."

"Where was that one bound?"

Charrington shrugged his shoulders. "Cape Town to New York, perhaps."

Later, Boyd relieved Toby at the helm and told him to join the others at supper.

Toby moved away from the tiller, closed his notebook and put it away in the cockpit locker, but he showed no inclination to go below. His hair was by now extraordinarily long, hanging lank and black on his thin, weathered cheeks. Half naked as he was, he might have been an Old Testament shepherd boy. Watching little hurrying clouds, or watching herds of sheep—what was the difference?

"When you saw that ship pass, what did you think?" Toby asked.

"About my laboratory and my books," Boyd said at once.

"I thought so. I knew you understood."

"Why—have you left a job unfinished too?"

"It's not that. I was sure you would feel the connection with home."

Boyd smiled. "I'm sure Marcus felt it too, and Jack. But since there is no chance of short-cutting things in any case they said nothing."

"I suppose you're right. But tell me, would you like to short-cut things—get home at once by some means—if you could?"

Boyd did not answer at once and Toby added, "He can't hear. He's in the saloon, not his cabin."

"No," Boyd said, ignoring the last remark. "Even if a liner or a flying boat came alongside and offered to take me home I wouldn't go. A week ago, perhaps. Then I felt cured and idle. I had a longing for my work like the longing for tobacco. But I don't feel that now. I've eaten of the lotus, and I'm content to find my interests within our own little world."

For a minute or two they remained without talking or looking at each other.

Toby said suddenly, "I don't mind talking to you."

"What would you like to talk about?" Boyd asked.

"I've sometimes wondered if the Skipper was really taking us to Bermuda."

"You don't doubt that now," Boyd said.

"No, as a matter of fact I don't. The Skipper talked to me for a long time the other night. I didn't help the conversation much I'm afraid, but he was perfectly friendly and open. . . But tell me, why did *you* ask if he was dissatisfied with us or did not trust us—when we were off Madeira, I mean?"

"I wanted to clear the air—and I did. Are you worried about anything, Toby?"

"Worried? If I can't make a success of this—I've never had such a chance in my life. It's magnificent."

"Then why this talk about leaving the yacht, and of crises and so on?"

Toby looked slightly self-conscious. "I don't mind telling you. I'm intending to write a book, so I want to know what people think and why they say things."'

The last incident during this second two-weeks period in the Trade Winds occurred when Marcus was at the tiller at 1 P.M. and the rest of them below. Charrington came from his cabin into the saloon where they were having lunch and said:

"I've just worked out the noon sight. We've reached our furthest South. Twenty-two degrees, fifty-five minutes of latitude."

"The Torrid Zone," Boyd said.

"Yes, we're into it. And from now on we begin to trend north."

"Does that mean we're halfway across?" Toby asked.

"More."

"Damn! We ought to have celebrated mid-ocean. Surely that is a special occasion."

"Too conventional. But I'd give a party if Jack decided to go naked like the rest of us in honor of the Torrid Zone."

"I don't feel right undressed," Jack said, looking embarrassed.

"Besides it gets quite fresh in the evenings. I'm always worried you'll take a chill."

At that moment there was a loud commotion on deck, bangs and thuds and a staccato drumming noise.

They bumped into each other to get up the companionway.

Marcus was on the floor of the cockpit, wrestling with a big dolphin. Its all-muscle body was twisting, flailing, bouncing about.

Charrington who had been first on deck reached forward over the companionway and drew the tiller of the dinghy—a two-feet length of hard wood—from the place where it lay lashed together with the oars under the dinghy's upturned stern. He pushed Marcus aside and struck several times on the dolphin's head. The creature shivered convulsively. Its vivid colors changed as it died, glowing and then fading.

"It worked perfectly—once I guessed the secret," Marcus said, tremendously pleased with himself. "You know they wouldn't take bait when I trawled. So I put a flying fish on and cast it like a fly. He came at it like lightning—and my God what a fight! He must be three feet at least. I suppose you haven't a spring balance aboard, have you, Richard?"

CHAPTER 17

TOBY was sitting on his bunk, writing up his notebook by electric light.

"The Skipper says we are more than halfway between Spain and Bermuda. One accepts that of course—one has to. But, myself, I appreciate the meaning no better than I did as a child when an adult told me I was halfway to manhood. I only feel that we are driving further and further into the middle of the ocean.

"One by one, as regularly as the spokes of a revolving wheel, the members of the crew come up and take their turn at the tiller and then go down again. All the time the water creams and bubbles at the bow: the dial of the log ticks off mile after mile;

but we don't seem to be getting anywhere. The view is the same. By day there is the circle of horizon and the lid of sky. But by night these limits are removed and there is nothing between us and the stars.

"People say that adventuring in the lonely places of the world makes you feel humble and unimportant. Nonsense—just the reverse. In London you don't expect God to notice or hear your prayers because of the bustle and row and church bell ringing that everybody else is creating. But here—if God is watching the world even casually he can't have failed to see the little yacht in the middle of the Atlantic. When I am alone at the tiller on a calm night I feel as if there is nothing separating me and God. Whatever I say he'll hear. That isn't blasphemy, it's common sense.

"And if that is common sense it becomes quite reasonable to talk to a person who is dead. I ask her why she did not obey the unmistakable sign that we were meant for each other, why she did not come away with me and be safe in another part of the world as she came to my car. I ask why she did not even answer my letters, but traveled into the west and dropped into the sea.

"Her answers are indistinct but I'm certain she is not far off. In the sea perhaps, but near. I can't explain, but I'm quite sure about it."

"Toby," Yeoman called from the hatch, "it's your watch."

"All right, I'm just coming."

Toby read through the last paragraph. He wondered, as so often before, what her answers would have been. . . .

"Toby, the Skipper's in the cockpit. He wants me to go and do that repair on the topsail."

"All right, I'm just coming."

Two hours later Boyd relieved Toby and found Charrington still on deck. When Toby had gone below they sat for some time without speaking while *Heather Mary* glided swiftly over the dark and placid water with a noise like rustling silk.

Then Charrington said: "Toby and I have been having a philosophical discussion."

"Based on what?" Boyd asked.

"Microcosms. Toby was comparing the yacht with the heavenly

bodies. According to him she is another inhabited planet, slightly nearer to the Earth than Mars is, but not much."

"Yes," Boyd said.

"I suggested that she was more comparable to the whole Universe, with each of us representing a separate world. We work to the same rules but haven't much idea what goes on in each other's mind."

"No," Boyd said.

"You and I, for instance, are as different as we could be. I'm inquisitive and violent in my reactions—and nobody ever tells me anything. You don't care. No, that's not right—you seem interested but I don't believe you would ever be surprised. Therefore people confide in you. Isn't that true."

"I do get confided in—unfortunately," Boyd said.

"Why unfortunately."

"When people confide they generally want advice."

"I don't want advice," Charrington said.

Boyd smiled, "I'm sure you don't."

"But there is something I would like you to tell me. Will you?"

"If I can."

"You know that when I finally got back from Germany I found that my wife was in America. I cabled to her, and for a day or two was in the depths. Then I heard from the Foreign Office—they are an impersonal lot but can be kindly. They said she was coming back on the *Prince Rupert*. One couldn't find out the details of sailings in those days, but I realized that Mary must have dropped everything and started immediately when she got my cable. Can you realize how happy I was? I managed to discover where she was docking and went to meet her. . . . Mary did not come off the ship. Everybody was busy and it was some time before I found out why."

Boyd listened in a state of almost physical discomfort. He felt deeply sorry for Charrington. But what could he say to comfort him? He waited with anxiety for the form that his question would take.

"In war one learns to accept the danger of bombers and U-boats," Charrington said. "But to be lost like that! How did it happen? Why did it happen? Was it some extraordinary accident or—I have been driving myself half crazy ever since through puzzling about that. And you can help me solve it once and for all by answering a single question. You got to know her on the *Prince Rupert*. You saw her often. Tell me, was she happy?"

Boyd hesitated, but not for long, for Charrington's eyes were fixed urgently and impatiently upon him. And the form of the question made it so easy.

"I noticed her as soon as she came on board because she looked so happy," he said.

Charrington's intent expression gradually changed.

He climbed out of the cockpit and walked to the bow. He stood there for some time, staring forward over the dark water. Then he turned and came slowly aft again. Without even looking at Boyd he went below.

Boyd did not feel pleased with himself. To tell only part of the truth was as bad as to lie. And yet—why cause pain if it can be avoided? Heather would not have wanted that, surely. She had suggested that he might "help" her husband. But had he, by that answer, driven out Charrington's devil? The last glimpse of his face as he went below made Boyd doubtful.

Heather. . . . Looking at the smooth water sliding away astern, he recalled that part of her story which he had not told to her husband.

Heather, in the stern of the *Prince Rupert*, had described only a few incidents of her stay in America. Probably, Boyd thought, nothing else had impressed itself on her tired mind. For she had been doubly strained before she sailed, by her work and by her private worries.

At the back of her mind she had hoped to escape her problem, at least for a little while, by crossing the Atlantic Ocean. But it caught up with her when she woke in the ship on the last night of the voyage. For a moment she thought that Richard was in the bunk above her. Then she became convinced that he would meet her on the quay. She lay trembling, fragile as glass, while the ship swayed and trembled as it rushed her though the dark water.

When daylight came she was no longer haunted by these fancies but much worried that she had experienced them so vividly and with such fear. She believed her brain to be logical and straightforward. What did it mean—that a sort of fifth column in her mind was trying to avoid meeting Richard again and facing the struggle of wills this would entail? She didn't want that. The sooner the struggle was over the better. But—but first she must find an opportunity to rally her strength.

She did not find it in Washington. The work was hard and the recreation harder. They would not leave her to herself, and they asked so many questions. She realized that her health was failing and became frightened, because it was essential she should be well. No doubt this extra anxiety hastened her collapse.

She gave no description of her illness. Nature, Boyd thought, has her own anaesthetic and those who have suffered from a nervous breakdown may be saved all the memory of it. What Heather next spoke of was her convalescence. It was spent in a series of visits which might have been endless—for the warmth of invitations never failed—to an ever increasing chain of new friends. Officially she was free to do exactly as she liked. In fact she found it so difficult to refuse pressing kindnesses that she allowed herself to be carried from one sympathetic home to another.

"The war will soon be over. Then your man will come back to you." They all said something like that.

One evening she managed to escape for a walk by herself. Without thinking where she was going she wandered into the poorest quarter of the town. She was passing a saloon when she stopped in her tracks. Somebody inside, with a fine sensitive voice, was singing one of the songs of the Hebrides.

> *When I'm lonely, dear white heart,*
> *Dark the night or black the sea—*

The song came to an end and was replaced by a buzz of talk. A man came out. The buzz swelled and diminished as the door swung. The man said something to Heather but she was scarcely conscious of him. She was waiting for the singer.

He began again. Heather's skin pricked all over and tears started to her eyes. The lovely voice was asking her—

> *Will ye no' come back again?*
> *Better lo'ed ye canna be —*
> *Will ye no' come back again?*

Here was a person from her own land! Without hesitation she pushed open the door and walked into the saloon.

The room was shabby, crowded and vague with smoke. Some of the men stopped talking and fixed their eyes on Heather. She ignored them. She was looking for the singer. She saw him in a corner, leaning against the wall with his white teeth flashing as he sang, as oblivious of the company as she was herself. . . . He was a Negro.

For a moment she remained staring and bewildered. Then she turned and walked quickly out through the swing door. All the way back the words and the black singer haunted her. And gradually the shocked disappointment she had experienced at not finding a fellow countryman gave place to a mood of exhilaration. She had received a message. The strange way in which it had come to her accentuated its importance as if it had been in a secret code. The meaning was unquestionable.

She must go home. How simple a solution! A month even a week or two at Amulree and she would be herself again, ready to face Richard calmly and with assurance. Where their romance had started they would bury it together without bitterness.

There was no difficulty about obtaining permission—she was on indefinite leave as it was—but passages were hard to find. However, since she was still officially an employee of the Foreign Office, and since everybody was anxious to help her, it was arranged that she should sail for England in the *Prince Rupert* which would leave for England via Bermuda in a fortnight's time.

Those two weeks were for Heather a period of daydreaming. She saw Amulree in the crystal clear weather of spring, when there was still snow on the highest hilltops and, lower down, the new green growing stronger every day against the fir trees, among the bare woods and the ocher patches of dead bracken. She could hear the waves talking to her by the shore, the cries of sea birds. . . . She lived in a state of trembling excitement, scarcely believing in the arrangements which were going forward so smoothly, frightened that something would go wrong. Not until the ship sailed did she breathe free and deep.

It was then that Boyd had seen her—and smiled with appreciation. She was so pretty and so happy. Her body seemed almost too frail to face the breeze which was blowing from the open Atlantic, but her eyes appeared to see something better than this world. He supposed that she was going to meet somebody she loved. He would have liked very much to speak to her.

An hour later, going into dinner, he saw an empty chair at the table where she was sitting, and on the impulse sat down there. They began to talk immediately. Boyd had been in Washington and they discovered acquaintances in common. After the meal they strolled together on the blacked-out deck, looked down at the dark water and listened to its petulant sigh as it fell away from the hurrying ship. Often during the next two days they walked or watched the sea together. They were at ease in each other's company as lifelong friends. Boyd was perfectly happy merely looking at her, listening to her rapid, rather breathless speech as she poured out what was in her heart. He learned that she was returning not to a person but to a place she loved, but little more at that time. She told him about Amulree and her childhood there.

The liner made a brief call at Bermuda. When they were at sea again, watching the low-lying islands fade into the blue, the signals officer joined them, saying he had been looking for Mrs. Charrington everywhere. He handed her an envelope. She took it, smiling her thanks, still talking to Boyd while she tore it open. The signals officer smiled back and walked away.

Then Heather glanced at the message—all the animation drained from her face, leaving it white and blank as a mask. Boyd found himself staring at her, and looked away to give her time to recover. The message must have slipped from her hand for it drifted into the sea where the broken water pounced on it. He turned back to Heather. She was grasping the rail with both hands, her eyes moving from side to side—a sick and frightened child.

Boyd began to talk. He had no idea what he said, and certainly Heather did not understand him. But his gentle voice had its effect and gradually she became calmer.

"Peter," she said. "Will we call anywhere else before England?"

No, Boyd told her.

"If I gave the Captain a thousand pounds, would he put back to Bermuda?"

"I'm afraid not," he smiled at her. "But why do you want him to, Heather? Is there anything I can do?"

She shook her head.

"If it had come two hours earlier, when we were at Bermuda, I could have waited for another ship. I'd have had time. I wouldn't have minded then."

He did not question her. They began to walk slowly up and down the deck, she clinging to his arm. He persuaded her to let him take her down to dinner. And there he was proud of her, for she talked as usual and no one could have guessed from her face what she was feeling. Afterwards they returned to the deck and leaned over the stern, watching the sunset.

"You are the easiest person to talk to that I ever knew," Heather said. "You're a stranger for one thing and we'll never meet again. . . "

Boyd, at the tiller of the yacht *Heather Mary*, remembered that phrase which had first come back to him as he stood alone on the deck of the yacht in Brixham harbor. Looking at the oily water in which the stars shimmered from side to side he had first thought of Heather's story as a film, actuated by her voice and projected by his imagination on the phosphorescent screen. Thus gradually he had run through it all—from her childhood until the evening on the *Prince Rupert* when she had received the cable from her husband relayed from Washington, saying that he had escaped and was back in England, that she was to return immediately and that he was waiting for her impatiently.

It was very late when Heather finished her story. She turned to Boyd and asked: "Peter, what shall I do?"

Often since then Boyd had wondered what he would have answered. But she gave him no time.

"No, no I must not ask advice. It's too big a responsibility to put to anyone."

"I want to help you if I can," Boyd said.

"You have helped me. You can't know how much you've helped. It's all so much clearer. I can see—"

She was staring down over the rail.

"I think you had better go to bed now," Boyd said.

"No. I want to go on looking at the water, and listening to it. . . . .

Peter, I wish Richard knew you. If you want to help me, will you get to know him? I don't want you to do anything special, but he will need a person who is calm and wise. Please get to know him and help him."

"I will do what I can. Let me take you to your cabin now."

He took her arm and led her unresisting through the blacked-out ship where none was awake except the watch. He took her to her cabin and went to his own.

At the court of enquiry the woman in the next cabin stated that she had awakened and heard Mrs. Charrington's door open and close at about half past four. None of the crew or passengers remembered seeing her since dinner time when she behaved normally. Boyd said only that he had taken her to her cabin at three o'clock. He did not feel justified in repeating her confidences or telling any more. It was known that she had recently suffered a nervous breakdown. The Captain of a ship in a hurry towards the end of a war was content to approve the evidence and record in the log, "Lost overboard and presumed drowned."

The tiller pressed gently against Boyd's side rousing him from his memories. He glanced at the binnacle to make sure that the yacht was still on her course. Then looking forward, he noticed that the light was still glowing through the skylight of the Skipper's cabin.

He felt a wave of sympathy for that lonely man. The aggressive manner which showed itself in all his moods—jovial, friendly and even sad—made his hearers withdraw into themselves. They could not confide in him even if they wanted to. They couldn't even express sympathy for fear of his reaction. So he was left to torture himself with his own troubled thoughts. Was it that which kept him awake so late into the night?

Boyd had an idea. He would be relieved by Marcus very soon. Why not take a cup of cocoa to the Skipper? That would not keep him awake, and even if he did not want the drink he might recognize the friendly intention. . . But suppose he had fallen asleep with the light on. That would spoil the gesture!

Boyd left the tiller and leaned out of the forward side of the cockpit. He could not see through the opaque glass of the skylight, but both sides had been lifted, like the two halves of a cucumber frame, to let in as much air as possible. With his head close to the deck, Boyd looked through the six-inch aperture on the port side.

From there he could see the bunk, and that Charrington was not in it. Slightly surprised, he moved to the starboard side. He saw Charrington's broad and naked back as he leaned over his chart table. The big chart in front of him must be of the Atlantic for on its eastern side the coasts of Spain and Morocco were indicated. But nothing else caught Boyd's eye except for a penciled X in a red circle somewhere out in the ocean.

Suddenly interested, Boyd looked with care. Did the X mark their position? Charrington's elbows hid the American coast, so it was difficult to get one's bearings. But it did not seem right—too far across.

The yacht, left to herself, had swung off course. As the wind took her almost a-beam she rolled. Charrington looked up at the telltale compass. His face clouded. He caught sight of Boyd and shouted furiously:

"What the devil are you doing? Get back to your job."

CHAPTER 18

BOYD was on watch again from six till eight. Generally, feeling so well, he spent a good proportion of these two hours thinking about breakfast. But on this occasion he was preoccupied. His precise mind insisted that he must find out the significance of that cross on the chart. But he did not want to provoke Charrington any further in mid-Atlantic.

When Yeoman relieved him, he went below and found them all at their porridge. He helped himself from the saucepan in the galley, and sat down. He chose his moment.

"Sorry to have peeped in at you like that, Skipper," he said. "I wanted to see if you were awake before bringing you some cocoa."

"That's all right, Boyd. But if you want to call on me I'd rather you did it by the door. Having been a prisoner makes one jumpy."

"I'm sorry."

"That's all right. I'm sorry I swore at you."

Charrington finished his porridge and reached for the tea. The incident seemed to have made no impression on him. Boyd hesitated how to put his question.

Charrington looked up at him and asked: "Did you see any marks on the chart?"

"Yes, a cross—"

"Damn. I hoped you hadn't."

"Why?"

"Do you remember when I threw that bottle of gin overboard and said we wouldn't drink the stuff except on special occasions? I'd decided that when we reached that Point X we'd have a party. But I meant it to be a surprise."

Boyd considered this.

"I see. But why should your Point X mark a special occasion? It wasn't placed in any particular spot as far as I could see."

Charrington laughed. "You've discovered half my secret. You must not ask me to tell you the rest. You know there is going to be a party but I can still surprise you with when and where it is going to take place."

He was in a particularly good humor. Instead of leaving the saloon directly he had finished eating, he spent a leisurely half hour over his tea. He described, as a good joke, the midnight incident. He fetched a chart—although not the same chart, which was pinned on the table—and showed them their position.

On the rare occasions when Charrington talked, as he did now, semi-technically about the navigation and their progress, they listened as intently as if they were being briefed for a battle. And afterwards their conversation broke out, highly strung and lively, just as it might have after the confidence of Orders. But, as they already knew, the maintenance of any mood depended chiefly on the weather.

For a few days longer the weather was very kind indeed. The Trade Winds, blowing gently and refreshingly, seemed to take *Heather Mary* by the finger tips as she skated gracefully along. Nothing disturbed the smooth blue ocean except its own inhabitants—a joyous pack of dolphins bounding on the hunt; a covey of silver flying fish flushed by the dolphins or the yacht; squids, useless and ugly as burnt fireworks landing on the deck with a thud; that fantastic creation, the nautilus or Portuguese man-of-war, sailing the Atlantic with the pomp of a Lilliputian argosy, capsizing and laboriously righting itself again; or the white bird which still accompanied them. These were the details of the view by day, the endlessness of blue the background; while at night there was the carpet of phosphorescent water, and above a sky like jewelry's velvet with diamonds glittering on it. Life was idyllic.

Each of the crew, at one time or another, had felt in his heart that there was something strange about this voyage. It was not remarkable that the yacht made them think constantly about the person who had bought her and sailed on her, and after whom she was named. They believed that they were being guided true, that a part of the round horizon would at last crystallize into the islands of Bermuda. They had no specific anxiety. But it was a unique voyage none the less and, in Yeoman's phrase, there was something odd about the Skipper.

In the idyllic conditions of friendly Trade Winds this did not worry them at all. If anything it heightened the romance. As has been said, their mood depended on the weather. They were prepared for storms, but the weather turned traitor on them in another way.

The wind vanished. The sails hung limp. There was nothing to mitigate the heat. The deck was like a frying pan, the glue bubbling in the seams and the planks scorching. Below, it was an oven, even at night, for then the heat of the day was given off again by wood and metal. The ripples had gone from the sea's surface, leaving an oily swell. On this *Heather Mary* did not rest motionless, but rocked and pitched slowly and unhappily like a person who cannot sleep.

The physical discomfort for the crew is obvious, but still more important was the effect upon their mental state.

A sailing yacht hurrying along with the invisible wind gives a sense of power and freedom to those on board her. After two months they take this magic for granted. But when in mid-ocean the wind is removed they feel deserted and helpless. That was the first reaction, and one which grew with each hot, breathless day. Then, since there was no point in taking the tiller, their routine was destroyed. They sat or lay about the deck, getting in each other's way and on each other's nerves.

Then—and this was the strongest reaction of all—they began to feel imprisoned. The circular horizon was a frontier over which they longed increasingly to escape. But there was nothing they could do.

In spite of a vague fear of sharks they started bathing. At first they only took dips from the bobstay. Toby was the first to adventure any distance. He dived off the bow. He went deep and swam for some distance under water with his eyes open. It was a bright green world. He passed a fish which took no notice of him.

He came up and shook the hair back from his forehead. The sun blazed but was no longer hot. The water was stimulating. He lay on his back and kicked it up in a fountain. He duck-dived, rolled and swam—he was a good swimmer. For a minute or two he gave himself up entirely to the sheer physical pleasure.

Then he trod water and looked about him—at the shoreless ocean and the little yacht. He had not realized how small she was, and it was to this toy that he had become bound.

He became conscious of an extraordinary sensation. He did not know what it was. He thought he was elated. For the first time in two months he was free of the yacht—no need to balance, hold on, be careful how he moved, fit in with crowding other people. He was alone in the ocean and supported by it, three miles of water under him and hundreds of thousands of square miles all round.

And then he noticed that the yacht, which he had thought stationary, was actually moving. It was drawing away from him. The sensation he had already felt became overpoweringly strong, gripping his heart. He put down his head and swam as hard as he could.

When he had climbed up by the bobstay he sat on the deck panting. As his skin dried the sun grew hot again. Although the yacht was almost steady he put an arm round the mast.

"You look a bit done up," Yeoman said. "Did you get scared of sharks?"

"No," Toby said. "Not of sharks."

He had been scared all right. But the strange thing was that it did not prevent him bathing again, making a habit of it and each time swimming a little further from the yacht. Frightening though it was, it was still more fascinating.

The others left the yacht too, not far by swimming, at which none of them was much good, but in the dinghy. Charrington had noticed goose barnacles adhering to the hull. So they launched the dinghy and tried to scrape or pull them off.

That started the custom of going for a row—taking a turn on the Serpentine as Marcus called it. They all thoroughly enjoyed this. It was satisfactory to get along by their own exertion. They used to go off in couples and row round the yacht. They rowed with tremendous energy and very little skill. If the little boat had not been so steady they would have capsized her.

Once Boyd and Yeoman were in her together. At the same time Toby was swimming some distance from the yacht.

"I wish he wouldn't do that," Yeoman said. "I like to keep near him in the dinghy when he does, but he shouts at me to go away. It's only showing off."

"Whatever it is, aren't we doing much the same?" Boyd asked.

"We? We're just having a little holiday from the yacht. It does you good, this sort of thing."

Boyd leaned back smiling in the stern while Yeoman rowed.

"You know, Doctor," Yeoman said, resting on his oars, "I feel more at home in a little boat like this than in the yacht. She's more what I'm used to. It wouldn't be so difficult to rig a mast or sails—"

Boyd comfortable as a cat, looked at the yacht round which they were rowing and Toby was swimming. Charrington was standing on the deck. Marcus was below. Boyd pictured him moving anxiously, notebook in hand, round the lockers in the saloon.

"You aren't planning to leave us, are you?" Boyd asked, smiling under his eyebrows at the big, red, serious man in front of him.

"Of course not, Doctor. I don't mean anything talking like that . . . I suppose it was the Colonel started it, asking me if another steamer showed up and didn't look like coming close enough if we could possibly intercept her and get some fresh food and water. He's worried about the stores since this calm."

"Would you really do that, you and the Colonel, row off to intercept a ship?" Boyd asked.

"Well—Not if it meant going out of sight, or too far before night—not unless the Skipper came with us."

Boyd looked at Charrington again and saw he had not moved. He was naked except for a pair of shorts, a brown, strong figure. He was in the attitude natural to him, which reminded Boyd of a boxer in the ring—waiting. For what—an opponent to attack, for applause, or to be told that his services were no longer required? That was the question about Charrington. What was he waiting for? He had said that he wanted to be told about his wife. Well, he—Boyd—had told him something. Presumably they had all told him something. He could scarcely expect more from people who had had far less chance of knowing her than he had himself. He could not be waiting for anything more from them.

Boyd looked at him as he stood watching them. How well did he know him? He was a born leader. One could not imagine him doing anything except lead. He was a first-class Skipper of a yacht. He had the reputation of an aggressive fighting Captain— one could believe that very well—and of a persistent, immensely ingenious escaper from prison. Whenever you were with him you were under his spell. You accepted his reputation. You felt his magnetism. . . . And yet—seen from a hundred yards away, was he so impressive? Had he, by bad luck, missed his chance in life? Had Fate miscast him?

While Boyd had been thinking, Yeoman had been pulling more on one oar than the other and drawing nearer to the yacht. Charrington greeted them.

"What have you two been talking about?"

"Microcosms," Boyd said. "We can't escape from our sun."

Charrington had sounded almost angry when he called out to them, but he was in a good humor as he helped them pull the dinghy on board.

The calm ended at last. The sails fluttered like a child's balloon you are blowing up, then gradually filled. The water at the bow made a noise like crinkling paper. *Heather Mary* was on her way again.

Everything on board fell into the old routine and the log ticked off a hundred miles a day. But several things which seemed dramatic happened. First the boom swung over from the port to the starboard side. They had been so long in the belt of the Trade Winds, and here was proof they had come out on the other side of it at last. They were bearing up into the North Atlantic. Anything might happen now.

The next event was that they passed an acre of yellow seaweed—a startling color in that world of blue.

"Sargasso weed," Charrington said.

Yeoman's round face lighted up at once. "Are we going to sail through the Sargasso Sea? I've read about that. It's a big whirlpool—isn't it?—where there's nothing except seaweed and strange monsters and wrecks."

Charrington punched him on the shoulder. "You're perfect, Jack. The Sargasso was debunked by the Michael Sars expedition, but you are quite right that it's an empty quarter. We must cut through it to get back to the steamship routes and Bermuda."

While they sailed on northward, with a fresh breeze on their quarter, the ocean heaved with an unusually big swell, and the northern sky at night was splashed with distant lightning.

Charrington said: "The barometer is playing funny tricks. The weather can break up at this time of year, patches of storms everywhere."

"I don't care where the storms are so long as they aren't here," Marcus said.

Left alone at the helm, Toby thought: "It is strangely impressive to feel the heave of a storm yet little or nothing of the wind that causes it. I remember the same sort of thing when we were on the other side. It is another instance of the vastness and homogeneity of the ocean. But thank God we are moving fast enough. Before long we might even see something other than water."

That was worth writing down. He opened the cockpit locker to take out his notebook. But it was not there.

CHAPTER 19

ALL next day there were the signs of distant battle in the sky and water, and that evening there was an extraordinary sunset. Huge jet-black clouds were piled up solid as a stack of coal on the western horizon. When the sun touched them they caught fire. Their edges glowed red hot. As the sun bored in you had the impression of a furnace blazing through vents behind the mass. The whole sky glowed with it and the little clouds drifting high above were set alight.

Then the sun dropped into the sea and the fire went out. Night came down, sucking the color out of everything, and the coal-black mass began to move forward across the sky.

It came slowly. It was almost dawn before the storm arrived. Those below heard a rattling of the blocks and shrouds as the wind rushed up from a new quarter. Those on deck saw the dark water stippled by white waves, felt the sudden strength of the tiller and heard the strain and whine of the rigging. Another storm—they all knew what that meant, a damned nuisance. Those below turned over in their bunks and tried to sleep again, determined to get what rest they could before the shout, "All hands—"

As it happened they were allowed to finish their rest. With the help of the watch on deck Charrington shortened sail and settled the yacht as nearly on her course as the headwind allowed. Everything movable had already been secured and the hatch covers lashed in place. There was nothing more to do.

Morning showed a gray, unfriendly scene. The wind had broken up the smooth swell and was sweeping the lumps of water along anyhow. Except when their tops were cut off they were the color of lead. The air, full of spray and rain, was blowing by like smoke, hiding the sky. It occurred to Toby that although on clear calm days they could see much further, it was bad weather like this which brought the feeling that the ocean was limitless, without shores. *Heather Mary*, struggling through the waves, seemed to be getting nowhere.

All day it was the same—so different from the recent colorful days in the company of birds and fishes. The barometer was dropping slowly, promising nothing spectacular but equally no change in the present squalor and discomfort. They knew too well what the coming night would be like. During the dog watch they were all together in the cockpit, silent and depressed.

"Tonight the yacht can sail herself," Charrington suddenly announced. "We'll all go below and have a damned good dinner. No steamships ever come hereabouts."

He lashed the tiller and led the way into the saloon. He put gin and sherry on the table and then shut himself in the galley.

"It always seem miraculous to me," Yeoman said.

"What?" Marcus asked. "The way Richard manages to produce a pleasant surprise when it's most needed?"

"Yes that, of course—but what I meant is the way the table tips half upside down and yet the plates and glasses don't fall off."

"Jack," Toby said, "doesn't it ever strike you that it is we who are half upside down and liable to fall off?"

Marcus gave his laugh and changed the subject.

"This is exactly like our first night on board," he said.

The slow smile came into Boyd's eyes.

"Not exactly. Jo was not at the tiller then and we had not heard of Point X. I suppose it is our arrival there that we are to celebrate."

"If Point X stands for one of Richard's special dinners I don't see what anybody is grousing about."

"Nobody is grousing, Marcus," Boyd said.

"But you've got something on your mind," Marcus persisted.

Boyd looked thoughtfully at the galley door through which came the roar of the pressure stoves.

"We are nowhere in particular. Why should Point X be here?" he asked.

At that moment the galley door opened and Charrington came in with a steaming frying pan.

The meal which followed had a remarkable effect. It completely changed their mood. They had expected "a good dinner." What they were given was something far above the average by any standard. First there was an omelet from eggs which Charrington had concealed and preserved until now, then steaks of dolphin cooked in wine, and finally a fruit salad with fresh apples and oranges in it—another surprise. With the food they drank champagne and after it a very good madeira. The totally unexpected touches were exciting: the trouble which had been taken was complimentary. At the back of all their minds had lingered the resentment caused by the Skipper's refusal to put into port before crossing the Atlantic. Suddenly the perfect host was offering them as good a meal as they could have bought in the best hotel. And now it was not a vigil-of-hardship dinner, but a celebration with most of the ocean behind them. Let the storm blow—it only heightened their appreciation. Also, the fact that they were leaving their fate in the hands of Jo—or Heather Mary—suited their new mood. There was no sign that Charrington had anything on his mind. They talked about nothing in particular with the greatest possible vivacity.

"You know, Skipper," Toby said, trying to hold his glass in front of the swaying lamp, "it's a lovely color, madeira."

"The sailor's wine," Charrington said. "The only wine bar sherry that is improved by rough voyages."

"They always used to carry their barrel, didn't they, Skipper," Yeoman broke in. "The old trading Captains, I mean. They said it was better for the tropics and a few storms and sea battles. I've read about that."

"I know I'm better for this voyage," Marcus said. "If you had told me two months ago that I'd eat a dinner and enjoy it on a boat tossing like this, I'd have called you a liar. But here I am—"

Boyd's eyes were shining with appreciation but he did not speak. He realized that all of them were a little tipsy, and he wondered why, for the amount they had drunk did not account for it. Presumably it was reaction, after the long weeks of monotonous strain —healthy and hungry bodies suddenly satisfied, minds which had expected another weary night startled by companionship and pleasure. How charming the Skipper could be when he wanted. The celebration was doing him, and all of them, a world of good.

"Mary liked it best when it was rough," Charrington said.

Suddenly everyone was quiet. Charrington filled the glasses, recorked the bottle and put it carefully back between the cushions on the divan. He went on speaking without apparently noticing any difference in the atmosphere.

"When it was windy—and I was steering of course—she used to go up to the bow and sit there with her hair streaming back. I used to tell her she was acting the figurehead. The old sailing ships we've been talking about, if they had women's names, generally had figureheads which typified them. I expect the tough sailors idealized them as their loves—although such as I've seen appeared remarkably unresponsive . . . You have a habit of sitting in the bow when there's a breeze, haven't you, Toby?"

Charrington sipped his wine, looking round the saloon at the suddenly startled faces.

"She didn't do that when it was calm," he went on. "Then she used to climb the mast—to look over the horizon, I supposed. Did you see over the horizon, Jack, before you fell? Or, more often, she'd sit in the stern against the mizzen mast—just as you have been doing, Marcus. But she wasn't fishing. It fascinated her to watch the water flowing by. That's right, isn't it, Boyd? . . . You have each played your part in reminding me of her."

Outside there was a continuous surge and boom as *Heather Mary* drove forward. In the saloon it was quiet as a storm center.

Marcus cleared his throat. "What are you getting at, Richard?" he asked.

"Getting at? I was about to ask you to drink to Mary's memory."

"Of course we'll do that." Marcus tried to rise, but a sudden movement of the yacht threw him back on to his seat again and spilt half his wine.

"We drink sitting—even to kings and toy princesses," Charrington said. "Heather Mary Charrington!" He raised his glass and the others did the same.

A minute or two later—they all remaining silent—the Skipper asked, "Well, who is going to reply?"

"What do you mean, Richard?"

"Reply to the toast, of course."

"I think *Heather Mary* is doing that," Boyd said quietly. "We would be better employed attending to her on deck."

"Don't shirk the issue. You each have something to say. You helped to fill the cup with—that's what I want to know!"

"Look here, Richard," Marcus broke in. "You've given us a damn good dinner. Don't let's get philosophical or something now."

Charrington turned on him. "Philosophical? It's facts I want. Don't pretend you can't understand. It is two and a half years ago that Mary died. But you know that of course. What you may not know is that within a few hours we shall be sailing through the very water in which she is buried."

"You told us just now that no ships ever used this part of the Atlantic," Toby said.

"Liners did not keep to the shipping lanes in wartime. In this case *Prince Rupert* went south. I searched out the Captain. He could show me his course exactly. The only thing he did not know was when it was during the night that the thing happened.

One of you could have told me that but—never mind. Tomorrow at latest we shall reach her grave. There is no more time for evasions. You shall each tell your part of the story tonight."

Charrington paused, his flushed, bearded face thrust forward.

"I suppose you mean that you want us to talk about Heather," Toby said wearily. "We all knew her and were fond of her. Isn't that enough? Can't you let her rest—if there is any rest in the sea."

Charrington looked at him.

"I had already realized that you would prefer everything to be buried," he said. "But you left one or two things above ground."

"What the devil—"

"Steady, Toby," Marcus said quickly. "Look here, Richard, for God's sake don't let's quarrel now—or talk about anything serious for that matter. We are all too damned tired and on edge. You can't have had a proper night's sleep for weeks."

There was a crash of water and a shrill scream of wind. The yacht checked, shivered, then leaned right over and began to gather speed again—faster and faster, jumping the waves or boring through them.

"Would it not be wise for some of us to go on deck?" Boyd asked.

"The vessel can look after herself," Charrington answered. "I am not quarreling as Marcus suggests. I am only asking for a clear statement—which was your own request on the other side of the Atlantic. Then I told you frankly why you had been invited—to show me some lost pages of my married life. Have you? I have spoken to each of you alone and in confidence. All I got were evasions, silences, attempts to change the subject—"

"Good God, Richard, you talk as if we had something to conceal."

"Haven't you? What else can I think? Boyd, you're a scientist, isn't that the logical deduction?"

"All I know, Skipper, is that we would be better either on deck or in our bunks. Can't we leave this till the morning?"

"By morning we shall have reached the place. Are you or are you not going to make a clean breast of your relations with my wife?"

"Since you put it like that I am not going to utter a single bloody word," Toby said.

Charrington swallowed his wine and put the glass down beside the others which seesawed up and down, up and down continually on the swinging table. His face was red and his dark eyes had become small.

"Very well, I shall tell you the story myself," he said. "You will of course correct me if I am wrong . . ."

He began a description of his married life, repeating much of what he had said before, making an idyll of it. Even the stormy passage southward from Amulree he spoke of as part of their "adventurous life together." Boyd thought of the struggle to the death of personalities which he had glimpsed from Heather Mary's story. But he kept silent. Since Charrington could not be deflected it was probably best to let him talk on unopposed. He appeared to be calmed by the roseate picture he was painting. It absorbed him. He was oblivious of the creaks and yearnings of the hardpressed yacht and the threatening howl of wind and water. He behaved as if he were in the smoking room of a club.

He refilled the wine glasses, and talked about his war service. He described several actions—the long hunt with eyes straining through the darkness, then the thunderstorm explosion of noise and speed and tracer bullets. Death or glory, and brief but intoxicatingly happy leaves on shore were the impressions that he gave.

Although he had the knack of description it was obvious that he was exaggerating. Was he trying to compensate himself for the briefness of his active war? Boyd wondered. If so, that was harmless enough. But they all wished that he would hurry up and finish talking and go on deck to ease the yacht. She trembled at each blow of water and the noise of the wind was a continuous howl.

"Then I was captured—in a damn fool way. They got my ship too. They came on board and fixed a line and towed her away," Charrington said. "Everything went wrong. I expect you wonder why I've gone through all this. You had to have it as a background to the story you would not tell yourselves.

"I did two things as a prisoner—three if you like. I tried to get back to my wife, I wrote letters to her and waited for her replies. I told you off Madeira that one couldn't expect a creature like Mary to express her true feelings in censored letters. Until that time that had been my explanation of the coolness and superficiality of her replies. But while you on our night watches together have been evading my questions and thinking your own thoughts, I have been thinking my own thoughts too. I've told you that we never quarreled. But once it did cross my mind that she might have—tender feelings for someone else. I put it away from me like a blasphemy. Even when I saw many of my fellow prisoners deceived by their wives I was convinced that mine was pure. What was she made of except purity? But if she had—why funk the word?—if she had lusted after someone else that would be a complete explanation of her strange manner, of her running away to America—of everything."

When he said that, Charrington looked like a man in torment.

"Isn't that logic, Boyd?" Charrington asked. "Marcus, you know the world. Jack, you are a wise old bird. Toby, you have read books at any rate. Look at it coldly. If you can, for Christ's sake tell me that I'm wrong!"

There was silence in the cabin while the wind roared outside. Then Yeoman blurted out, "You can't talk of lust in the same breath as Miss Heather."

"Can't I? Prove it, kill the devil that has been eating my heart so long. But how can you? What did my wife do when I was taken prisoner? I expected her to return to her highland home. If you knew how much she thought of that place! No, she stayed in London on the excuse of some artificial job. As if a lady of her upbringing were capable of war work!"

"Meg told me she did it very well," Marcus said. "You know Meg is a good judge."

"I know she is kind hearted—and that women stick together. But in any case that is only one small point. . . . To go back, the month or two before I was captured was the most active period we had in Coastal Forces. Almost every night we were out, and generally in some sort of scrap. But when we did get an unexpected night off it meant shore leave. Mary knew that. Would you not expect that she would wait for me—or for news of me if the luck had failed? No. On my last visit I found that she had gone out—to tea, Meg said. I waited as long as I could—until six o'clock next morning. But she did not return. That was a long tea party, Jack Yeoman."

"I've told you, it wouldn't have been right to let her go. We didn't know about you coming."

"We? Oh yes, your wife was alive then. But not the next time—if it was the next time—when she stayed with you for a week."

Yeoman's big hands clenched.

"You know about that too. I've told you. It was sheer kindness."

"It was a pity that letter was washed away in the first storm," Charrington said, his small eyes fixed on Yeoman and the point of his beard towards him. "I would have been interested in your explanation of why you called her your 'mistress sweet and kind' and a dozen similar endearments. She came to you from sheer kindness. Your wife had died suddenly—of an unknown disease, you said."

While Charrington was saying this Yeoman looked as if he meant to rise and lay hands on him. But the last phrase stunned him. He fell back on the settee, his mouth working but no sound coming out.

Charrington turned to Marcus.

"And you—you whom I thought my friend—spent a fortnight with Mary in the privacy of Amulree. There was no reason why either of you should have gone there at that time except—to go together. Oh, I know that officially you lived ten miles apart. But I have been back there and—with difficulty I admit—unearthed some interesting facts . . . I know why you have never mentioned Mary's name to me, and why when I confronted you with her photograph you goggled like a stranded fish and pretended not to have seen it."

"Richard!" Marcus shouted. "You are going too damned far. Stop this or—"

Charrington snorted.

"What will you do? I suppose the lot of you might overpower me, but if you did you'd drown. The yacht has driven too far into this storm for fools like you to handle her. Go up and try. One mistake and you'd dismast her or turn her on her side. Listen!"

The wind had risen to a pitch of frenzy and the sea sweeping the deck sounded like a river in spate. They could all imagine what it would be like up there. They would be numbed and battered, groping in the dark—and uncertain what to do.

"Even if a miracle got you through the storm, what then?" Charrington asked, his small dark eyes boring into Marcus. "How would you get to port? You know the condition of the stores—just enough for a straight passage, but no more. You don't know where you are or what to do—"

"I don't believe you could manage the yacht now yourself," Toby said.

"That's a lie. You've seen what I can do. I've never yet been beaten by the sea and never shall—"

"Let him finish," Boyd said. "We are only prolonging this by answering back."

"That's right, Mr. Scientist. And I'm coming to you. But Toby first. Toby, you should not leave your diary lying about, and you should not have written with so little restraint to a person who never destroyed a letter or even locked them up. I wonder how you will explain your references to that moment when you held her trembling in your arms. And what was the unmistakable sign from Heaven that you and she were meant to be together?"

"I've told you that I am not going to utter a damned word now," Toby said. "But when we get ashore—"

"Ah, when you get ashore. That depends on your justification when you reach the place—"

"Tell me what I did," Boyd said.

Charrington swung round to him. He had been working himself into a passion and his face was now wild as the storm sounded.

"You—you ask that. You who forced yourself on a lonely woman returning to her husband. I've read the evidence of the Court of Enquiry, read between the lines. You were in the dark stern of the ship with her for most of the night. What you did is between you and the devil for you made sure that she would tell no one of it—"

"Stop that and listen to me," Boyd said. He spoke no louder than usual but his voice was cold and hard. "You pretend you started this voyage with the most sympathetic motives and that it was we who drove you to this fine frenzy. But you gave yourself away when you admitted that you read and carried with you your wife's letters, and when you told us that you went back to Amulree—a place you hated—to spy on her. That is how you really spent the two years of freedom and sailing alone—in avoiding the truth and grubbing in the gutter of your mind for another explanation.

God knows what you intended, but you had condemned us before we even came on board. The only true word you have spoken is that I lied to you the other night—"

Charrington jumped to his feet. Boyd never moved except to raise his hard clear eyes to Charrington's face. He went on speaking slowly and distinctly.

"I lied to save your feelings, but you are not worth consideration. You shall have the truth now. Yes, your wife came on board the liner happy though very weak—ecstatic even. She was going home to rest—to Amulree where she was truly loved and appreciated. She had not had your cable then. We were at sea before that was relayed. It meant that instead of gaining strength at Amulree she would find you waiting on the quay. Her spirit snapped at last. I know what I am saying for she gave me her full confidence. Now I have heard the other side, and I can judge. . . . You killed her—you with your overwhelming conceit, your blind animal egoism. She was never unfaithful but she preferred death to being touched by you again. Now stop your posturing and go sail the yacht she gave you if you can."

All the blood had drained from Charrington's face. Slowly it came back until the veins were standing out like creepers on a brick wall.

"If what you say is true I do not care—By God I'll take you to face her all together. I—"

Charrington fell sideways with his legs in the air. The light went out. There was a snapping of wood and a shrill clatter of broken glass. Water poured into the saloon. They felt *Heather Mary* being picked up and thrown down violently on her side.

CHAPTER 20

Heather Mary must have been on her beam ends for only a few seconds. The wave passed and left her in the trough. She righted herself, and the men inside her slipped down the wall on to the floor.

They lay there in a foot or so of water. They could not distinguish each other. But their eyes were drawn to the patch of comparative brightness—the gaping hole of the smashed portside skylight. Through it, high above, they saw the glint of moving foam. They must already be below the surface, and they were helpless with that open wound on the weather side. This was the end. They waited, without emotion and without knowing if their limbs were moving.

Another wave struck them. *Heather Mary* scarcely rolled to it, she was so heavy. But more water came jetting in, frothing and hissing, pouring down on top of them.

They were all on their feet now. One of them plunged splashing through the after door of the saloon, which was open, and up the ladder steps of the companionway. They heard him grunt as he tried to slide back the hatch.

It was stuck. He could not move it. And there was only room for one man on the companionway. He realized this and jumped down again. The rest had been pressing behind, and he landed among them, causing more confusion. He ploughed through it— it was Charrington—and tried to open the galley door.

It was jammed.

Their instinct was to get out on deck. The storm—anything— was better than this trap. And as conscious thoughts began to form they realized that this was their only chance. They must reach the tiller and turn the yacht so that her wounded side no longer faced the wind. As it was—only two or three more waves pouring into her and she would founder. But they were shut in. The whole yacht must have been twisted and warped by the strength of the blow.

A long thin figure tried to scramble out of the hole. He got his head, one arm and shoulder through. Pieces of glass still adhering to the frame broke off with sharp reports. He struggled, his legs kicking in the air. But there he stuck.

Meanwhile 'the others had thrown themselves behind Charrington against the galley door. It splintered. They charged through the galley, into the forward cabin.

The vertical iron ladder was there, roofed by the forward hatch. This hatch was a two-feet square piece of mahogany which opened on hinges like a box lid. But it would not open. They punched upwards, breaking their knuckles and not feeling it. It did not move. At the beginning of the storm they had lashed the canvas cover over it.

Yeoman began scrabbling about in the water and the darkness looking for an axe among the scattered tools.

In the cabin Toby was withdrawing himself from the broken skylight hole. There was a sound of tearing cloth as he splashed back into the cabin. He was the slimmest, and since he had failed nobody had a chance that way. Another jet of water surged after him.

"The Skipper's cabin," Boyd said.

These were the first words anyone had spoken during the hundred seconds since the freak wave struck. There had been plenty of noise, of course—their movements, their breathing, and above all the storm. But a human voice was like a new creation in the chaos, and it rallied them.

Of the crew only Marcus had been in the Skipper's cabin before. But they all knew the double skylight which was just forward of the cockpit. Like the forward hatch it had a canvas cover lashed over it. But it was made of plate glass, not mahogany. They could break out there.

In fact, they found one of the panes of the port side broken already. Charrington opened his knife, reached above his head, and slashed the canvas cover. Then he caught hold of the sides of the frame and pulled himself up. Marcus and Boyd put their shoulders under his feet and pushed.

It was hard work. Charrington seemed to be stuck. Wetness dripped on their heads. But they were used to that. They were in a good position and pushed hard. They got him out. His legs vanished.

At that moment Yeoman joined them with the axe. They broke the other pane of glass and cut through the separating wooden frame before they scrambled on deck, one after the other.

Until now they had only heard the storm from under cover, as if they were inside a drum. Now they were outside, under the blows of the drumsticks. It took a few moments to recover from the shock.

It was dark of course, with spray blowing past in a horizontal stream, stinging their eyes and making it difficult to breathe. There were no sails. The mast was there, swaying from side to side, although it seemed less tall than usual. The deck was piled like a rubbish heap with spars and canvas.

Charrington was in the flooded cockpit leaning his weight against the tiller. But nothing was happening as a result. *Heather Mary* wallowed deep as a sponge in a bath.

Charrington shouted his orders—"Marcus, Boyd—pump! Yeoman, plug that hole. Toby, stow that gear or cut it away."

They obeyed at once, unhesitatingly. The accusations, bitterness, jealousy and threats were quite forgotten. Those were abstract things, swept away by the great wave. Now they were all fighting for their lives against a common enemy, and Charrington was the leader.

Marcus and Boyd worked the hand pump. They had to work together because with the strain and difficulty of keeping balance a single man had not enough strength left over to push the piston in and pull it out. They hung on to the T-shaped iron handle, constantly on the wet rocking deck, often falling, sometimes being swung bodily around, but always managing somehow to push in and pull out, hundreds and hundreds of times. It was the sort of work which is described as back breaking. The actual sensation was as if their backs were wire cables which were continually being bent into an inverted U and straightened and bent again, until in spite of the universal wetness they became dry and hot, and first one strand and then another cracked and broke.

This may sound too colorful and exaggerated, but there is no torture more agonizing than that which strong-willed people can inflict upon themselves merely by continuing some quite ordinary action long after the automatic warning which pain gives.

They drove each other, each determined not to be the one who stopped first. They were in constant danger of being washed overboard, but there was no time to rig a rope. In their imaginations they saw the saloon waist deep in water, with much more pouring into it than they sucked out. The yacht was sinking and then there would be nothing except water.

They kept on pumping. They did not know that Yeoman, uncertain how to plug the broken skylight quickly, had lain down over it. He clung there with fingers and toes, taking the waves on his back and stopping most of the water. Actually nobody ever knew about this. It was too dark and the air too full of spray to see clearly. Toby stumbled over him but was preoccupied and did not realize what Jack was doing.

Toby was preoccupied in trying to clear the wreckage. The mainsail had come down, with the tip of the mast. The roughly folded envelope of canvas lay upon the deck, overlapping it on the lee side, and full as a gigantic blister with water. Rather, since the sail was crumpled, there were a score of different blisters making up a topheavy deck cargo. He tried to pour or flatten them out, but nothing is heavier to handle than wet canvas.

Charrington lashed up the useless tiller and came forward to help Toby.With his knife he stabbed the sail and let that water out.

Still the yacht lay inert, passively offering her wounded side to the waves.

Through the shrill scream of the gale the noise of the pump went steadily on—like the noise of feet plodding through deep mud, squelching in and sucking out.

Charrington joined Marcus and Boyd. "Faster. Lighten her!" he shouted. Then, "Come, Toby."

The gaff was over the lee side, hammering it with each rise and fall, threatening to pierce it. Lying face downwards half over the side, struggling, pulling, they at last got it in.

Next Charrington was in the stern. Although the mizzen had not been set, its boom had snapped in half. The part-furled sail was trailing astern, still further deadening the yacht. Charrington, holding with one hand to a stay and swinging out recklessly over the water, cut it free with the axe.

Still *Heather Mary* would not obey her helm.

The jib had been torn loose from the clew. It was streaming out like a flag, flapping itself to pieces. They lowered it, knotted what was left of it to the sheet and hoisted it again. It could not last long but for the moment it was bellying and quivering against the pressure of the wind. Toby had followed Charrington blindly, helping where he could. Now, resting for a moment, he had the impression that they had done all that was possible. He looked aft: Marcus and Boyd were no longer bowing to the pump. They must be resting too. The yacht seemed lighter in the water. Something ought to happen.

A wave swept over them from a new angle. Toby glanced at Charrington for confirmation. Charrington had both arms round the mast and his head was drooping.

"She's coming round," Toby shouted.

Heather Mary rolled through seventy degrees or more, first one gunwale dipping right under water and then the other. Charrington's head lolled from side to side and struck the mast. He straightened up and Toby saw him blink and stare as if he had been asleep.

Charrington ran to the cockpit, staggering and swerving along the tilting deck. He unlashed the helm, ran the yacht off down wind and held her with the waves dead astern.

"Get those holes stopped," he shouted.

Boyd found the electric torch in the locker. Then he and Yeoman crawled forward and examined the port skylight. Not only had the glass been shattered but the wooden coaming was split from end to end. It was a shipwright's job. Even to patch it they would need planks. Where the devil could they find planks? The best they could do at the moment was to cover it with canvas.

Yeoman went below with the torch for hammer and nails.

While he waited in the darkness, crouching on the wet wind-washed deck, holding on for his life yet feeling light headed, Boyd experienced a detached glimpse of himself as the one-time Professor Boyd might have seen such a creature.

"Why, little fly, did you crawl into the wind tunnel?" the Professor asked.

"From curiosity, Sir."

"And what do you think you are achieving?" the Professor asked.

"At the moment I'm only trying to exert an equal and opposite force," the creature answered.

"What about this man Charrington you were so worried about?"

"I'm still worried about him. But I'd be even more worried if he were not here."

"Then hold on and do what he tells you. This sort of storm ought to blow away little things like jealousy and suspicion. In any case, whatever happens afterwards, you can't be worse off than you are now."

Yeoman returned with the tools and they set about the repair. One man had to stretch the sail over the hole while the other nailed it in place. Both tasks were essentially two-handed—but one hand must always to be used for holding on. The torch, steadied under a knee or elbow, was generally pointing in the wrong direction. The canvas was constantly ripped out of place by wind or surging water; and if the nails did grip they bent under the hammer rather than pierced the hardwood. Bangings, wallowings and curses from the Skipper's skylight, two or three paces away, suggested that the other pair were having equal difficulty.

Meanwhile *Heather Mary* retreated through the darkness, rolling and plunging with her speed, and the wind, racing up after her, howled and booed as it swept past her empty rigging. The dark waves reached forward with the wind. They caught up the yacht, hissing as they came, and slapped down on top of her, reaching out white fingers from stern to stem. Then the fingers seemed to clench into a fist behind the stern, and the yacht drew ahead—until the next wave came. It was, if anybody had had time to think about it, a nightmare progress—like a bad dream of running from the breakers on a beach and never escaping on to dry land because they followed up the shore. The crew were much too busy to think about it, but they were conscious of *Heather Mary's* fugitive speed and the necessity to get their jobs done somehow and at once.

Boyd was tapping in one of the last nails—he had let go with the other hand to direct the torch on to it—when somebody shouted, "Look out!"

Turning he saw a huge mass of water hanging over them. It fell. They were half crushed, blinded, stifled. Then they felt the wave pushing and tugging at them to get them over the side. And then they heard water pouring below and surging about in cabin and saloon.

It was fortunate that nobody had been washed overboard, but that did not occur to them. They only realized that their work had been destroyed and that they were in the same danger of foundering. But why, now the yacht had come alive again?

Charrington lowered the remaining half of the jib. Then he got a sea anchor out of the sail locker and trailed it astern on a pair of stout warps. They had been running too fast, trying to race the wind, disturbing the water.

With *Heather Mary* properly restrained they set about pumping and patching her once more. They worked silently, too tired even to swear. But gradually they began to feel that they were gaining—until another wave came aboard and they had to start all over again.

They were not, strictly speaking, being pooped any longer. The wind seemed to be shifting all over the place, or the waves to be acting independently. Perhaps the yacht was in the center of the depression. God knew. This was no copybook storm. It was impossible to see anything clearly, but often they glimpsed white water where a star should have been. And every now and then one of these seas thundered on board to put them back again where they had started.

Each time this happened the effort of recovery was greater. What was the use? They began to think more and more about the saloon, even with water in it. Why not go below and wait for the overwhelming forces to settle things one way or the other?

They could not do that because of Charrington. He gave a minimum of orders—he hardly spoke. But he was always there. Since the wind had begun to shift he was no longer most useful at the tiller. He was at the pump, at the holes patching, in the cabin baling, on deck again hanging oil bags over the side. He was everywhere. He had no word of praise or encouragement for any of them. All his tireless energy was directed against the storm. Damn the man! They were not going to be beaten by him in endurance. They worked on in a cold and dogged fury.

At last they became conscious that it was not quite so dark. There was no sign of sunrise—nothing except spray and cloud. They couldn't tell where the water ended and the air began. But the night must be coming to an end at last.

Nothing really heavy had fallen on the yacht for half an hour or more. Sails had been draped over the holes, and the bilge was only a few inches above the cabin floor. Yeoman stretched his agonizing muscles and felt that he could rest for a moment. . . . And then he began to shiver. He looked down at himself. In the gray light he saw that he was dressed only in trousers and a sleeveless vest—what he had been wearing at dinner in the cabin. He was horrified. Presumably they were all like that. They would catch their deaths! But it was too late to think of putting on oilskins now. The only thing which might save them was a good hot cup of tea.

The torch was being used so he borrowed Toby's lighter. By its small flame he found his way below. It was quite difficult, even apart from the rolling and pitching, to get through the saloon. It was cluttered with the shattered table, broken bottles and glasses, all the books, remains of the barograph, biscuits, cereals, and other food, pillows and bedding and heaven knew what else. Among this wreckage a quantity of brown and bloated cigarettes floated in the bilge water, rushing aimlessly from side to side and disintegrating as they did so.

The galley was in an even worse mess. The batteries, housed under the locker, had carried away with the first wave. Many of the china cups, once suspended on hooks, had broken free of their handles. A whole pile of plates, which had been contained in a sort of wooden well, had somehow smashed themselves to pieces and jumped out. A jug of coffee, prepared by Charrington, had disappeared but left stains even on the ceiling. The demijohn of paraffin was rolling about. The top must have struck something and turned itself on. Most of the fuel had run out. All the crockery used at dinner was somewhere in the mess. Quantities of food tins and every pot and pan was on the floor. With each movement of the yacht these clattered over each other and everything else making a fiendish racket.

By now the lighter was so hot that it burned Yeoman's fingers. He extinguished it. Then he opened the forward door and threw or kicked most of the rubbish into his own cabin. (God knew when he would use his bunk again.) That done he set about getting a stove burning.

One of them was still on the gimbals. It was filthy of course; but after a thorough wiping and then a liberal burning of methylated spirit he pumped it up and the flame purred. (That was the first pleasant sound.) He filled the kettle with water and put it on the stove. Then he leaned back against the wall and went to sleep.

Charrington also had been below. He had collected the weather boards which they had used to keep themselves in their bunks when the yacht rolled. He was nailing these over the broken skylights, making a proper job of it, with canvas to cover the cracks. Two of his crew were helping him while the third steered. There was just enough light to work by. The sea was definitely calming but the blanket of cloud and spray was so thick that the sun, if it had risen, could scarcely penetrate it.

Yeoman was wakened by the noise of the kettle boiling over. He made the tea, hot and very strong, and carried it on deck. There, the work being finished, they drank together. They spilled a good deal of tea because they were shivering so much from cold and that extreme of reaction which brings tears into the eyes. But each scalding mouthful revived them further. They were no longer intent upon a task of the moment but could notice things as a whole.

In the growing light they saw the immensity of the ocean. The waves were forming themselves without any apparent reason, rising up into cones like slag heaps, then collapsing and rising somewhere else, barging about without enough wind to discipline them. They were just like the waves—Toby thought—which are caused by stirring a bath. People could only change their size in fairy stories. But when waves did it it was true. Perhaps that was why they could be so frightening. . . . How wonderful it would be to have a hot bath.

And the toy yacht in the bath? Her deck was a shambles of broken spars and torn canvas. All that remained of the dinghy was a length or two of curved planking. Toby felt literally sick with retrospective fear, realizing how near the yacht must have been to complete destruction. Brave little *Heather Mary!*

What had kept her alive? The group of tired men drinking tea, Charrington in the middle of them. Or—

"Good God, Skipper, what's happened to your trousers?"

They were tattered and a dirty rust color.

Charrington did not answer. His face was gray and his eyes heavy.

Boyd dropped on his knees, pulled open one of the rents and examined the bare leg while Charrington sat like a statue.

"Skipper," Boyd said. "Come below."

Charrington did not appear to have heard him.

Marcus and Yeoman lifted him to his feet and took him carefully and slowly to his cabin. They laid him on his bunk and cut away what remained of his trousers.

On his buttocks and on the outer sides of his thighs were long deep cuts which were still bleeding. He must have lost a great deal of blood.

––

CHAPTER 21

––

STUMBLING and slipping first one way and then the other in the water on the rubbish-covered floor of the Skipper's cabin they only got in each other's way. So all except Boyd went on deck.

There they sat under the attic ceiling of gray sky, the lowest cloud fragments trailing close above like cobwebs. They sat across the cockpit, their feet thrust against the opposite side. With the rolling they were sometimes in effect standing upright and sometimes almost upside down. And as the yacht dipped her sides under water, fragments of the smashed dinghy, pieces of spars, canvas or cordage—anything left loose upon the deck—was licked overboard. They watched this happening with indifference. They were exhausted and the whole thing was such a mess.

"If we could set a sail it would steady her," Yeoman said.

Toby said: "We'd have to climb the mast."

They looked at the mast swaying from side to side. It was broken off at the crosstrees and swinging through sixty degrees. The rigging was waving in tangled streamers. That was the end of that conversation.

In a hoarse voice so low that it was scarcely audible Marcus said: "I had such a good leverage. I heard something tearing—I remember—it must have been his legs, but I fairly shoved him up."

Neither of the other two said anything. They sat together rocking up and down.

Marcus added, with the misery of weariness: "Perhaps he'll die, and I killed him."

"Good show," Toby said.

"That's damn bad form—"

"Bad form?" Toby was thoroughly roused. "To hell with bad form. He was out to murder us, wasn't he? What else could he have meant? He stole my notebook and read other people's letters. He—"

"Don't get so bloody hysterical," Marcus shouted. "Who got us through the storm?"

"He did," Toby shouted back. "We were on the same side then. I helped him do everything. He's all right so long as he's frightened as well as us. But the storm's dying and it's damn lucky for all of us if he's dying too."

"That's cowardly."

Marcus and Toby were yelling at each other at the tops of their voices. Yeoman sat unhappily between them.

"That's a lie. I did everything for *Heather Mary*." Toby's voice rose to a squeak. "She deserved it. She saved us by running into that wave. She's probably mortally wounded but she's ready to save us again, and none of you seem to realize anything. You think I'm hysterical but I feel as if I'd taken benzedrine or something and can see everything perfectly clearly. He beat the storm but he couldn't beat Heather—"

"Oh, pipe down," Marcus said.

Toby opened his mouth to shout an answer, but his voice broke. Tears began to run down his face while he stared angrily at the heaving sea. The other two sat without looking at him. They did not trust their own nerves very far.

It was then that Boyd came on deck.

"How is he? Is he going to recover?" Marcus asked.

"I don't know. I'm not a medical doctor. I only did what seemed necessary."

Boyd was strangely abrupt.

"What's the next move?" Marcus asked.

"Sleep."

"There's a good deal to settle—"

"Exactly. But it is important. So sleep first—and then, I hope, clear heads."

Toby took a grip on himself. "What happens if he comes to meanwhile?"

"He won't," Boyd answered. They looked at him enquiringly but he said no more and led the way below.

They swept the debris off their bunks and squelched down on them in their oilskins.

Boyd woke first. In spite of his weariness he had not slept deeply, and only for four hours. The first thing he noticed was that the water on the floor had risen an inch or two. The yacht must be leaking, but only slowly. That was a minor worry. At the door of the Skipper's cabin he hesitated, then turned away from it and climbed the companionway. He put his head and shoulders through the hatch. Lead-colored waves were still heaving aimlessly about under a low ceiling of smoky rain clouds. The wind was blowing again, nothing like a gale, but hard enough. The crippled yacht pitched and heaved, straining at the sea anchor like a tethered animal which has been frightened and tries to get away. Boyd gave an involuntary shudder and went below again, closing the hatch.

He called the others. They ate damp biscuits in silence.

Marcus asked: "How's Richard?"

"I haven't looked," Boyd said.

"What!"

"He will still be unconscious."

"How do you know?"

Boyd shrugged his shoulders. "Come and see if you like. But it's much more important to decide what we're going to do."

Charrington lay on his back. His face was colorless and his mouth open.

Quickly and clumsily Boyd thrust a hand on to his chest under the blanket.

After a moment or two he gave a kind of sigh and said quietly: "He's alive."

Toby turned and left the cabin.

"Look at this," Yeoman said.

In the water on the floor was a sodden mass of books, charts, biscuits and papers. He had picked up the photograph of Heather and was wiping it carefully with his sleeve.

"To think anyone so gentle should be the start of so much trouble."

Marcus and Yeoman stood looking at the photograph while Toby's feet clumped up the companionway.

Toby's excited voice broke out above them: "Come quick—quickly!"

As soon as they reached the deck they saw the vessel. She was only a few hundred yards distant but moving rapidly away from them, a wall of white foam at her stern and black smoke trailing out across the water.

They waved frantically. They could distinguish no one on the deck but an angry light began to flash dots and dashes at them from the bridge. It paused, as if waiting for a reply, then flashed again. When it stopped the vessel itself was almost out of sight, for it was impossible to see far in that weather.

"Anybody read Morse?" Boyd asked.

"Not at that speed," Marcus said. "She was a destroyer, wasn't she? What the devil was she doing out here?"

"Naval exercises, I suppose."

"They might have stopped to investigate. After all, a little yacht without sails—"

"That kind of sailor doesn't know some boats need sails," Toby said.

"It's no use crying over spilt milk," Marcus said with an attempt at briskness. "We'd better start setting our ship in order. What do you think, Boyd?"

"She is riding well enough to the sea anchor. We must keep her pumped out, of course, but otherwise I think the first job is to settle the party line."

"You mean for when Richard comes to?"

"Yes. There is not much wrong with his legs. They were flesh wounds in the buttocks mostly. It was just the blood he lost. Once he has slept off his weakness he will be able to get about. How are we going to treat him?"

"Tie him up with the thickest ropes on board," Toby said. "And I suggest we do it before he wakes."

"We can't do that," Marcus protested.

"Mutiny I suppose—"

Boyd put in quickly, "Never mind what you call it. It would mean the end of all co-operation, and we've got to decide whether we can do without him. If we decide we can't, what do we do— let him take command again as if nothing had happened? With the storm between, those hours in the saloon seem unreal. But they were real enough at the time."

"Do you think we might reason with him?" Yeoman suggested.

"No. I'm sure that the relationship of each of you with Heather was the same as mine was—affectionate and absolutely harmless. But Charrington's brain is his own Iago. It twists facts in the most abominable way."

"He got excited once before," Marcus said. "But by talking of ordinary subjects and keeping off Heather—"

"We did not mention Heather first, he did."

"Why risk it? Tie him up," Toby said.

Marcus's sunburned face became redder than ever. "Get this clear. We are not going to tie up a wounded man. If I can't persuade you, I'll order you. I'm in command now. But look at it sensibly. Here we are, four strong, fit men scared about what one casualty may do to us. Surely to goodness we can keep a watch on him and look after ourselves. Isn't that common sense?"

"I don't agree but I won't argue," Toby said. "I don't want to cause trouble. I'd like to hear Boyd's judgment."

"I agree with Marcus," Boyd said, "but for a reason he has not given. Before the storm the Skipper had a line of retreat. Whatever he intended, he could have got away in the dinghy. She was seaworthy as a lifeboat—isn't that right, Jack? But the dinghy is gone. We literally sink or float together and I don't believe Charrington means to sink."

"All right then," Marcus said. "Everyone agree?"

"Just one suggestion," Toby said. "Of course we can look after ourselves—so long as he's not armed. But hadn't we better make sure about that?"

"It's a point," Marcus said. "Doing the food check I've been through the whole yacht except his cabin. I'll search that now. Will you come with me, Boyd? Meanwhile Toby and Jack might pump the bilges."

Half an hour later Marcus returned to the cockpit and announced: "No offensive weapons. I've conducted arms searches before, so you can trust me. But here's something for you, Toby."

Toby took the notebook and his face lit up with happiness. "Thank God fasting! I thought the whole voyage was wasted. Now—let anything happen."

Marcus said: "I feel justified in telling something else because it shows Richard has a soft spot in him. One thing we found was a woman's jersey. Boyd thinks he knitted it for Heather while he was a prisoner."

"Look," Yeoman said, pointing.

A rift had appeared in the clouded sky to windward, showing a patch of blue. The patch increased rapidly in area. The dirty clouds slipped down to the horizon. Suddenly the world was blue and dazzlingly bright in the afternoon sunshine.

The effect upon their spirits was immediate. They became cheerful and optimistic. Toby and Yeoman climbed the mast and managed to get the trysail set—after a fashion, pulling the head up after them and tieing it to the mast. Meanwhile the other two patched and reset the jib. An hour before sunset they were ready, they believed, to put *Heather Mary* on her course again.

"What course shall we steer?" Boyd asked.

"The same as before the storm," Marcus answered. "What was it then? Lord knows what has happened to the log but you've a good memory."

Boyd smiled. Marcus, as the man in charge with a clear job to do, was so much happier than he had been before.

"Northwest by west," Boyd answered. "But I take no responsibility for where it will get us to from here. We weren't aiming for Bermuda then, but Point X—and Heaven knows where that is or where we ran from it in the storm."

"Never mind. If we miss Bermuda we'll hit America."

"America is six or seven hundred miles beyond Bermuda. I don't suppose we'll go very fast with this rig."

"We can make a start in any case. It won't do Richard any harm at all to find out that we can get along without him for a bit."

"When do you expect the Skipper will come to?" Toby asked Boyd.

"I doubt if he'll be fully conscious before tomorrow morning."

"But, Good heavens," Marcus exclaimed. "He didn't get a crack on the head or anything like that. You told us yourself it was just flesh wounds. He must have bled like a pig rushing about as he did. But he's tough as old leather. Why should he be out for twenty-four hours?"

Boyd squatting like a lean Buddha in the cockpit, looked at the three hopeful men in front of him. How different they were from the tired and nervous people of that morning. Would they remember how they had then felt. Probably not, but they ought to know what he had done in any case.

"I gave him three of my sleeping pills," he said.

"Was that good medicine?" Marcus asked.

"For him? I don't know. For us—I thought it essential."

"Why?"

"As I finished bandaging him up he was grunting and heaving about. He was unconscious but talking to himself—or rather he repeated what he said to me just before the wave. I thought he might wake up and—well, be tiresome. At the same time I overheard you on deck, quarreling like politicians. So I gave him the sleeping draught. I knew it was a risk, but I felt we must have time for rest, and to settle our differences, and for morale—"

After a long pause Marcus said: "You might have killed him."

"I know. This morning I thought I had killed him. I still may have, but I don't think so."

Yeoman asked: "How will he wake up, Doctor? I mean, after all that sleep will he jump out of bed like a liver salts advertisement, or will he sort of grumble and come coherent slowly like a person who's had a night on the tiles?"

"I'm not a medical doctor. I can only describe my own experience, and people react differently. Those pills made me sleep whatever was on my mind. But I never took them unless I had a free day following. I spent most of that day waking up."

"Then we'll have time in the morning to make her ship-shape, that's a good thing. She's a disgrace now—sails hauled up anyhow like an old woman paddling. I wonder if she'll go into the wind."

It took a long time to persuade *Heather Mary* to swing around and face into the wind on her old course. When she finally did so she traveled very slowly. The log line towed not far from vertically. It was extremely disappointing, disquieting even, but there was nothing more that they could do with the night coming on. They settled down to sleep and regular watches. To conserve paraffin for cooking and the navigation lights they decided not to use the oil lamp in the saloon. It was a dark, discouraging night.

Next morning, thank God, the weather had improved still further, but there was little else to be thankful about. According to the log they had traveled only a dozen miles during the night. The yacht would not sail into the wind with her canvas crudely lashed to a broken mast. One read about jury masts but one couldn't make one out of nothing.

They started work trying to reset the rigging—but with little confidence. Hard facts, distances, were in their minds as they worked. They must be at least a hundred miles from Point X. The *Prince Rupert*, Boyd said, had steamed for twelve hours at about 25 knots before Heather disappeared. So Point X must be about 300 miles from Bermuda—on whatever bearing the *Prince Rupert* had been sailing. On that information they could have very little hope of finding Bermuda—and America was six or seven hundred miles further on. About a thousand miles at, say twenty miles a day meant over five weeks. The wounded yacht would not survive another storm, and at this season another storm was certain within that time. Besides, a quantity of stores had been ruined. Therefore they must somehow rerig the yacht so that she sailed faster, and they must find Bermuda. Although none of them expressed it aloud they each realized that they had no choice in their behavior to Charrington. At all costs he must be persuaded to navigate them to Bermuda. Thank God he was only asleep, not dead!

Marcus turned his crew's energies from the skilled sailor's tasks he did not understand to a busy, systematic tidying of the deck. They pitched the rubbish of torn canvas and splintered spars into the sea. But anything which might come in useful—whole lengths of wood, for instance—they lashed down where the dinghy used to be.

They were interrupted by a noise which puzzled them at first because they had not heard it for so long—the hum of an airplane. They broke off what they were doing and searched the sky for it.

They saw it, a silver insect traveling across the dazzling blue. They stood and stared until the sight and sound faded. They felt first excited and then disappointed. They turned back to their work.

"Never mind," Marcus said. "It must have been bound for Bermuda. Lots of air routes center there. We're getting near the hive. Somebody will see us soon—or better, we might arrive on our own."

At about eleven o'clock in the morning, the yacht still plunging slowly and with apparent unwillingness through the shoreless sea, Toby went below to make coffee.

As he went down the companionway he put a cigarette in his

mouth and took his lighter from his pocket. But a sudden whiff of
fuel stopped him lighting it.

Charrington was standing in the saloon with his back to Toby.
He had placed the oil lamp on the table, and at his feet was a four-
gallon jerrycan. It was not the blue paraffin container, it was the
red can used for filling the tank of Little Tich. In the surprise of
seeing Charrington on his feet and busy Toby did not realize the
significance of this. But he had at once a feeling that something
was very wrong indeed.

Charrington took a box of matches from the locker, and removed
a match.

Toby stared. Here was the familiar scene—Marcus' bunk, the
table where they ate their meals and which they had just repaired.
The old, rather dirty brass lamp—and the Skipper, who ought not
to have been out of his bunk at all, calmly engaged on this un-
believably terrible occupation. The whole place reeked with gasoline fumes. Toby stared, numbed and fascinated.

Charrington flicked the match across the striking surface. Its
head came off. He took out a second match, and did the same
thing—with the same result. Looking for another box, he turned
and saw Toby.

"Lend me your lighter. These matches are all wet," he said.

Toby came out of his trance. He dived at Charrington.

By the force of the attack Charrington was knocked on to the
gasoline soaked settee. But a moment later he had Toby by the
throat. Toby felt an agonizing pain as if he had been stabbed in
his neck, and a hot light blazed at the back of his eyes. Then he
was flung back across the saloon. He brought up with a thud on
the opposite settee and struck his head violently against the wall.
He sat there dazed and gasping, scarcely able to see for the water
in his eyes.

"Knocked something over?" Yeoman's voice asked from the
hatch.

There was no answer. Yeoman began to descend the companionway. Like Toby he was barefooted for their work on the mast,
so he made no sound. But, from the saloon, first his shins, then
body became visible. He entered the saloon.

His eyes and nostrils opened wide. He sniffed, staring from

Charrington to Toby who sat directly opposite each other.

"Fetch the others," Charrington said.

Yeoman disappeared without a word. In half a minute he was back with Boyd. None of them said anything until Marcus joined them, evidently excited.

"I heard you were up, Richard. Splendid," he began. "There is something away to windward—probably just a bit of Sargasso weed. But will you lend me your binoc—"

Then he became conscious of the fumes and sensed the strain.

"Sit down there on the other side of Toby," Charrington said. "He has just attacked me."

His eyes had a vague, dreamy look and his voice was muffled.

"You ought to be in your bunk," Boyd told him. "What were you doing?"

"I had just filled the lamp. I was going to light it and trim it. The matches were all wet. I asked Toby to lend me his lighter"—he held it up—"but he attacked me."

"It isn't paraffin, it's gasoline," Boyd said.

"Is it?"

"Yes. It wouldn't do for the lamp at all, and you have spilt it all over the place. You had better go back to your cabin while we tidy up. Let me help you."

"No, sit there," Charrington said. "Of course I knew it was gasoline really. And I soaked the bunk on purpose. If I lit this thing it wouldn't catch fire, it would explode. I was lying just now. But you discovered last night it isn't any good telling lies. Sit in a row and we will finish our discussion."

"We were not lying," Marcus said.

"That's what you keep on saying. But it's not worth while arguing about it now. Last night I gave you a chance to make a clean breast of it. It was a sort of confessional before reaching the place. But you declined it. Now we have arrived and there is very little more to say."

"Richard, you are a day out in your reckoning," Marcus said in his most persuasive tone. "It wasn't last night we were talking. There has been a storm in between, and then you were unconscious. You hurt yourself badly. You are still unwell."

"It is no good trying to deceive me," Charrington said, looking at Marcus with a fixed, unnatural stare. "I have thought about this much too long and carefully." As he spoke he kicked the jerry can over so that more and more gasoline welled out with slow hiccuping noises. The fumes became so strong that their eyes watered.

"You have always boasted about this lighter, Toby," Charrington went on. "But even if it doesn't light first time the spark will be enough. We don't want a vulgar scene. This is a solemn moment. We have reached the place where Mary is buried."

"No, that's not correct," Boyd said. "When we were talking you said we would reach the place next morning. But in the storm we had to turn and run away from it. Don't you remember how difficult it was to bring her round? Now we must be a hundred miles away from it at least. We ought to beat back to it before finishing the discussion."

"Do you think you know more about navigation than I do?" Charrington asked, a flash of anger in his sleepy voice. "This is Mary's grave, I tell you. This is where we settle it."

"How?"

"With this," Charrington held up the lighter.

The four men opposite him glanced sideways at each other, wondering if any of them had a plan. Toby thought, if it were a pistol we might rush him. Only one or two would get hurt. But with that—Oh, God, Elaine. You'll think we were drowned in a storm. You will never guess it was your present.

"Skipper," Boyd said. "The dinghy has been destroyed. If this yacht sinks we all sink with her—all."

"Exactly," Charrington answered. "You brought it to this, you know."

"I, how?" Boyd like the rest of them was trying to talk in a normal voice. That seemed the only chance of calming or diverting Charrington. With the table between them there could be no hope of disarming him except by words. This time they needed to prolong the conversation.

"You lied to me," Charrington said, "but you made me realize that I had been lying also—not to you, to myself. Listen carefully, and don't move. Since I escaped from Germany and found her gone all my thoughts about Mary have been anchored to the belief that she started back to England when she got my cable. I lived on that. Although it was difficult to reconcile the timing, I never allowed myself to doubt it. But you have convinced me that was not so. She was going back to her damned wilderness. When she heard I was waiting for her she killed herself rather than face me . . . That is not a pleasant realization for a husband. But why could she not face me? Because you—you four—had made it impossible. Oh, I know you will deny it still. But there's no need. We are going to blow this damned yacht of hers to smithereens. What's the use of lying now? We are going, all together, to face the little sanctimonious bitch and get the truth out of her herself."

Charrington had worked himself into a passion. None of them had any doubt that he meant what he said. In desperation they were all poised to jump at him directly he should shift his eyes. It was a million to one chance but there was nothing to lose by trying it.

Charrington paused, getting back his breath, watching their faces—cat and mouse.

"Well, Jack, a penny for them. I'm sure they will be worth it," he said.

Yeoman had not spoken a word. For most of the time he had sat listening, apparently completely overcome by a state of affairs so utterly removed from his experience, from his imagination even.

But now he said angrily: "You called Miss Heather a bitch. You have no right to do that. If she could hear you—"

"No doubt she can hear me. We are right on top of her grave."

"Are we? That explains it," Yeoman shouted with sudden excitement, shaking his finger in Charrington's face. "Yes, I suppose she *can* hear you. It must have been her calling out these last five minutes. Listen!"

His red round face was shining like the sun, his blue eyes were brilliant. "Listen!"

They all stared at him. He had become possessed almost as Charrington.

"Listen!!"

They had heard it before while Charrington was speaking—a sea bird crying plaintively every now and then. But Jack put a new character to it. Suddenly, in spite of Charrington, in spite of their sickening danger, he dominated the saloon with his wholehearted boy-like excitement.

"Listen—it's her!"

By the honesty of his conviction he changed the sound in their ears from that of a sea bird to something very like a woman's cry.

He got to his feet and leaned his arms on the table with his face close to Charrington's.

"Don't do anything silly like blowing us all up, Skipper. Nobody will ever know the truth if you do that. If Miss Heather is here she will want to talk to us alive."

Charrington stared at him. Something in his half-drugged mind seemed to respond.

"There really is a woman out there," Yeoman went on. "I don't understand how it can be Miss Heather. But I'm going to look."

Slowly and rather clumsily he stepped over their legs and went out of the saloon, up the companionway.

None of them knew what to make of it. They were so puzzled, so affected, that they followed Yeoman with their eyes until he was out of sight. Only then—although it was on this their lives depended—did they turn back to see how Charrington was reacting.

Charrington's aquiline face was working with excitement. But it showed another emotion also—or the lack of one. He was no longer sure of himself. He had half risen and was staring after Yeoman as if he wanted to follow but was held back by doubt or by the fear of something he did not understand.

Yeoman reappeared at the door of the saloon. He was beaming all over his face.

"I was right," he said, nodding at Charrington. "She's quite close. Come and see."

CHAPTER 22

CHARRINGTON still hesitated, but his mind had already followed Yeoman on deck. The others sat watching him. They were like members of an audience who feel the power and urgency of a strange music but are puzzled and uncertain in the presence of those few who can interpret and react to it.

The sea bird cried again. One had accompanied them since

about the time when they passed Madeira. They had not noticed it since the beginning of the storm, but before that, as far as they could remember, it had been with them almost every day—a white bird with long wings which glided low over the water, hung in the air, moved without effort. They had come to forget its presence because it was so usual. They could not remember if it had cried before.

Charrington began to follow Yeoman. He moved slowly and stiffly, as if he had wooden legs, holding on to things for support. When he was gone they had an intense feeling of relief. They wanted to burst out talking—but found nothing to say. They looked at each other questioningly, and shrugged their shoulders. They glanced at the floor where a sheen of gasoline floated on the bilge water. Marcus righted and closed the jerrycan. Then they hurried on deck—with very little idea of what they expected to find there.

Charrington was there, of course, but they took no particular notice of him, They looked eagerly round the circle of heaving ocean. They saw the white bird swooping gracefully along a wave crest—that was all. Their hearts dropped with a disappointment they could not have expressed even to themselves. Hope against reason is a private thing, and their minds were still shocked by the affair in the saloon.

"There!" Yeoman was pointing.

One of the valleys had become a mound of water. On it was a human figure. Although the distance was too great to see clearly they never doubted it as a woman's. She was lying face downwards with arms and legs spread wide as a starfish, supported by a patch of yellow weed.

The dead do float, after some while. That was their instant thought, awed but not horrified.

She disappeared into a valley.

Charrington had reached the tiller and unlashed it. He shouted orders. The woman was a hundred yards or more to windward of them and it was necessary to beat up to her by a series of short tacks. At the helm Charrington was a sailor again. Yeoman led the crew in obeying him, tugging and heaving the clumsily set sail from one side to the other. In the sense that they automatically trusted the Skipper to achieve their common purpose whether he were otherwise mad or not, it was a small-scale repetition of the storm. But in this case the difficulty was less the wind and sea than *Heather Mary* herself. More than once, in spite of Charrington's skill, when he put the helm hard down she refused to go about but hung in the wind with flapping sails. He cursed and shouted at her, and the crew. They tried as hard as he did, but they could not make the yacht move any faster.

The practical busyness involved helped to remove the experience from the supernatural sphere into which it would otherwise have tended. And as the distance between them lessened—for although *Heather Mary* scarcely moved the woman drifted down wind towards them—they saw she was supported not by seaweed but a rubber float.

By now Charrington had become accustomed to the yacht's new behavior. With a well-timed maneuver he swung her across the wind—and the pneumatic float butted against her side like a lamb against its mother.

Four men were kneeling in line with outstretched arms. They raised the woman in the float, for she was strapped to it, and so laid her on the deck.

Then for a moment they stood in a circle looking at her. She was sprawled face downwards. The strap about her waist and her wet clothes clinging to her accentuated the feminine outlines of her body. In spite of the man-made float it was so strange—the shoreless ocean and this woman, this real woman dead or alive, who had come out of it.

Boyd was the first to recover his wits. He dropped on his knees, felt for her heart and then unbuckled the strap.

Charrington pushed past the others.

"Don't touch her," he shouted. "Of course she's alive. Didn't you hear her?"

Kneeling himself, he swung the limp body across his shoulder and tried to rise. But with the wounds on his legs and the swaying of the yacht he could not do it without fear of falling. He laid her gently down again, still with her face hidden.

"Take her below," he said. "Carry her in the float."

They obeyed at once. They were still awed, and Charrington was the only one with a clear intention. Yeoman who had led them for a while had shrunk into a passive role again.

It was not easy getting the float down the companionway, but it was pliant and pneumatic and could be constricted.

"Take her to my cabin."

They had to squeeze the float almost double to get it through the cabin door.

"Lay it on the bunk. Good. Now stand back."

They had moved so slowly that Charrington had been able to keep up with them. He propped himself against the side of the bunk and slid the woman off the float on to the mattress. She rolled on to her back, and for the first time they were able to see her face clearly. It was ugly, gray and drawn—the face of a corpse. It was an unusual shape, triangular as a cat's but with a wide mouth and full lips. The eyes were shut.

Boyd, standing with the others against the chart table, looked from this face to the photograph of Heather on the shelf above the bunk. They were not the same—far from it. The only possible similarity was in the well-marked cheekbones. Thank God, the thing was explicable—a shipwrecked woman. Heather and she had nothing in common. Charrington was trying to get the wet clothes off her. It was nonsense that he should be the only one to touch her.

Boyd stepped forward.

"Get back. Get out of the cabin," Charrington said.

"I acted as your doctor—and you are alive," Boyd said in his quiet, matter-of-fact voice.

Charrington turned his head and looked at him closely for a moment. Then he nodded.

Together they stripped off the soaking garments and wrapped her tightly in one of the blankets which had been dried on deck the evening before.

"Make her a hot drink, somebody," Charrington ordered.

"But Richard, we can't—" Marcus began.

"Give her brandy," Boyd said.

Charrington took a bottle from the locker under the chart table. With his left arm round the woman's shoulders, he held it to her lips. The brandy dribbled out of her mouth again. Then she choked, and her throat worked violently as she swallowed.

"That's enough," Boyd said. Charrington laid her down again. For a moment longer she remained quite still. Then she stirred. Finding herself constricted she began to heave about. In a moment she was fighting like a wild cat in a trap, her eyes wide open and terrified. She flung the blanket away from her and would have tumbled from the bunk.

Charrington grappled her. An extraordinary struggle followed. He, for all his strength, handicapped by his stiff-bandaged legs which reduced his balance on the swaying floor and by his extreme care not to hurt her, and she, kicking and striking out in a desperate passion to escape from something which frightened her beyond all reason—he and she fought together.

The others crowded and stared—there was no room to help in any case. But they were most affected by the noises that she made, something between groans and squeaks, animal noises.

Without any warning she collapsed. She lay still except for the heaving of her breast.

With extreme care Charrington wrapped her up again. There was a strange expression on his face.

He said: "All she needs now is rest. There's little enough air— it would be better, if you don't mind—."

The others glanced from the woman to Boyd. He nodded, so they went out of the cabin. They were still thinking more about the woman than of Charrington.

But in the saloon, beyond the cabin door and the open hatch, the gasoline fumes hit them like a blow on the nose and returned them to the former scene.

"We ought not to have left him alone," Toby whispered. "He— Lord knows what he'll do."

"It's worth the risk," Boyd said quietly.

But out here he had lost his authority. Toby turned to Colonel Harding.

"You won't take an unnecessary risk. What shall we do?"

"There isn't much we can do about this except pump it out." Marcus gestured at the gasoline floating on the floor. "There isn't even a fire extinguisher, or sand. And with the skylight covered with canvas, it will just have to filter away through the hatch."

"Yes, but I mean leaving him alone with her. God knows what he may be preparing at this moment."

"That has changed. I think Richard has got his balance back."

"I'm going to look," Toby said.

"No. If anybody is going to look, I am."

Marcus left the saloon and quietly opened the cabin door. They could see him standing there, staring. At last he very quietly closed the door and rejoined them.

He asked Boyd: "What did you mean when you said just now it was worth the risk?"

"It's not much good passively keeping an eye on him. He's too clever. Our best chance is to help him recover his will to live."

"How the hell do we set about that?" Toby asked.

"By leaving him alone at this moment."

Toby turned away from Boyd impatiently. "Marcus," he appealed, "you've been in action. You don't believe that. We were within an inch of being blown up just now. The danger is the same. Surely you aren't going to leave him free now we've got a chance?"

Since he returned from the cabin Marcus had not looked like a man of action. He was evidently puzzled, at a loss. He did not answer Toby's question.

"How did you find him?" Boyd asked .

"He was—fascinated," Marcus said.

He sat down, and the others did the same doubtfully.

They waited. No sound came from the cabin. After some minutes Marcus took out a cigarette and tapped it on the case. Yeoman grabbed his elbow and he put it away again. The others had started violently. Their nerves were on edge.

There was a clatter of activity from the cabin, and the unmistakable noise of a warped drawer being tugged open and jammed shut. Marcus wondered which drawer it was and whether he had searched it properly. All four men in the saloon jumped to their feet. Charrington came out of the cabin in a stiff-legged hurry. He paused at the entrance of the saloon and asked impatiently, "Why didn't you tell me it was almost noon?"

He clambered up the companionway. He had the sextant in his hand.

Marcus said: "I'll go on deck too and have a smoke."

Boyd followed him.

Toby sat down—then got up again. He went into the cabin and stayed there for some while. He came out at last slowly and reluctantly.

Jack Yeoman had remained in a corner of the gasoline soaked

settee, absorbed by thoughts which were evidently unhappy.

At last he went on deck and busied himself pumping out the bilges—in the mood of one who digs his garden to take his mind off something else. The gasoline made rainbow colors on the sea.

Meanwhile Charrington was leaning against the mast, one naked hairy leg thrust out, the foot pressed against the gunwale to give him steadiness, his left hand holding the sextant in the exact position before his eyes, his fingers of his right slowly turning the micrometer screw while through the lenses he followed the sun up to its zenith. Marcus and Boyd watched him with close interest, while Yeoman steadily went on pumping. Charrington was intent. He was a skillful sailor, as he had been in the storm. Relieved, they went down to the saloon and brought up cushions and bedding to dry in the fresh air. Toby helped them.

Charrington made some notes on a piece of paper and went down to the bare saloon. Toby followed. The floor was now dry but the sigh and squelch of Yeoman's pumping still continued.

Charrington put down his sextant and notebook on the table and started for his cabin.

"What are you going to do?" Toby asked aggressively.

"I'll work it out here. I don't want to disturb her. But I must get the nautical almanac."

Charrington went out and returned with a battered and damp volume.

Toby sat opposite to him on the bare settee, watching the neat columns of figures being drilled.

"Where are we?"

"Only the latitude so far. We must have drifted a long way south. I will have to wait three hours for a longtitude." He yawned. "It's absurd, but I feel bloody tired. Do you mind if I rest on your cot? We'll have to go shares now—four beds between five men."

About this time Yeoman felt the bilge pump ease and heard it suck empty with a long wheezy sigh. He stood straight until his back had stopped aching. Then he walked forward over the gently swaying deck to the bow where Marcus and Boyd sat smoking and talking. The hard work had partly soothed his feeling, but he did not understand the smiles with which he was greeted.

"We were discussing where she comes from," Boyd said.

Marcus added: "She must have come from a wreck. The destroyer and the airplane may have been looking for survivors. That would make it less extraordinary her appearing when she did. But however it was, she saved our lives, she and your sixth sense."

Yeoman staring unhappily at the heaving sea did not respond.

Boyd said: "You of all people, Jack, have no need to be despondent. We are most grateful—and interested. Can you explain your part of the mystery?"

"There isn't any mystery," Yeoman answered. "I really thought it was Miss Heather. But it wasn't. That's why I'm sad."

Boyd and Marcus looked at each other. Marcus said: "Steady, old Jack. You know it couldn't have been."

"I suppose not. But after so long with such a lot of strange things happening you don't judge like you would at home, or I don't, not being educated." Yeoman was speaking sadly and dreamily. "I've thought such a lot about Miss Heather—more and more. I suppose it started with the yacht being like her—the way when you were advising her on a point of business, she'd be docile as a lamb and then suddenly, if she didn't approve, she'd take her own line and stick to it for all you said whatever the consequences for herself. . . But it was more than that. Thinking about her at night she came nearer alive every time. . . And then the Skipper mentioning the Sargasso Sea—All I read about it as a boy! I don't know—I was sort of waiting for her. . . I felt pretty sure she'd come because that was the only reason for all this. . . But it was someone else after all. Suddenly she's dead again. She was such a lovely person. She oughtn't to be dead."

Marcus and Boyd avoided looking at each other. Jack was sane enough. He had touched something which in their greater sophistication they had lacked the courage to share.

The white bird swooped by, beautiful and indifferent.

"Where did the cry come from?" Marcus asked. "From that bird or the woman?"

"It's a giant petrel, I think," Boyd answered. "I've never read that they are mute."

"It hasn't made a sound before."

"Are you sure? In the saloons we didn't notice the cry until Jack told us to listen. But we must have heard it and taken it for granted it was the bird."

"It can't have been the girl. She was unconscious."

"It might have been her last effort, seeing the yacht," Boyd said.

Yeoman said: "She made noises in the cabin anyway. And the way she fought—It wasn't human. She's a wild, savage creature. She has no right to be here."

"She must have been strapped on that float for a long time," Boyd told him. "There is a little mast and sail but she hadn't tried to use them. She had just lain there like a prisoner, hiding her face, through that storm. You mustn't judge her yet. She may surprise you."

"Why do you say that?" Marcus asked.

"We are all animals underneath. It doesn't take so very much privation or shock to remove the civilized covering. When she's rested you may find her charming."

"I don't like her," Yeoman said stolidly. "She will only cause more trouble. The best plan would be to put her back where she came from."

"Jack!"

"I didn't really mean that. I suppose I'm disappointed."

Toby came hurriedly on deck.

"I think she's dying. What can we do? For God's sake hurry."

Boyd asked: "Why do you think she's dying?"

"She opened her eyes. But she didn't answer when I spoke to her. She just slowly closed them again."

They went down to the cabin where the woman lay, as Charrington had lain, with Heather's photograph above the bunk. Her eyes were still closed but Boyd noticed that there was more life in her face. Toby's anxiety, whatever had caused it, was not justified.

Her eyes opened just a slit. When they closed again there was a hint of expression on her face. She was puzzled.

"Should we give her some brandy?" Toby asked.

"No, I don't think that's necessary," Boyd said.

The woman's eyes opened again, this time wide and big. They

moved very slowly from one to another of the four men who stood looking down at her.

Toby broke the silence. "Where do you come from? Who are you?"

She stared at him.

"I was in the sea," she said with a faint voice. "I was in the sea for ages and ages."

"But who are you?"

Again there was a pause, and then like the tired sigh of one falling asleep she said: "Mary—"

There was a sudden movement behind the four men. Charrington was standing in the doorway.

CHAPTER 23

WHILE she lay in the cabin she was not an individual but a woman who had come out of the sea, fraily and mysteriously alive. Physically she was a face above the bedclothes. Charrington cooked for her—over a stove on deck. Boyd was her doctor. But they all saw her once or twice a day, taking her food, clearing it away, or for some minor office. They came into the cabin on tiptoe. They glanced almost reverently at the face. If the eyes were open they made some conventional remark. "You're all right now," or "You'll be well soon." They were conscious that the eyes followed them. Sometimes, after the first day, there might be a ghost of a smile or a faint "Thank you." They tiptoed out again.

Spiritually she was a reminder of other women—the woman most important to each—and of another life. Of course they had frequently thought about going ashore at the end of the voyage. But they had been so long afloat that this other life had become almost as vague as paradise. Her presence reminded them of the conventions. They shaved, tidied themselves up and were more careful about the words they used. At least one of them would have liked to quip the others about this, but he was in no position to because, in spite of himself, he also had been influenced. When they spoke of her—instinctively in a low voice—their guarded re-remarks concerned her health and the way she had affected the Skipper. She was a woman and an influence, nothing personal.

Then, on the afternoon of the second day after her rescue, Boyd announced that she would come into the saloon for tea. Tea had never been an official meal but a refreshment snatched whenever anyone was free. Now all of them, except Yeoman who had insisted on taking the helm, were waiting as for a formal occasion. On the battered table there was a more or less clean cloth.

She entered wearing a pair of Boyd's trousers—he was nearest to her in height—and Toby's roller-necked sweater which had been shrunk by many wettings and which she filled very well although it was much too long for her. Her face though far from beautiful was quite attractive with the baby wide eyes and big generous mouth. She had tied a silk handkerchief of Charrington's over her hair, and this gave her a demure and simple look.

When they had sat down again, Marcus handed her a cup of tea.

"I'm sorry there isn't a saucer. We had some but they got broken —a storm, you know."

She smiled at him. Then she sniffed the air and remarked, "What a funny smell."

There was an awkward silence.

Charrington laughed. "My fault. I spilled some fuel the other day. But it's practically gone now and I promise to be more careful in future."

While he was speaking, Mary kept her eyes on his face intently but without particular expression. When he had done she gave him the same quick smile with which she had acknowledged Marcus' apology. Then she took a sip of the tea and bit the corner of a biscuit.

She turned to Boyd. "So you're on a yachting trip. How inter-esting!"

"Yes," Boyd said.

"Rather more than a yachting trip," Marcus broke in. "We are on our way from England to Bermuda."

"Bermuda," she said. "Oh—oh—"

Boyd looked interested. "Can you tell us now what happened to you?" he asked in his gentle voice.

"Please don't make me speak of it yet." Her eyes were glistening with tears.

"Certainly you need not talk of it if it pains you," Charrington said. "I'm Skipper of this yacht and you are my guest."

She gave him a grateful look and recovered herself in silence. None of them had much conversation.

"So you're the Skipper," she said. "It's silly but I don't know who anybody is."

They apologized and introduced themselves.

"I'm Mary Brown. I hope you will call me Mary, though. I always think people waste such a lot of time being formal. And since you rescued me—"

"Thank you, Mary," Charrington said. "I'm sure we would all be glad if you would call us by our first names. I'm Richard—he's Toby—he's Marcus, he's—"

"I call him Doc," Mary said. She went on. "I'm sorry I was silly just now. I was frightened for a minute. But you are all so kind. Of course I'll be glad to go to Bermuda. When will we arrive?"

"That depends on a number of things," Charrington answered. "Are you in a hurry?"

"Well—They will all be worried about me, the public I mean. It will be terribly exciting to arrive—" She noticed Charrington's somber expression, and stopped. "I'm afraid I'm a terrible nuisance," she ended sadly.

"A nuisance!" Charrington exclaimed heartily. "You are doing us all a world of good—making us behave like gentlemen instead of cave men."

Toby went on deck to relieve Yeoman at the helm. His feelings about this girl were not entirely clear. But she wasn't a bad little thing.

Next morning when he was alone with his notebook in the saloon Mary Brown came in.

"What are you writing?" she asked.

"Nothing much," Toby answered.

"I'm sure it is. Please tell me."

"Just an account of the voyage. I try to keep it up every day."

"How wonderful. Are you going to write a book?"

"I might. I hope so."

"How wonderful to be able to write a book—and to be in it yourself."

She sat opposite to Toby, her arms on the table, looking straight at him with glowing eyes and parted lips.

Startled by her enthusiasm he gave a sort of laugh.

"It's nothing much. I—" He became confused by the appearance of his old roller-necked sweater.

"What, Toby?" she asked.

"I—I was only going to say that of course you would be in it. You would be about the most important person. The way you turned up was just about miraculous."

"Seriously?" She leaned still further across the table.

"Before you arrived—" he began.

"It *would* make a wonderful story," she said. "Just like a novel. I'd been in Hollywood. I was coming home for a rest, flying of course. We got to Bermuda all right. We started on for—well somewhere. The weather was bad. I'm sure they'll say that's why we crashed—"

"What happened to the other people?" Toby asked.

"I suppose they were drowned—tragic. Perhaps they were saved. They had big rafts and things. I went off alone. I'm sure they'll say it was the weather. That's partly right, of course, but I know the pilot was madly jealous. He wanted me to sit beside him, but I couldn't—"

"What exactly happened?" Toby asked.

She began to explain—but Toby's mind wandered. He couldn't disbelieve her because here she was. She was here—that was the point. She was young and attractive and he liked her.

While he was looking into her face, nodding at her words but scarcely hearing them for his own thoughts, the door opened and somebody came in. The light in her face was switched off.

She turned to the door.

"That float of yours," Charrington said. "It occurred to me it would make the nearest thing to a comfortable seat we've got on board. So I've fixed it up on deck. It's a nice day and the fresh air will do you good. Would you like to try it, Mary?"

"Thank you, Richard." The light came on again. "I'll come at once. I was just chatting with Toby."

From that day onwards, since the weather was fine and the wind no more than a light breeze, Mary Brown made a habit of reclining in what she called her "throne" on deck where she could talk to the helmsman. Increasingly, when he was not busy with his navigation, Charrington made it a party of three. Thus rarely except at night was the man on watch alone. Once when Marcus relieved Boyd at four in the morning, he asked in a whisper: "What do you think of her?"

"I'm pleased with her," Boyd said.

"So am I. She doesn't seem to understand you, though," Marcus smiled.

"That has always been my worst fault with women, except with— It's strange how one hesitates to mention Heather's name now— like the name of a person who has just died."

"What do you mean by that?"

"Jack could explain better than I. But we were speaking of Mary Brown. Her arrival reprieved us. Since then she has certainly revived the Skipper's will to live, and she is encouraging him to hurry to Bermuda. Whatever one's personal feelings about her may be, one must consider her an asset."

"She eats a lot," Marcus said.

"What's the real state of the stores?"

"Bad. Worse than I've said. Quite a lot was spoiled by seawater and paraffin and the damned fish won't take any longer now we need 'em most. There isn't any fresh water to spare either. I had to start the tank in the Skipper's cabin yesterday."

"There are about thirty-five gallons in that, aren't there?"

"Yes. We'll be all right if we are careful. I'll tell you a strange thing, though. That photograph of Heather has gone. It would be cheek if that girl has hidden it."

"More likely to be Charrington."

"He hasn't taken it with him. He couldn't, sleeping in a different bunk every night—"

"He may have got rid of it."

"But good God," Marcus began and stopped, staring at Boyd. "You don't think he's falling for this girl. She's quite attractive, but he was married to Heather. She has never left his mind. He couldn't do a switch, not in a week."

"He might not admit it was a switch."

"He couldn't confuse the two. The only similarity is in their names, and Mary is the commonest name in the world."

"Don't you think he might believe that a more submissive, more appreciative Mary has risen like a watery phoenix from the grave of the first? I know little about madness—"

"But he's not mad," Marcus protested. "Of course some things drive him off his head—we know it only too well. But that was after a period of strain and sleeplessness. And we know the subjects to avoid. Damn it, no one who was really mad could have patched up a wounded yacht as he has and coaxed her along so well. Besides, he has been so open with us, keeping the chart in the saloon. He has even taught you to navigate, hasn't he? Whether it's the fact of having rescued this girl from the sea or what, I do believe he's cured."

"Would you like to make a bet?" Boyd asked.

"What about?"

"I'll be ready to buy you a case of whisky and your wife a new hat if within a week of our arrival in Bermuda Charrington hasn't sold *Heather Mary*, even to be broken up."

"Good Lord, he won't do that. He has often said *Heather Mary* is the perfect yacht. She can be repaired in a shipyard."

"His pride can't. Now he knows that Heather was not returning to him, that she killed herself to escape him, he hates her memory. Whether or not one Mary can replace another without a sense of unfaithfulness, he will get rid of everything that reminds him of Heather. But I must go to bed. Which bunk is vacant? I don't want to crawl in on top of Charrington in the dark."

Left alone, in no way encouraged by his talk with Boyd, feeling his responsibility as second-in-command, Marcus tried to appreciate the situation in proper military style. They were two hundred miles southeast of Bermuda, with food for a week and water for rather longer. The intention was to arrive before these stores were exhausted. So far so good. But when it came to the courses open to the enemy Marcus found it impossible to progress logically because he didn't know who the enemy was. He agreed with Boyd that it was not Mary Brown. Was it the weather? The wind was blowing gently from exactly the wrong direction—from Bermuda. They had to tack, moving through the water at a bare three knots and in the right direction at an average of less than one. If the wind would change direction and blow more strongly they could reach harbor within a few days. But on the other hand the lightness of the wind was saving the yacht. A storm would certainly finish her . . . Richard had been their enemy, but since the girl came on board he had been very much on their side—had behaved as their commanding officer, in fact, and had to be treated as such. You knew where you were in a good old straightforward war, but here—The only thing to do was to go carefully with everyone and everything, particularly with Richard. No naked lights, no matches lying about, the axe locked away, all dangerous subjects taboo—he was doing his best.

Marcus heard somebody coming up the companionway out of the black belly of the yacht. Was it Richard resuming the old habit of midnight talks, and if so what line ought one to take?

It was the girl.

"Oh, it's you, Marcus. I'm so glad," she said. "I couldn't sleep, and not having a light—Can't I really have light?"

"It is safer not. There may still be gasoline in the bilges. In any case we haven't any paraffin to spare. But I expect Boyd will get the electric lights working soon."

"Anyhow it's so hot down there. Have I really got to have this canvas over the skylight? I thought I'd sleep on deck."

She got into the float and made herself comfortable.

"It's frightfully funny," she said. "I thought I was absolutely terrified of this thing. I think I still am really. But you being here makes all the difference. I wouldn't mind sleeping in it at all."

Marcus made a noncommittal noise.

"Why are you going to Bermuda?" she asked.

"Personally, because my wife and kids are there."

"You've got children? How lovely. What are they—boys or girls?"

"Two little girls."

"How lovely. What are their names?"

Marcus told her. Soon he was telling her all about his family— and feeling strangely happy. He knew he had missed Meg and the brats but had not realized how much he had also missed talking about them to a sympathetic person, to a woman.

The end of the watch took him by surprise. Yeoman fumbled his way on deck. When he saw Mary Brown he stood and stared with his mouth open, looking alarmed and completely at a loss.

He remained like that for the best part of a minute. Then suddenly and loudly he said to Marcus: "We had better have a look at the navigation lights."

"We don't need to light them."

"We must look at them."

"Why on earth? They are quite unnecessary. We are still in the empty quarter."

"Come and look at them, please."

Marcus followed him to the bow.

"Don't leave me alone with that woman," Yeoman whispered urgently.

"Why? She's a good sort."

"I wouldn't trust myself," Yeoman said in the same agitated voice. "I would push her overboard in that float of hers."

"Jack, really—"

"She tried to vamp me while she was getting a splinter out of my hand. She called me Uncle Jack. She has no right to be here on Miss Heather's yacht—a woman who acts in films and goes flying about on her own. She had better take herself off as she came and find someone else to look after her."

"Get a grip of yourself, Jack."

"Don't leave me alone with her, Colonel, please."

"You won't be alone," Marcus said.

While they had been speaking Charrington had come on deck.

He called out to Yeoman. "You can go down again, Jack, if you like. I'll stand your watch. I'm going to do some star observation. Boyd is coming up to try his skill."

"See you later," Mary called to Jack. "I want to look at your hand again."

Before morning the wind had died away completely. The water glowed in the early sunlight with the varied colors you see in puddles filmed by oil. It was as calm as that—except for the wide and gentle undulations of the swell. *Heather Mary* tipped and tilted helplessly, with no life in her.

Charrington set them to work on the hull and rigging. There was not much more that they could do effectively, for lack of materials. But the work occupied their minds and the day passed quietly enough. Mary Brown had spent it sprawling luxuriantly in her "throne," watching with interest and talking in her vivacious way to anyone who happened to be near her. She told Toby she didn't really mind the delay. It would make her arrival all the more exciting. In the evening she suggested that they should have supper on deck.

"I wish I could give you a feast," Charrington said. "But Marcus is too strict a quartermaster. I tell you what, though—we'll have a rum issue."

"No," Marcus said firmly. "I think we had better not."

"Why?"

Marcus hesitated. "I think we are better without," he said lamely.

"What do you think, Mary?" Charrington asked.

"I agree with Marcus. Drink is bad for people. I never touch it."

"Oh, very well," Charrington said.

The others looked at him in surprise.

It was a plain but pleasant supper, enlivened by the now usual duel for Mary's attention between Toby and Charrington. Toby was in high spirits, telling of their early misadventures—the egg basket and the salt water drinking. Mary laughed delightedly.

They finished eating as the sun sank below the horizon in a golden burst of glory, leaving the little yacht alone in the middle of an opal-colored sea. There was not even the white bird to keep her company.

Mary sighed. "The only thing I miss is a campfire," she said. "It's so romantic telling stories round a campfire."

In the startled silence which this remark caused she went on, "Last night Richard was telling me about his war adventures—his tremendous fights in gunboats and things, and then when he was wounded and taken prisoner how he tried to get back to his wife. It was lovely. But you didn't finish, Richard. Won't you tell us how you actually got back to her?"

There was a crevasse of silence.

"We have asked him that before but he won't talk about it," Toby said.

"I'm sure he will for me, won't you, Richard?"

Again there was a silence.

"Certainly I will tell you how I came home," Charrington said.

CHAPTER 24

IT would be difficult to imagine a more peaceful scene than that in which Charrington began his story. The water was smooth as silk. The colors were fading out of it as the clouds which it reflected turned from red and gold to gray. The whole world—the round ocean and the doming walls of sky—seemed to be closing like a flower to sleep. Charrington spoke quietly, for his hearers were close about him on the deck, some of them smoking, all of them quite still.

But Marcus felt his heart thumping. It made him angry with himself as that uncontrollable reaction always did. . . . He knew why he was scared. He had recognized the start of the same old drum dance. He had done what he could, as they all had, to prevent it—obeyed Richard's orders, behaved as if there had never been anything strange or strained between them, kept off dangerous subjects. But this newborn woman had barged in, walked into the holy place with her boots on. Even then, when he had seen the trouble coming and wanted a drink like hell, he had vetoed Richard's offer of alcohol in the small hope of keeping him calm. But Richard was off now like a nigger with a tom-tom. Forcibly to interrupt him would only precipitate the climax. To hell with it and let it ride. Listen for the danger signal and be ready to jump first, that was all they could hope to do. Perhaps in any case it was best to get it over.

To some extent the other three of the crew felt the same. They sat like coiled springs, listening to the tone of Charrington's voice rather than the words. But since the pitch did not rise they began to hear the story.

He was telling of an escape plan he had hatched at the beginning of 1944. He had not described this previously and his hearers were at first uncertain whether it had been the start of his final and successful bid or not. He had just been transferred, he said, to a camp from which, the Kommandant boasted, no one had managed to escape. It was in a plain, with no sort of cover within miles. That was its strength. But Charrington had only one idea in his mind when he examined his new quarters.

"There was no chance of getting out through the gate, either disguised or in a coal or ration truck. They were prepared for that sort of thing," Charrington said. "It was a case of under the wire, through the wire or over the wire."

"Which did you do?" Mary asked.

"I spent a few days deciding. To burrow is the natural instinct of prisoners—so the guards had taken steps to prevent that. Besides, any tunnel would have had to break in the open. Crawling through the wire—there was a double fence with coils of wire between. Still, it might have been possible, for one can make wire cutters. But to tell the truth I didn't trust my nerves after all that time. There were watchtowers and searchlights. If your clothes caught you had to lie still. I doubted if I could do that. Over the wire—I was in the mood for something quick and desperate. But I needed a ladder because of the overhang on the inner fence, and even if I got out there was that open country to be crossed. I didn't want to be caught or shot directly I was outside. I meant to get back to—" He hesitated.

"Please tell me quickly what you did," Mary said, sitting bolt upright in front of him.

Charrington paused and looked at her in the dusk.

"You musn't hurry me. You can't hurry an escape. . . .While I was still thinking over the problem the Kommandant sent for me. He was patronizing and sure of himself. He said that he knew all about my record—that was why I had been transferred to his camp—and he wanted to save me the trouble of trying to get out. He had studied the records of every break in this war and the last and had taken measures to prevent a repetition of any of them."

"How horribly discouraging," Mary said.

"It was helpful. From people who had been caught again I also had heard, first or second-hand, about every important break. I had to think of something new. But there wasn't anything new— not at that stage of the war. Then I remembered an escape from Warburg a couple of years earlier when about thirty officers climbed over the wire using home-made assault ladders. The ladders were beautifully constructed, sliding on themselves and opening like an inverted L so that the men could climb above the first fence, cross the gap to the next and swing outside. Of course the Kommandant would know of this escape. But he would believe, as the authorities in the camp had believed, that the ladders could not have been made by the prisoners but had been dropped by the R. A. F. during a near-by raid a few nights earlier. Therefore, if I could imitate their stealth and carpentry I had a chance. And a mass break was what I needed. A man alone would probably be caught by the patrols outside the wire. But if there were a lot of us scattering in different directions I would have a very good chance. . . ."

Charrington's voice, urgent and intense, went on and on in the quiet night. They had good reason to fear him in such a mood. But he was talking to the girl, not to them, and surely he meant her no harm. Besides, what sudden damage could he do—on deck, with the four of them surrounding him, on a calm night? So they listened, quiet and watchful—and more and more interested.

In great detail, so that they saw every step, Charrington described the secret preparations of the next three months. There were ladders to be made—out of bedboards and slices from the library shelves. (The people concerned had to be persuaded that they could sleep without bedboards and the books must be balanced on half shelves.) The hinges of the ladders were made from window catches forged in a converted stove. (People in other huts had to be persuaded to part with a proportion of their small coal ration.) The ladders could not be kept assembled but must be taken to pieces and concealed, for the most part in the places where their components came from. But one ladder was put together nearly every evening for practice in the music room, using two wires stretched nine feet above the floor to simulate the double fence. The escapers went on practicing until the teams of ten could go over with packs on their backs, in the dark, in under half a minute. The noise they made was covered by music and there was, of course, a screen of watchers outside the hut.

That was only part of the organization. A meteorologist must calculate the best evening, the minute even, for the attempt to start. Maps must be made and routes worked out, for the essence of the second phase was dispersal. Diversionists must be enlisted and trained for their thankless task of getting themselves into trouble with no hope of escaping. Someone must discover how to fuse the lights, and do it without rehearsal at the exact moment. Three or four men must undertake to hold the ladders steady against the wire, a most dangerous task if shooting should start as it was bound to do sooner or later.

Security was vital. When there is nothing else of interest to talk about it is cruelly difficult to keep a secret. Therefore, though every man must be thoroughly briefed in his own task he must know as little as possible about the rest—ideally, not even the names of men outside his team. And above all there was the problem of maintaining interest and morale during the long months of preparation.

Charrington had dealt with all this. He alone carried all the responsibility, all the details in his head.

While he was now telling his story the darkness closed in like a black wall around the yacht. His voice dropped to a whisper. They leaned closer to him, listening like conspirators.

At last the chosen night arrived. The sun had set but there was still a little time before lights out. The escape teams were waiting in a hut, their packs on their backs, their faces blackened, socks over their boots. The diversionists were in position, the electrician at his post. Meanwhile—as far as possible—the ordinary life of the prison camp was going on. The lights blazed all along the wire and the silhouettes of the helmeted sentries could be seen in the watchtowers.

Charrington waited impatiently for a signal from the men who were shadowing and detaining with talk any prowling German guards. It was exactly ten minutes until Lights Out when any movement outside the huts would cause investigation. And in half an hour the moon would rise. If the All Clear signal were long delayed it would be too late to make the attempt that evening. And it was too complex an operation to be easily or safely postponed. Disappointment is harder to conceal than anticipation.

At last an officer, strolling to his hut, could be heard whistling "Pack Up Your Troubles." Charrington gave the word which he had been living to give through sixteen weeks of ceaseless strain. The lights went out all round the camp and over the wire. From the far side of the camp came a sudden furious shouting as if a fight had broken out. English voices bellowed contradictory orders in

German. Just beyond the nearest watchtowers there was a twanging noise as grapnels were thrown over the trip wires.

Charrington waited until he judged the sentries would have turned. Then he said: "Go."

The black caterpillars of the escape teams emerged. The ladders were thrown against the inner fence, the cross pieces extended... Forty seconds later firing started in earnest and the lights went on again. But by then thirty-nine British officers, in parties of two or three, were scattering in every direction across country.

"And you?" Mary asked breathlessly. "Where were you, Richard?"

"I was leaning against the hut with a couple of crutches under my arms," Charrington said in a flat voice. "During the last practice I fell and wrenched my leg."

"So you didn't get out?"

"No. I couldn't walk—and I couldn't postpone the thing."

"I thought you had escaped," Mary said with tears in her voice.

Charrington lit his pipe. For a moment they saw his tired and angry face. They felt half sorry for him but they were glad that he was still a prisoner. They felt safer so.

"But you did escape. You told me you escaped," Mary insisted, on her knees in front of him.

"I got out of Germany in the end."

"How?"

"I would rather not speak of it."

"You must, you must. You can't stop like—like a magazine. I can't sleep till you tell me how you got home."

"Don't, Richard," Marcus said quietly. "Leave it alone."

But Charrington seemed not to hear him, as if his ears were tuned only to the woman's voice.

"I went on trying," he said. "But I was so tired. And I got more letters from home. I think it was a private punishment by that damned Kommandant. He was mad with rage but couldn't pin the escape on to me... I went on trying, but they were watching me like cats and I didn't get anywhere. It was a year without news and almost without hope.

"And then in March '45 they moved the camp. The allies were getting too close. We could hear the guns when the wind was right. They moved us at short notice. I took nothing in my pack

except some chocolate and biscuits—and the two personal posses-
sions I always carried. The rest went on the baggage carts which
we had rigged up, using pram wheels and heaven knows what.

"They took a long time organizing us. But at last we were quit
of the camp and marching along the main road eastwards. The
column was three or four hundred yards long. The guards weren't
thicker than one every thirty yards, but in that open country with
the corn hardly showing there was no chance of slipping away.
They were taking us further from the frontier, but there was a
sense of freedom in being outside the wire. It was a lovely spring
morning, soft and warm, not a cloud in the sky.

"We had been going for not more than half an hour when a
reconnaissance plane came over and we identified it as one of
ours. It flew up and down the column and we were sure it had
recognized us by our uniforms and comic transport. We were
sorry when it went westward. It was a link with home.

"Then the planes wheeled in formation.

"Someone shouted: 'My God, they're coming at us!'

"We dived for the ditch and the little piles of stones at the
roadside. For the next twenty minutes the planes made a systematic attack on the column, flying at two to three hundred feet and
firing with all their guns—point five tracer, explosive and armor
piercing bullets. They made runs down the road, across it at
right angles, and diagonally—while we lay there without any
proper cover, cursing or praying. Some officers tried to run for it,
and one of the thunderbolts chased them and shot them up. There
seemed no reason why they should stop before everyone was dead.
After all those years of prison, with the end of the war in sight,
we were being systematically murdered by our own people. It
was the most dreadful thing that has ever happened to me—bar
one.

"The man beside me was hit by an explosive bullet. Of course
you haven't seen a man hit by an explosive bullet. I was splashed
all over. On the other side of me was one of the guards lying with
his face pressed into the earth. His helmet had tilted forward and
I could see his neck. I didn't suppose he would bother me but just
to make sure I picked up a paving stone and brought it down on
the back of his neck. It seemed better to make sure. Then I got
up and walked away.

"I don't know if they tried to shoot me—the other guards or the airplanes. There was still a lot of noise going on, I remember. I didn't feel frightened or brave. I didn't feel anything. I just walked in the direction of our lines. After about an hour I remember stopping and trying to light a pipe. But I couldn't do it—literally couldn't do it—because my hands were shaking so much."

"Oh Richard, poor, poor—What did you do?" Mary cried.

"Do? I walked on. I had to get back to England and sanity, that's all I knew. I suppose I took precautions. I'd been taking them so long that it was second nature. But I don't remember what I did except walk on. They told me that I walked through a battle to get to our lines."

"It was fated, Richard. It was fated that you should come safely home," Mary whispered, close in front of him.

"Yes, they flew me back at once."

"To someone who could comfort you and make you well again."

"To an empty house. She hadn't waited for me. She had gone. It wasn't I who had escaped."

Mary stretched out her hand to Charrington. He took it and sat silent for some time. They could not see his face in the darkness.

At last he rose to his feet and went below.

CHAPTER 25

TOBY and Yeoman were off duty between midnight and four o'clock. For most of this period they thought their own thoughts in silence or dozed in the cockpit or the float. (The girl was sleeping in the cabin because of the mist which had formed after sunset.) But when the hour approached when they must go below to stand their watch, Toby moved close to Yeoman and began a whispered conversation.

"This is stupid. Don't you think so?"

"The Colonel knows what he's doing," Yeoman answered. "He's had more experience than you."

"Oh yes, Marcus is sound enough. But he's too cautious. Defense never won a war."

"We aren't at war yet."

"We will be. He was right off his head at the end."

"What is it you think we ought to do?" Yeoman asked.

"Tie him up. I've always said so."

"The Colonel won't have that. Nor will Boyd. I wouldn't like it either. I want a job in Bermuda, not a lawsuit or some nasty publicity."

"What would you do then?" Toby asked.

"What I'd have liked to have done before now is put Mary Brown back where she came from."

"Why?"

"She has no right here. Since she came we've lost the wind and the white bird and it feels as if this yacht had nothing to do with Miss Heather. I'm only saying what I'd like to do, mind. I'm not really going to push her over the side."

"It would be a little severe," Toby said. He was too used by now to Yeoman's other-world mood to show surprise at it.

"But someone else might go off in the float."

"Who would do that?"

"I would. No, I'm not crazy either. Jack, the yacht is helpless in this calm. But one could paddle that float even if one couldn't sail. The emergency stores are still on board it. It's two hundred miles to Bermuda. At three miles an hour that's less that three days."

"You want to save your own skin?"

"And everybody else's. I'd send help. Within four days a launch could be here. And Charrington wouldn't dare to try anything in the meantime. Don't be an ass, Jack, I'm not planning to run away. You can do it if you like. I'm only anxious that somebody should do it."

"We had better talk to the Colonel or Boyd," Yeoman said.

"They wouldn't agree."

"Then I won't either."

"Oh hell—"

Boyd came on deck.

"Your turn now," he said. "But there is nothing to worry about. He hasn't moved all night."

"Where is he?" Toby asked.

"In the portside bunk of the forward cabin. Marcus is in the other. He will come up as soon as one of you takes his place. The other stays in the saloon. We've got a small lamp burning there."

Toby and Yeoman went below, and a minute later Marcus came on deck. He lit a cigarette, inhaled deeply and blew the smoke out in a long sigh of relief.

"I don't mind admitting I'm glad to be out of there."

"He was quiet enough," Boyd said.

"Too quiet. You weren't actually with him, and you had the light. I kept thinking of that German guard he killed with a paving stone."

"I'll get the electric light working during the day. I only haven't done it before because of using gasoline. But if you think it's worth that risk—"

"Darkness is a worse risk. So long as we can see him, and watch him—"

They sat smoking in silence for half an hour or so. It was absolutely still. The white mist seemed to pad and support the yacht. It felt as if they were floating in it rather than on water. They could see no stars but they might have been on a star themselves—a new one so far off that the light of the other stars had not reached it yet.

At last Marcus said, speaking quietly as before, "One feels different up here. It's weird, but much better than in the cabin. One almost feels as if we were overdoing things."

"You aren't suggesting that we need not watch him?"

"Of course I'm not. But we will have to devise a less exacting method. No one has had any sleep at all tonight."

"It's an original routine—watches below instead of on deck to guard against a mutiny by the Captain. It takes a little getting used to. But it may not last for long."

"How do you think he will behave, or won't we notice a change?"

"The one thing I'm sure about is that he will be changed," Boyd said. "He is a brilliant actor, but he wasn't acting last night. He was carried away by his own story. He was living it."

"Don't you think that it might have done him good?"

"In what way?"

"Those psychiatrist fellows take your money for making you

tell them your nastiest secrets. They say it does you good. Mightn't he have cured himself?"

"One naturally hopes so."

"But you don't believe he has?"

"We have got to prepare for the worst. He wasn't telling a story last night. He escaped—and this time found a woman waiting for him."

"Then, if he has escaped—"

"Can he continue to believe it? You remember that last calm, how we all felt like prisoners."

"What exactly are you afraid of?" Marcus asked.

"Violence."

"I'm less scared of that than cunning. Always have been. But why do you say that?"

"I never used to think about people's characters," Boyd said. "But I've done a lot of it lately. 'The proper study of mankind is man.' I believe that the key to Charrington's character is violence."

"You aren't suggesting tying him up?"

"No. Someone would get hurt or killed in the process. He's strong as a gorilla. We have got to avoid violence, which may not be easy. Think of his life. It was his—call it emotional violence—which killed Heather. He was a master at the violent art of gunboat fighting. Heather told me about a night on leave when he shouted in his sleep: 'Drown them, kill the swine'—"

"And there was the guard he killed with the paving stone," Marcus said thoughtfully.

"Just to make sure. And do you remember when he told you that Samson did the best escape in history?"

"I never quite understood that."

"Samson killed more Philistines in his death than in his life."

"If we are the Philistines we must avoid that."

"Exactly. Having made that point I want to suggest something."

"What?"

"It might take as much as a fortnight to reach Bermuda, half starved and quarreling. We have got to get in touch with the outside world before that."

"But how—even if a ship or airplane came close enough? None of us understands flags or Morse. I don't think Richard would signal. No true yachtsman can bear to be salvaged. And he has

the memory of Germans salvaging the gunboat he did not destroy—
the only time when his violence failed him. No, we must signal
ourselves without his knowledge—with the float."

"I don't quite follow—"

"No doubt they have given up searching for Mary and the other
survivors of the airliner. But if a yellow float were seen, somebody
would come to investigate. Since the air routes converge on Bermuda there is a good hope that something will pass close during
the next day or two."

"Even if an aircraft passed right over us would they notice it
on the deck?"

"No. But as soon as we see a ship or airplane that looks like
passing within range, one or two of us—you and I, say—must get
into the float and paddle as far from the yacht as possible. We
would take with us that flare from the front of the cockpit—there,
where the lifebelt used to be. We'd catch their eye by igniting
that. But it would be the float itself that would do the trick. Even
if they thought the yacht was rescuing it, somebody would come
dashing out from Bermuda to get the story. Film stars—even ones
nobody has heard of—are not allowed to vanish without investigation."

Marcus gave a ghost of a laugh. "Suppose we arrive in Bermuda
under our own steam, and we are greeted by cameras and re-
porters—all for Mary Brown. I can't see Richard enjoying that."

Then he became serious again and said. "I don't like it, Boyd.
Suppose we failed, didn't attract attention—what about Richard
then?"

"We would be wisest to keep away from the yacht."

"We couldn't leave the others."

"It sounds callous, but somebody must, I think. And the others
need not suffer. The Samson mentality has passed. Charrington
means to live. So he wouldn't scuttle the yacht if he hadn't got
the float."

Marcus still looked troubled. "There is another snag," he said.
"I remember how that float fairly waltzed over the waves when we
were scarcely moving. If there were any wind we might not be
able to get back to the yacht."

"It would ride a storm. There is a risk of course. But I didn't
think that would be the snag,"

"Oh, I get scared," Marcus said. "You'd be surprised how scared I get—particularly on a strange element. But actually I was thinking it would look so damned like desertion. No, it isn't possible."

After a little while Boyd asked: "Have you a better plan?"

"Frankly, no. Boyd, old boy, I don't want to shoot the scheme down entirely. You've got a brain and this trip has done you good. You would make quite an efficient soldier. But it has got to be modified. We must bring the other two in on it."

"Charrington himself told us that the fewer people who know about an escape the better."

"I can't help that. In the course of the day I'll explain to Toby and Jack. And we'll draw lots. Before evening the two who are to go will have been chosen and briefed. But they don't go without my order. It's an emergency scheme."

"You don't feel there is an emergency already?"

"Until I see Richard I can't say. But after all, what can he do? We watch him, we keep fuel and anything like a weapon under guard—"

"One reads of people opening the sea cocks—"

"I wouldn't know a sea cock if I saw one. But I don't believe there are any on a yacht. No, it's an emergency plan. I'll only launch it *in extremis*, or if it looks certain of success."

"Very well."

"Personally, Boyd, I don't think it will be necessary. I've known Richard longer than you have, and I dare say my life has given me more chance of seeing all sorts of men under all sorts of strains and stresses. Even the best ones can lose their heads sometimes, develop fixed ideas. But they never go wrong altogether. Richard is one of the best at heart. This woman is a softening influence he has missed since Heather died, since he was taken prisoner in fact. It's my personal bet that his confession will have done him a world of good. Given a breeze we'll sail into harbor all right and I'll be able to report to Meg—'All present and correct.'"

It was beginning to grow light. They could see the sails hanging limp as tarpaulins, the patches of mist writhing on the water like the white smoke of slowly burning garden fires.

"There is another thing I hope," Boyd said. "I hope that Heather comes back."

Marcus started. "I didn't expect you to say a thing like that."

"I'm learning from Jack. But it is not really so unscientific a remark. Without a breeze no yacht could show character. Wind is the spirit of a sailing boat." He put his hand on the tiller which moved up and down like a limb out of joint. "Without wind *Heather Mary* is dead. If I'd felt the old companionship I would not have suggested clearing off and not telling the others. We are all here because of Heather. We stand or fall on our attachment to her."

"I'm glad you said that," Marcus whispered. "I've felt the same. If the yacht were a live thing again—well, there might be a crisis but it would be an appropriate one, like the storm . . . I suppose we would all be rather insensible if we had not got into this mood after so long aboard. After all, we were each of us very fond of Heather—and she of us, I think."

They sat in silence while the light grew, the mist patches vanishing like ghosts before the sun. Boyd thought of that morning on the *Prince Rupert* when they had told him that Heather was missing. . . . Suppose the night before he had advised her, persuaded her, to go on and meet Charrington. Suppose he had stayed with her, not left her to herself. It must have been very near to where they were now—Point X again.

There were sounds below. Toby came on deck.

"Any wind?" he asked.

"Not a breath. What is the Skipper doing?"

"He hasn't moved yet."

"You ought to go back. We'll relieve you in a minute."

"I wanted to talk to you first," Toby whispered. "I looked in with the lamp several times these last four hours. Jack was awake of course. But the Skipper was sleeping like a child."

"Is he still asleep?"

"No. His eyes are open but he is just staring at the ceiling."

"Does he look—unhappy?" Boyd asked.

"Why do you ask that?" said Marcus.

"I remember him telling us, off Madeira, of prisoners who failed to escape and finally became melancholics who only lay and stared at the ceiling."

"He doesn't look melancholy," Toby said. "He's—calm. It's hard to express, but he reminded me of a warrior lying in state. I wonder if he is putting it on."

Before anyone could say more, Charrington came on deck, followed by Yeoman. As Toby had said, it was difficult to define his expression. His face was drawn and tired but there was nothing hard in it.

More slowly than usual he looked at the sails and round the circle of the horizon.

"Still no wind," he said.

"Do you think the weather will change?" Marcus asked.

"The glass is steady. But it must blow soon. My God, I want to arrive. Where is Mary?"

"Still sleeping."

"Let her sleep. Meanwhile we must get the yacht shipshape, and breakfast cooked. Can we have it up here, Marcus. It's freer on deck."

For some time after that they hardly spoke. There was the purr of the pressure stove. Marcus was cooking, Boyd had begun dismantling the engine, Yeoman was doing a long splice, tapping it smooth with the dinghy's tiller as a mallet, Toby was polishing the brass binnacle. All of them were busy to hide their interest in Charrington who was sitting on the wood and canvas covered top of what had been the saloon skylight.

Suddenly he asked: "Did we drink a lot last night, Marcus?"

"Nothing. Do you feel bad?"

"As if I'd had my whole inside cut out. What did we do last night?"

"Nothing much. We were yarning."

"What did I talk about?"

Marcus hesitated. "You told us how you escaped from Germany," he said at last.

"Did I? I thought so, but wasn't sure if I'd dreamed it. I've never spoken of that to a living soul . . . I'm glad I've got it off my chest at last."

They looked sideways at him while they worked. All except Marcus felt it was too good to be true.

Charrington filled his pipe, his fingers working automatically while his eyes stared forward over the yacht's bows.

"Can anybody give me a light?" he asked.

Toby held his lighter for him, and then pocketed it again.

"Thank you," Charrington said. "There is something I want to speak to you about before Mary appears." There was a hint of embarrassment in his voice. "We have been shipmates nearly three months now. As you know it's the first time I've had a crew since the war. If I've behaved strangely sometimes, kept things from you or lost my temper, I want to apologize. I have a hell of a temper. You now know what I've had on my mind. But I want to finish this voyage well. It's rather important."

They said nothing. They were puzzled. Charrington sat watching them or looking out over the still sea which was now clear of mist. He was behaving, Boyd thought, like a convalescent who looks at everything with a new interest.

"There's a ship," he said.

On the horizon to port were little smudges of smoke. They all stopped working and looked at them.

"She won't come any nearer," Charrington said.

"What route is she on?" Marcus asked.

"New York to South America, I dare say. But we are still a long way from all the shipping lanes—south of New York to Cape Town, north of the West Indies to England and France, south too of England to Bermuda. But not many ships go to Bermuda from the east."

"It's the hub of several air routes," Boyd said, watching Charrington closely.

"Yes, but we are off the main ones, I think. We are well south of Bermuda to the Azores or Lisbon, for instance—in the middle of the segment between that and Bermuda to Jamaica."

He paused, drawing on his pipe. "We are unlikely to see a human being until we sail into harbor," he went on. "That's as it should be—a sudden arrival. Your little girls will have the day of their lives—eh, Marcus?—and Meg too."

A few minutes later Mary Brown came running up the companionway and stood in the middle of them.

"Good morning, everybody, am I late?" she said, turning herself about like a mannequin.

Her auburn hair, for the first time uncovered since they had lifted her from the sea, hung to her shoulders glossy in the sun. Her face was bright and confident. She was no longer wearing men's clothes. She had made her own skirt presentable and she had on a jersey which might have come straight from Bond Street.

It was navy blue. It fitted her almost too well and had a white M embroidered over the heart.

She stood in front of Charrington, showing herself off, caressing the jersey with her hands.

"I found this in a drawer. You don't mind, Richard? I think it must have been made for me."

Charrington stared at her while the others waited. At last he said: "Sit down, you little minx, and have your breakfast."

Marcus and Boyd exchanged glances.

When the meal was done, Charrington said. "You must amuse yourself, Mary. Everybody is going to be busy today, except me."

"Aren't you well?" she asked.

"Very well indeed—but tired."

"Of course you must rest. The boys will do all the sailor jobs and I'll wash up. When are we going to reach Bermuda?"

"As soon as we get a wind. But we must smarten her up a lot before then. Would you like to sail her in?"

"Oh no, I wouldn't know how. You must do that. She's your boat."

All morning they were busy. Boyd worked on the little engine. The rest of them were not engaged, as formerly, in trying to strengthen the yacht, but in tidying, polishing, splicing. It gave them a curious sensation doing these little beautifying tasks to a yacht which lay dead on a dead ocean.

Marcus, true to his word, found an opportunity to speak to Toby and Yeoman in the bow. He explained the plan and made each of them draw from his hand a folded strip of paper. On some excuse, under the eyes of Charrington who still sat in the middle of the deck, Boyd came forward and did the same. By noon each of them knew what was to be done in an emergency, or at the perfect opportunity, and whether he himself were to do it or not.

While they were eating lunch on deck an aircraft passed, a silver speck moving along the sky. But it was too far off. Marcus shook his head. It would have been difficult in any case, for the girl was in the float and Charrington near her. Besides—everything was going so well.

Towards evening, when Boyd had re-assembled the engine and Marcus was throwing buckets of water on the deck while Yeoman scrubbed, they felt a breath of wind. Marcus licked his finger and held it up. The breeze was coming from the southeast—from the perfect direction—but it was too weak to fill the sails.

"It will grow stronger," Charrington said. "Tomorrow we will move."

This hope made them halt in their tasks, light cigarettes and talk. Toby, into whose head a few neat phrases had come, sat down to write them in his notebook.

Mary came over to him. "Are you writing about me?" she asked.

"No, but I will if you like. What shall I say?"

"Be serious, Toby," she laughed. "I'll have to give lots of interviews when I arrive. I won't have the least idea what to say unless you tell me."

"Tell them about your early life—they always lap that up. Did you ever run away and get lost when you were a child?"

They sat together, the youngest pair by many years, joking and laughing. Toby knew how to make her laugh. Charrington watched them.

The little engine burst into life, making them all start. But Boyd had eyes for nothing else. He worked with absorption until it was running smoothly.

With the approach of evening patches of mist began to form. They glided slowly over the smooth water although the yacht still lay motionless, her sails too heavy for the gentle breath.

Boyd went below for a moment to connect up the batteries in the galley. Marcus followed him and asked, "How are you getting on?"

"Well enough. You shall have light tonight."

"Good. Are you sleepy?"

"A trifle. But I'll finish this job. So if you want a rest, take it now."

"Are you sure? Right-oh, I'll stand easy till sunset. Yeoman is coming down, but Toby will stay on deck."

"Good. I'm just going back on deck too. I want a few more revs out of Little Tich."

Boyd returned to the cockpit and tinkered with the engine for half an hour—until it was working harder than it had ever done before. Then he stood up, put his hands in his pockets and smiled down at it, his head slightly on one side. He lit a cigarette and became conscious of the evening—a little more mist but no more wind, and no sign of the airplane or ship.

"I'm going to have another glance at the batteries," he said to Toby.

"O.K.," said Toby, who was talking to Mary.

Passing through the saloon Boyd saw that Marcus was already asleep. He went on into the galley and dropped on his knees beside the batteries. The engine sounded loud and industrious even from here. There was nothing wrong with Little Tich. He tested the batteries. They were charging at last. In a couple of hours—before it became dark—there would be at least a glimmer of light in the bulbs.

Boyd relaxed. Still on his knees, he looked through the open door at the sleeping soldier on the bunk. Marcus' stern and clean-cut face was twitching. Boyd wondered why.

In fact, Marcus was dreaming. It was a reminiscent dream about an incident which he did not like to remember when he was awake and which returned as a nightmare when he was particularly tired or nervy. Its origin was a civil riot in the Far East when he had sent his men out armed with pick helves. There was a confused surging and shouting. From out of the darkness a native rushed at him with a knife. Marcus had no time to do anything. He saw the long blade flash and braced his chest to receive it. But at that moment the native collapsed. Marcus could not see what had happened, but he knew by the noise.

A pick helve brought down on a bare human head makes a noise unlike any other—something like a cricket ball being struck by an unoiled and badly sprung bat, yet different. One could not mistake it even in a dream.

But he was no longer dreaming.

He swung off the settee. He saw Boyd kneeling in the galley doorway.

"What was that?" he shouted.

"Someone closed the hatch," Boyd said. "And I think they must be resetting the sail. Toby is on deck—"

Marcus turned away from him and ran for the companionway.

CHAPTER 26

MARCUS tugged the hatch open but found something else blocking the way—the whole weight of the trysail. He struggled with the hard and heavy canvas. Meanwhile Boyd ran back through the saloon and the galley where he collided with Yeoman. Together they tried to open the forward hatch—until Yeoman remembered that he had put the cover over it before he and Marcus washed. Back to the saloon—it was as it had been in the storm except that the exit they had then used was battened down. And the danger was different. There was no sound of wind and waves. The noise of the engine had stopped and in its place was the crackling roar of fire.

The only chance was the main hatch. Marcus' legs were disappearing as he squirmed under the canvas. They followed. It was stiflingly hot—and they didn't know which way to go. The weight pressed them down. They wriggled like rats in a sack. At last they emerged, one after the other, on the edge of the deck, almost falling overboard.

A column of yellow and orange flame was spurting like a volcano out of what had been the engine casing. Marcus was already tugging the sail over it. Boyd and Yeoman helped him.

The flames went through the sail as if it had been paper. The three men dragged the forward part into place, but that went brown and black and vanished too.

"Water," Yeoman said breathlessly, looking at the sea.

"No good. More canvas," Marcus jumped for the sail locker.

There was another jib and the topsail and the balloon staysail. Dragging canvas out of a confined space quickly must be one of the most exhausting tasks there is. In their desperation they did it in a moment. But instead of being stifled the pillar of flame consumed this also.

They had no time or breath to speak, but they were all conscious of the water, the endless useless water, waiting for them when they had to jump from the heat.

Then the flame drew back like a tongue into a mouth.

"That's the end of the gasoline," Boyd gasped. "Thank God I didn't put much in."

But it was not the end of the fire. The woodwork all around the engine was well alight.

"Water now!"

It was difficult to get the sea water on deck in any quantity. Somewhere there was a canvas bucket on a rope—Marcus had used it that afternoon—but they could not find it. They fetched pots and pans from the galley, lay on the deck and scooped them full. But the effect was pitiable. They could scarcely even hear the hiss. Then Boyd, running through the saloon with the swill bucket, noticed Marcus' blanket. He snatched it up, and others from under the mattresses. They dipped these over the side and dropped them on the fire. They had an effect, checking the burning while the men threw on more water. Smoke poured up where flames had been.

"I think it's under control," Marcus said.

"One or two more blankets. There must be some in the Skipper's cabin."

Yeoman went to fetch them. He was back in a moment.

"It's burning there!" he shouted.

That was much harder to deal with because it was further from the sea. They tried to stifle the flames and glowing wood with dry bedding, but the cloth smouldered and became so hot that they could not handle it. Then Marcus thought of the spare fresh water tank. He turned on the tap and soaked a pillow and the mattress. That was enough to check the fire. By then the others had fetched buckets and saucepans of sea water. The cabin was so full of smoke that they choked and their eyes ran—but they could see no more fire. They went on deck again.

There they found Toby sitting against the mast. He looked at them with eyes screwed up and forehead deeply wrinkled.

"What the hell's been going on?" he asked.

"What happened to you?" Marcus asked. He looked at Toby,

as they all did, with interest but without sympathy. They had been through too much themselves.

"The Skipper told me to reset the trysail in case the wind—did something," Toby said slowly. "I loosed the halliards. Then something exploded in my head."

Boyd examined his head. The skin was broken and a bruise was coming up like a balloon. But it was not bleeding much. His thick hair had saved him.

Yeoman had picked up the dinghy's tiller from the deck and was pointing with it.

"There they are. Good riddance."

The float was a hundred yards ahead. Its little sail was set and with the zephyr of a breeze it was drawing away from the helpless yacht. They could see Charrington and Mary lying aboard it. It appeared to Boyd that the girl was strapped down, but he could not be sure.

"Do you suppose he forced her over the side?" Marcus asked.

"That wouldn't be difficult for him—particularly when the fire started," said Boyd.

This extraordinary sight—the Skipper running away from his ship and crew—affected them remarkably little. Their eyes were red and sore, they were still coughing the smoke out of their lungs, their burns were beginning to hurt. They didn't care much about anything else. Charrington had tried to murder them, but in spite of his cunning he hadn't succeeded. Yeoman was right: it was a good riddance.

They were more impressed by the position of the sun—still well above the horizon. It seemed as if they had fought the fire for hours, but the whole thing must have been over within a few minutes . . . Then one of the slowly drifting mist masses engulfed the yacht, and they could see nothing more of their surroundings.

They helped Toby down to a bunk in the saloon. They cleaned themselves up a little and dressed their burns. Then, in the last of the daylight, they made a thorough examination of the cabin and cockpit, breaking away the charred wood to make certain that the fire was dead. Under the engine Boyd found the blackened tin container of the flare. That was how Charrington had started the fire—with the life-saving flare.

While they were thus engaged they heard an airplane. It must have passed almost directly over them but they could not see it for the mist.

They discussed for a little while what Charrington had done and why he did it. He had fooled them properly. While they had been absorbed in their own secret plans he had been quietly waiting to put a similar plan into operation.

"You have got to admire his single-mindedness," Boyd said. "He went straight on from where the wave, and then Mary, interrupted him—with improvements."

"What improvements?"

"He has made sure of the woman in this escape."

"I can see why he knocked out Toby. But why try to burn the yacht?"

"The gunboat, Heather Mary, his four deceivers—he would have destroyed them all together, except for your quick reaction, Marcus. Another half minute and a red-hot engine would have dropped into the cabin. Then nothing could have saved us."

They paused and thought about that, feeling frightened. It had been enough to put out the fire in the cabin as it was. If the sides of the yacht had caught—

"Do you think he has escaped?" Marcus asked.

"It's what we discussed. He has a better chance than we have, now. If he doesn't reach Bermuda himself he will be spotted and picked up."

"But *Heather Mary* is still afloat, in spite of him," Yeoman said.

They were too tired to think of the details of their situation. When darkness came they fell asleep.

Dawn came, gray and bleak. The state of the yacht shocked them. There was a black hole where the cockpit used to be. The drooping jib accentuated the lack of other sails. Tendrils of mist groped through the empty rigging, and around the broken mast. The masses of the mist writhed and rolled over on themselves as they slid, slow and ghostlike, along the smooth surface of the water. Even the familiar ocean appeared strange and sinister. Mist changes everything.

"There is nothing we can do," Marcus said. "Might as well have breakfast."

Boyd asked, "Don't you think somebody should remain on deck and pump her dry?"

"I will," Yeoman said.

Marcus felt that morale was top priority. Lighting the pressure stove in the galley he said, "We are going to have a bloody fine breakfast, even if we are hungry later. I've got a tin of bacon and two of sausages, and a tin of mushrooms, and some New Zealand butter. There is plenty of coffee."

Boyd and Toby sitting on the settees in the saloon, did not reply.

"Will you get some water, Boyd—from the tank in the Skipper's cabin?"

Boyd took the saucepan and went out.

Marcus asked: "Were you in France in 1940, Toby?"

Toby, his forehead still deeply wrinkled by a headache, answered, "I was at school."

"Yes, of course, you told me. That's when we first met a real big-scale armored attack, and I appreciated the importance of a good breakfast. You can't face tanks—or any other danger—on an empty stomach."

Boyd returned with the saucepan full of water.

"Here you are. Almost the last of it, you know."

"What do you mean the last of it? There were nearly thirty gallons."

"It's sucking dry. There can't be more than a few pints left. You used some last night, you remember, to put out the fire."

"Only a few gallons."

Marcus stood in the galley doorway trying not to look dismayed. He went to the cabin, and returned.

"That damned woman must have been washing. She must have had a bath," he said angrily.

"Hadn't we better go easy with what's left?" Boyd asked.

"Yes, yes of course. We can have the food—but not coffee. We must drink the water neat—just a drop each."

"No wind—no sails—a few pints of water—a leaking yacht that wouldn't stand any sea at all. Two hundred miles from land, we think—from a little island we probably couldn't find anyway. It's a pity we didn't act first," Toby said.

"We can find Bermuda," Marcus said. "Boyd learned how to navigate these last few days, didn't you?"

"Yes, but he must have taken the sextant. It was on deck and it's gone."

They sat in silence. Marcus looked for something cheerful to say but could not find it.

Yeoman came running down the companionway and burst into the saloon, his round face beaming.

"It's come back," he said excitedly.

"What—the float?"

"No, the white bird."

"Oh!"

"What is the weather doing?" Marcus asked.

"Thick as anything. But it came quite close—the bird. I mean. It's flying round the yacht."

"Any minute now we'll hear a woman crying," Toby said.

Yeoman stared at him, then broke out. "Don't you understand? Can't you feel it? It's not just the bird, it's Miss Heather. Now that woman's gone she's come back. She has suffered more than anyone could stand but she's come back to look after us. The jib is full and the yacht's moving. It's alive. She's at the tiller—you can feel it. We used to call it Jo, but it's her."

They looked at him in silence. No one felt inclined to say anything cynical.

"I don't suppose we are moving very fast," Marcus said at last, gently. "We are a long way from land, you know, or a shipping route even."

"It wouldn't matter if we were in the middle of space—"

An overwhelming noise burst on them, blaring, deafening, breathlessly aggressive as the tumbling snow of an avalanche, filling the yacht, their ears, their heads. It swept them, stunned and terrified out of the saloon ... A thing like a cliff was bearing down on them.

This is how it appeared from the deck of the big ship.

The little yacht appeared out of the mist so close that the officer on watch only had time to blow the foghorn and order "Hard a-port." Even so he might have avoided a collision if the yacht had held her course. But as her crew came tumbling on deck, and before they could reach the helm, she veered to starboard and raced straight at the liner's side. One had the impression of a desperate but deliberate act.

As her bowsprit struck she rose straight upright and then disappeared as an entity. The men were catapulted through the air.

Next their heads and startled faces were framed in tumbling water. They seemed to race away astern. Very soon they were only dots on the smooth surface far behind. Then they were lost sight of in the mist.

A big ship at full speed takes over two miles to stop. But the officer of the launch which was lowered and sent back had no difficulty in finding the swimming men because of a giant petrel which glided to and fro above them.